ORACLE

MUTANT WOOD

C.W. Trisef

Trisef Book LLC

How to contact the author
Website – OracleSeries.com
Email – trisefbook@gmail.com

Oracle – Mutant Wood
C.W. Trisef

Other titles by C.W. Trisef
Oracle – Sunken Earth (Book 1 in the Oracle Series)
Oracle – Fire Island (Book 2 in the Oracle Series)
Oracle – River of Ore (Book 3 in the Oracle Series)
Oracle – Solar Wind (Book 4 in the Oracle Series)
Oracle – Waters Deep (Book 6 in the Oracle Series)
Oracle – Cure the World (Book 7 in the Oracle Series)

THE INFINITY TREE

Tunguska, Russia. June 30, 1908. 7:14 am.

It was a day like any other. The old couple moved about their farm house slowly but dutifully. While the wife cleaned up the morning meal, the husband headed down the front porch. She washed the plates first, then the silverware. He grabbed his boots first, then his shovel. She watched him through the window as he paced away toward their little field, the same twinkle in her eye since the day they met so many years ago. Yes, it was just another typical day at the uneventful farm on the remote hill, tucked away among the dense woodlands of the vast Siberian wilderness.

And then the sky split in two.

She saw it first: a shiny spec off to the right, high in the sky, falling at a very slight angle toward the earth. It was moving fast, leaving a trail of bright light behind it. A shooting star, a Chinese firework, a gift from the gods—whatever it was, the country woman found it to be a delightful display...until the window started to rattle, followed by the dishes, then the entire house.

Alarmed, the wife threw down her dishrag and rushed outside to alert her husband. She burst through the rickety door, yelling for him and pointing at the unidentified flying object, now much larger than a spec. He paused mid-shovel and gazed curiously at his wife, then spun around to see what she was motioning at. His jaw dropped at the sight: a second sun, plummeting to the ground.

As lifelong Russians but cash-strapped farmers, the old couple had heard about a lot of things but actually seen very few of them. They stared at the oddity, mesmerized by its majesty, paralyzed by their perplexity. Although it was far away, its luster was almost blinding, only increasing as it plunged further and further through the atmosphere. The man stood spellbound until he felt the ground trembling beneath his feet. He glanced around: the field's foliage was agitated, the smallest dirt clods were bouncing. When he looked back at the sky, the flaming fireball had slipped from view behind the treetops.

There was dead silence on the farm for a moment as the couple anticipated impact. The husband turned to retreat to the house for shelter. He could see his wife already hurrying back up the porch, but then the world went blank. A blinding flash of white light snuffed out everything from view for a split second. No sooner had the flash blinded their eyes than a supersonic bang deafened their ears, followed by a mighty wind that pushed everything to the ground. The sound of a million trees being snapped in two filled the air. The woman screamed as every window in the house shattered.

But there was no time to recover from this 1-2-3 punch—no time to prepare for what came next: the heat. A wave of wicked warmth washed over the land, withering the crops in an instant. Still on the ground, the man began to squirm. He clawed at his shirt, which felt like it was on fire. He rolled along the grass, hoping its dew-smitten blades would provide some shred of relief. They did, and then the heat abated. Panting, the old man rolled onto his back, expecting more trouble. But none came.

When it seemed the danger was over, the worried wife fled down the hill to help her husband. He wasn't moving; she hoped he was still alive. She found him staring up at the sky. There was a massive plume of grayish white smoke, rising like a mushroom, where the point of impact likely had been. She helped him to his feet. They looked around: as far as they could see, the forest was leveled. Every tree, its branches unharmed, had broken at its base and fallen on its side, all in the same direction away from the epicenter. Their farm was ruined. The barn had collapsed. Their house was still standing, but a portion of the roof had caved in. Amid so much destruction, the two of them were grateful they had survived.

Word spread quickly among the small towns up and down the nearby Tunguska River. Rumor had it that the mysterious explosion was the work of deity—punishment for wrongdoing, chastisement for misconduct. As such, none of the locals dared to even get close to the condemned area, and no one ever did for many years.

With one exception.

In fact, just hours after impact, the first footprints were made at ground-zero. They belonged to an old man whose beard was as long as his hair, both as white as a ghost. He wore a black, flowing robe and kept one of his talon-like hands wrapped around a spirally-twisted cane. His enemies called him evil; his servants called him Lye.

He moved with unnatural swiftness for such an old person, slowed down only by the occasional snag of his cloak on a branch. He was anxious to learn the result of the explosion, which had been the product of many decades of hard (and secret) work.

While any normal creature would have required some kind of full-body suit for protection from the many harmful substances on the ground and in the air, Lye used nothing of the sort. His simple remedy was the occasional sip from a personal flask he kept hidden inside his robe's chest pocket.

The land had become swampy and boggy, and fallen tree trunks made for more climbing than walking. A mix of dust and smoke hung in the air, adding an eerie ambiance to the surroundings. It was like strolling through a twilight zone, somewhere between the world of the living and the realm of the dead. The warbling of birds had been replaced by the burbling of chemicals. Instead of scattered sunshine, there was radioactive luminescence.

But Lye cared nothing for the damage he had wrought. Only the outcome mattered now. He moved with ever greater speed, eager to see if he could finally claim victory over such a stubborn situation. His hopes were high, as this was the first time he had employed the help of what he termed the ultimate weapon.

He knew he was nearing the place of impact because of the trees. So far, all of the trees had been lying on the ground, their trunks snapped but branches unbroken, each one having fallen in the same radial direction away from the epicenter. Now, however, the trees were still standing upright, but their branches had been snapped off. This was because the force of the explosion had been vertical at first, then became horizontal and pushed out in all directions as it made contact with the ground.

But Lye was only interested in one tree in particular. It was the biggest, the oldest—the tree to which all others could trace their roots. In a sense, it was the mother tree. And, if all had gone according to plan, it should have been obliterated.

Lye came to an abrupt halt. He couldn't believe his evil eyes. There was the tree—still standing and still intact. In fact, it looked totally unfazed by the blast. The Tunguska Explosion had been a complete failure.

His cold blood boiling with hot displeasure, Lye shook his fist at the twentieth-century sky and exclaimed, "Curse this tree!"

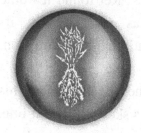

CHAPTER 1

OF GAMES AND GOALS

Something was missing. Ret could sense an emptiness somewhere, either in his life or in the world (or perhaps both). There was a void—a gap—that needed to be filled, not just by anything but by a specific thing. It was an important part of something as a whole, like a member of a family whose unique role no one else can quite carry out. In his mind, he could see a system that wasn't complete, still able to get by but continually suffering because of the absence of this one key component. It was irreplaceable. It was unsubstitutable. And it was missing.

This emptiness gnawed at Ret. It made itself preeminent in his thoughts. The incessant feeling of something lacking made it difficult for him to ever feel fully content about anything. Frustration set in, striving to fill a space without knowing what belonged in it. Was it a person he needed to find? a place he needed to go? the next element? Whatever it was, Ret found it ironic that although the thing itself was never present, its absence was ever-present, constantly nagging him from sunrise to sunset. Eventually, like reconciling a checkbook with a missing entry, he had to abandon his search and try to be at peace with a skewed bottom-line.

One thing that *wasn't* missing, however, was Ret's list of problems, which had been growing ever since he returned home from Antarctica and found a large group of protestors gathered along the southern tip of Tybee Island, directly across the creek from Coy Manor. It didn't seem like anything too serious until Ret learned what they were upset about: him.

"You've ruined our world!" they ranted.

"No more elements!" they chanted.

The locals said, "Shame on Coy!"

The posters read, "Save a pyramid, arrest Ret Cooper!"

The protest quickly evolved into a sort of occupation. Tents began to appear on the beach, placed among the signs and banners that had been staked in the sand. Activists came and went, intensity ebbed and flowed, but at least a few picketers were always present, refusing to back down until the Manor gave up.

The Coopers and Coys had figured it would only be a matter of time before animosity began hitting closer to home. They were grateful to live on Little Tybee Island, which provided some measure of security since it was inaccessible to the public (unless you had a kayak or had ever *Ben Coy*). The two families did their best to ignore the unpleasant rally that had taken up residence on the shore next-door, but even their most cursory glances at the daily headlines or nightly news reminded them that anti-Oracle sentiment was engulfing the entire globe. In a way, this was nothing new; people had been complaining since the days of Sunken Earth. But now that the world knew exactly who was to blame, the accusations had become extremely pointed and personal.

Every human being had at least one reason to be upset with Ret. Demonstrations were popping up in nearly every major city. Corporations were promising big bucks for people to take action. Economies were buckling, industries crumbling, and governments suffering. The whole world was in commotion, not to mention that the rapid climate change was throwing everyone's lives up in the air. And, thanks to Lionel's big mouth at the United Nations meeting, everything was Ret's fault. Although the physicist had made an attempt to explain his actions before the two of them parted ways in Antarctica, Ret still felt like his number-one fan had made him out to be the world's number-one enemy.

As bad as all of that was, however, Ret was more displeased by the fact that the game of collecting elements was distracting everyone from the goal of changing people. While the *game* was to find natural elements and restore them to a ball in order to achieve world domination, the *goal* was to find social elements and restore them to the earth in order to achieve world peace. But the longer the game went on, the less Ret wanted to play it. It was turning the Oracle into a sort of Happy Meal, which kids either accept or reject based not on the chicken nuggets but on the toy, thus letting the lesser purpose of fun overshadow the higher purpose of food. It was the same with the Oracle; Ret could sense these dual purposes (one lesser, one higher) more and more whenever he recited the prophecy, which was often:

> *What now is six, must be one;*
> *Earth's imbalance to be undone.*
> *Fill the Oracle, pure elements reunite,*
> *Cure the world; one line has the rite.*

The lesser purpose pertained to curing the world *as a planet*—reuniting landmasses and purging waste-places. After being divided for centuries, the earth's continents were now on track to come back together. Meanwhile, a global cleansing was underway: the Great River flushing out the Sahara Desert, and the great thaw making Antarctica inhabitable once again in its northern drift into warmer climates.

And although there was much more to this lesser purpose, it would all be utterly wasted without the higher purpose, which pertained to curing the world *as a people*—a reversal of culture rather than continents. While this was the *goal* that interested Ret most, it also happened to be a concept that repulsed most everyone else and sent them back to the *game*, allowing them to pass GO and collect more elements, singing 'too hard to correct it, so I'll just neglect it,' to borrow a phrase from Leo's song.

Why? Well, it's easier to cure a ham than to cure a heart; in other words, the higher purpose is more difficult than the lesser one. The lesser is carried out by Mother Nature, but the higher comes by way of human nature—the former originates from without while the latter must come from within. While the lesser might require us to buy earthquake insurance, the higher requires us to ask ourselves tough questions.

Unfortunately, this idea (nuggets before toys) has never seemed to sit well with generations past or present. But Ret belonged to a different generation—the one that would rather sweep problems off the earth than under a rug, the one that would rather dig into difficulties than get bailed out of them, the one that would rather attack the roots than whack the weeds. Unlike those before it, Ret's generation would rather make a difference than make a fortune; they would rather get somewhere than get something. He knew our issues as a whole were not any bigger or stronger than us as a people, for, in fact, that was the very issue: *us!* It was our hearts that were at the heart of the matter—our natures that were the nature of the problem.

Ret had a major dilemma on his hands. The unstoppable execution of the lesser meaning of 'cure the world' meant that the carrying out of the higher meaning needed to be kicked into high gear. If lesser were to finish before higher, the results would be disastrous. Clearly, the coalescing of the two was going to take some mad skills—the kind of stuff that heroes are made of.

For what good would it do to bring the continents together if nations still want to nuke one another? It would do no good at all; in fact, the fruition of 'what now is six, must be one' would only make matters worse. Or what good would it do to bring every nation side by side if people still want to keep their borders strictly closed? And what good would it do if the northern half of Africa turned into a very fruitful land tomorrow if that region is still plagued by the greed of today?

Ret was quickly coming to the conclusion that if he wanted everyone's focus to shift from the *game* to the *goal*—from 'fill the Oracle' to prepare a people—then he had better do the same. He figured 'pure elements reunite' would happen with or without him; if the Oracle didn't see to it, then Lye and another one of his clones would. But what about 'earth's imbalance to be undone'? How was he going to convince people to believe him and trust him?

That was a tall order for someone who was wanted in 29 countries. No, when it came to relationships with others, Ret wasn't doing so hot in that department these days (just ask the protestors across the creek). While most people might describe him as a loner, that was neither fair nor accurate. Ret was truly a people person—one who wasn't afraid to look you in the eye, one who liked to crack a joke and share a laugh, one who would rather listen to you than talk about himself. Yet, the world rarely saw that side of him. They saw the wallflower, not the social butterfly; the guy with countless acquaintances but few, if any, friends; the recluse who preferred to keep himself aloof from people, even though inwardly he had volumes that he wanted to share.

The reason Ret kept to himself was because he was different. He was not ashamed of his differences, but the world told him he should be, so he seldom shared them. He had learned long ago that to confide in people was to run the risk of being ridiculed—to be called crazy, that his dreams were too unlikely and his ideals too progressive. In many ways, Ret felt ahead of his time, like Sapiens among Neanderthals. He didn't expect everyone to understand but just wished everyone would try to. For him, opening up was like a duck hunt, where the fowls are shot down as soon as they come up.

You see, the thing that bothered Ret the most was how the *game* of modern life was distracting everyone from the *goal* of helping people. Because of the places he'd been and the people he'd met, Ret now lived in the real world, but everyone around him still seemed to live in their own little world. At the very least, he wished society was more mindful of the hordes of people on the earth who were in such great need. He wasn't advocating we forfeit our own blessings, only that we use them to bless the lives of others.

As much as Ret wanted to live a normal life, he possessed a gift that made it impossible for him to do so: vision. He could see things that most people couldn't—not apparitions but aspirations, things that could and should happen. This was both a blessing and a curse: a blessing because he knew what needed to occur in order to 'cure the world'; a curse because whenever he told the world he wanted to cure it, they usually called him a crazy.

Ret could think of only one person who seemed to have the same kind of vision that he had: the wondrous Mr. Coy, he himself crazy and proud of it. Although Ret couldn't cure the world alone, he might be able to with Mr. Coy. But how? Ret knew the battle for the hearts of mankind had to be won individually—one-on-one, one by one. However, given the current state of things, that was likely going to be a real challenge. Sure, he had plenty of vision, but he also had plenty of enemies. How was he going to make friends out of foes?

Most days, this was all too overwhelming to think about. It never failed to make Ret feel lonely and depressed. It didn't help that he was a marked man. His works, as misunderstood as they were, followed him everywhere, especially at school. As he walked the halls of Tybee High, he often felt like an American revolutionary among British lobsterbacks. Students avoided him. Teachers overlooked him. Yet everyone noticed him—this he knew because he could hear in the airwaves everything they said about him, no matter how softly they thought they were whispering. Such was the glamorous life of one with the scars. Sometimes Ret would spend an entire day without saying a word.

The first day of November would have been another such day if it weren't for something that happened during gym class. As part of their unit on track and field events, the teacher had her students running relays. She split the group into six teams, handed out as many batons, and then asked them to take their desired positions along the track.

Standing at his mark, Ret watched the relay as it got underway. In the lead were Justin and Lauren, followed by Briana and Hector, with Alan bringing up the rear.

Wait. That only made five runners when there should have been six. Ret counted again. Something was missing. Where was the sixth runner?

Ret looked back at the starting line. There, not far from it, was Kristina. She was having a hard time because she was overweight. Although she was obviously giving it all she had, her sprint was more of a shuffle, and the other runners left her in their dust.

The sight warmed Ret's heart. He admired Kristina's determination. She could have sat out, given up, or simply walked the whole way. But instead she was trying her best, and even though she was dead last, in Ret's eyes she was in first place.

Unfortunately, not everyone saw it in quite the same light. By the time the relay entered its third leg, Kristina was just wrapping up its first one. Ret could see her teammate still waiting at his mark, standing with some of the runners from the first leg who had long since finished. They were all watching Kristina, which was hard not to do, and yet it looked like they were cheering her on. Ret bent the sound waves to his ear and tuned in from across the track, eager to hear their encouraging remarks. He was shocked by what he heard:

"Come on, tubby!"

"Move those cottage cheese thighs!"

"Sometime this year please!"

"Gotta work off those honey buns!"

"Jiggle, jiggle!"

Ret swelled with anger. He gritted his teeth and clenched his fists. The dirt at his feet began to dance. His fingertips started to spark. In his rage, he unintentionally bent the metal goal post that was closest to him on the football field.

Just as the wind was beginning to pick up, Kristina shakily stuck out her baton. With a final jeer, her teammate took it and took off. Laughing, the other scoffers left, and Kristina collapsed on the ground, breathing heavily.

Ret's fury melted into sadness. His heart sank, and tears filled his eyes.

Just then he felt a jab at his side. He turned to find his teammate holding out his baton, anxious for Ret to take it and commence the final leg. Their team was in the lead, and Ret was their last runner.

Ret grabbed the metal baton, crushed it with his bare hand, and threw it into the next ZIP code. Then he entered a full sprint, but, much to his team's disappointment, it was not toward the finish line. No, the *game* was not his *goal*.

While the rest of the class crowned the winners, Ret went over to comfort the loser. He knelt down and gently lifted Kristina to her feet, her hair disheveled and clothes dusty.

"I'm sorry they were mean to you," Ret said

sincerely. She was too exhausted to be startled by who was helping her.

Amid sniffles and tears, she rasped back, "Me, too."

"I thought you did a great job," he told her as they walked toward the locker room.

"Thanks," she replied, unconvinced.

More than once, Kristina looked at Ret with a curious expression on her face. She wondered how public enemy number-one could be treating her so kindly. Maybe the things she had heard about him weren't entirely true.

Arriving at the building, Ret said pleasantly, "See you around," and they parted ways.

While changing out of his gym clothes, Ret reflected on what had transpired. Whatever it was that he had done, it left him with a warmth in his chest, proof that his heart liked it. It also left him with a numbness in his hand, which meant a scar must have liked it, too. Ret smiled, for the feeling was coming from the scar on the far left side of his right palm, which was the only scar left that had yet to be revealed.

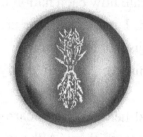

CHAPTER 2

POWER SERGE

"Welcome to Russia, Dr. Zarbock," said the man standing on the airstrip as Lionel stepped out of the helicopter.

"Thank you, President Topramenov," Lionel greeted him with a firm handshake. "It is an honor to meet the newest leader of this fine Federation."

"Yes, well, if it weren't for my election campaign, I would have attended the United Nations meeting last April and heard your stirring address in person."

"I understand," Lionel told him. "After all, you *are* quite the celebrity these days."

"Second only to you!" the president rejoined. "I hear you practically run the UN now."

"It is a responsibility that I take most seriously," Lionel affirmed, "hence my meeting with you today. As you know, the Security Council has asked everyone to aid in the obstruction of Ret Cooper, and they have assigned me to personally investigate how each nation is complying with that request. And, I might add, we are expecting great things from the Russian Federation."

"You will not be disappointed," the dignitary promised.

The pair left the helipad and headed for a nearby car, its driver standing ready to receive them. Although it was midday, a thick blanket of gray clouds veiled the sky, and the temperature was well below freezing. The guest followed his host into the backseat, and the company departed.

President Sergey Topramenov was your typical middle-aged Russian elite. With dark hair and a square face, he was thick in body but not in brain. He wore a black suit under his trench coat, and he smelled of fermented barley. His shifty eyes (and the bags under them) seemed to say he was up to something, and Lionel wondered if the man had ever smiled.

Their route was a dirt road, the kind that is created for a single and temporary purpose. They were deep in the heart of the country, at least a thousand miles from any coast. Rural woodlands dominated the landscape. Every now and then, they would come to a small clearing, but never once did they pass by any kind of town.

The forests gradually became less dense the further they went. Fewer and fewer trees were alive and upright while more and more were dead and fallen. These were not freshly felled trees but decaying ones, some that looked as though they had been laying there for over a hundred years. Lionel noticed how they were all resting in the same general direction, opposite the way the car was traveling. He was greatly intrigued.

"President Topramenov," Lionel began, "if I may ask—"

"Please, call me Serge," the politician interrupted.

"Very well," Lionel grinned. "If I may ask, why are there so many fallen trees all around? Lax logging laws, perhaps?"

"Not quite," Serge chuckled. "Are you familiar with the famous Tunguska Explosion?"

"I believe I've heard of it, yes," Lionel replied. "What was it exactly?"

"It was an enormous explosion that occurred over a century ago—still the largest impact event on or near earth in recorded history," said Serge, with a hint of pride. "It leveled some 80 million trees over an area of 2,000 square kilometers." Lionel took out his phone and converted the number to about 800 square miles, a unit which was easier for him to visualize. "Although no one knows for certain what caused the explosion, some believe it was an asteroid or comet."

"That could easily be determined by a simple test of the crater's soil," thought the physicist.

"Yes, except there *was* no crater," Serge returned, earning him a quizzical look from Lionel. "Others claim the explosion was caused by the air burst of some weapon that detonated before it hit the ground. The most generous estimates put the energy of the blast at a thousand times that of an atomic bomb."

"Impressive," Lionel observed, "but it would still be several years before nuclear energy was weaponized."

"And so it remains a mystery," Serge said with a satisfied shrug of his shoulders. "But hopefully not for much longer."

"Oh?" Lionel wondered. "Why is that?"

"At the time of your UN address," Serge began, "the Cooper criminal had already found three of the so-called elements. As we all know, he has since found a fourth. Correct me if I'm wrong, doctor, but if each of the earth's six landmasses is hiding one of these elements, which has been the case thus far, then that leaves only Australia and Eurasia."

"I would agree," said Lionel.

"I have been in frequent contact with leaders from several other Eurasian countries, all of whom agree we need to work together to beat Ret at his own game before we become the next Antarctica. We have identified several locations throughout our lands where Ret might strike next: ancient ruins, natural wonders, tourist attractions—every nation has some. And, for the nation of Russia, one of those is the Tunguska Explosion."

"Keep talking," Lionel beamed.

"A few months ago, I commissioned a team to go to the site of the explosion to see if they could learn anything that we didn't already know. In addition to the usual geologists, I included botanists, chemists, and experts from other professions that had never been included in a Tunguska expedition before. Given the staggering size of the site, this team decided to start their investigation at the epicenter and work their way out rather than start out and work in. They all agreed that if the explosion was not a random act of nature but actually had some special meaning, then there might be a reason why it occurred in the spot where it did."

"Smart team," Lionel remarked.

"They began at the epicenter," Serge said, "where they found a tree."

"Shocker," Lionel muttered to himself.

"But not just any tree," the president carried on. "No, this one was larger and older than all the others. When they attempted to take samples of it, however, they couldn't. Its bark was so tough that it broke their instruments—its roots so deep that no shovel could reach them. What's more, its limbs were barren of any leaves, and they couldn't find a single seed. The thing was indestructible, and it clearly did not want to be researched."

"Interesting," said Lionel.

"After hearing their report, I sent the team back but this time with much more substantial equipment. They tried all kinds of knives and saws, but each failed against the impenetrable wood, which simply bent the teeth of every blade without so much as leaving a scratch on the tree. Even chemicals were futile. Our only other option was to start digging."

"Your intention was to dig it out?" Lionel asked.

"Under it, around it—I don't know, what would *you* do?"

"To be honest," Lionel sighed, "it sounds like a job for one with the scars."

"That's what I'm afraid of," Serge confessed. "We're almost to the site now. We'll be able to see how things are coming along."

"I can't wait," said Lionel, his gaze returning to the window.

The landscape had changed. The ground was no longer littered with rotting tree trunks. The forest was alive and standing tall, which meant they were nearing the epicenter.

And then the car stopped. Through the trees, Lionel could see why. A few yards ahead, the dirt road took a nosedive. It seemed they were parked near the edge of some kind of cliff.

Serge got out of the car and began to walk toward the edge. Lionel followed. When he reached the end of the forest, he was amazed at what he saw.

They were standing on the ledge of a massive excavation site. A giant hole in the ground, it was an open-pit mine, similar to the kind used for unearthing things like copper or diamonds. Like giant stairs, the sides of the pit had been terraced, each level acting as either an access road or a pit bench. The many workers resembled tiny ants, and the beeping and honking of backhoes and dump trucks echoed against the tiered walls. Load after load of waste rock was being hauled away. It was like peering into the Roman Colosseum.

And there, in the center of it all, stood the tree. In a word, it was striking—a marvelous mixture of beauty, majesty, and terror. Unlike most trees with their straight trunks and smooth stems, this one was gnarled and twisted, like many strands of taffy spun together. Its few but fibrous limbs snaked outward like great tentacles, bent and contorted in the most unpredictable manner. With branches so sharp and pointed that they appeared to have been whittled, this tree's bark *was* its bite. The wood was light in color, a combination of soft yellows and slight browns, with occasional dark streaks, the bark so riveted and sinuous so as to have been shaped with a thick-bristled paintbrush. There were loops in its boughs, corners in its curves, yet not a single leaf or needle was to be found.

Already large in stature, the tree appeared even grander now that some of its roots had been exposed. Like the legs of a great bridge, these thick and sturdy roots fanned out in all directions, not one of whose ends had been reached. With the arch and awe of brontosaurus necks, the underground system served as a sort of ribcage that protected the tree's main taproot, which shot straight down from the trunk into the farthest reaches of the earth.

Against such a solitary backdrop, the great tree commanded attention and silenced discussion. Its shape told of slow growth, and its structure bespoke of ripe age. Built to last, it seemed the living thing could withstand anything, from the driest drought to the greediest lumberjack. No matter who you were, whether you loved it or hated it, there was no denying you had to respect it.

"So what do you think, doctor?" Serge asked, brimming with pride.

"I think it's very good," Lionel answered, "for a preventative measure, that is."

"What do you mean?" Serge questioned, sounding a bit deflated.

"Your determination is commendable, president. Your idea to outsmart Ret and beat him to the punch is creative. And there's no question you are not afraid to throw your resources behind that which you strongly believe in. But," Lionel leaned toward him, "how does any of this stop Mr. Cooper?"

"Well…uh," Serge groped to defend his efforts, "if, in fact, this tree is—"

"And what if it's not?" Lionel butted in. "This is not a time for ifs, my friend. When it comes to the elements, the Oracle gets straight to the point. It doesn't mess around, and neither does Ret. In fact, *he* could excavate this entire pit with a mere wave of his hand." Serge's eyes widened at the thought.

"Then what do you suggest we do?" he put forth, feeling a bit put out. "You don't expect us to just abandon this entire operation, do you?"

"Of course not," Lionel advised. "Keep on digging, full steam ahead. You've already come this far, it'd be a shame to stop now. Besides, whether or not that tree has anything to do with Ret and the elements, it is still a mystery worth figuring out."

Relieved, Serge asked, "Then what of Ret?"

Lionel took a deep breath before proceeding with his recommendation. "The United Nations is looking for something more direct in the fight against Ret. We're asking world leaders to aggressively pursue him, not passively wait for him. If we don't make the first move, then he surely will, and we will all suffer for it. We need to hit him where it hurts, cut off his strongholds, paralyze his plans."

"What do you have in mind?"

"Cooper's unofficial headquarters—his base of operations, if you will—is a state-of-the-art facility in the southeastern United States," Lionel explained. "He and his associates call it Coy Manor, named after Ret's right-hand man Benjamin Coy. This is where they devise all their plots and store all their supplies—boats and planes, computers and electronics, even miraculous inventions called subsuits and black mirrors. Its loss would all but ensure our victory." Then, as if confirming what Serge was already assuming, Lionel declared, "The Manor must be destroyed."

"What role would Russia be expected to play in this endeavor?" Serge inquired.

"The United Nations has neither the manpower nor the firepower to successfully carry out such an attack," Lionel said. "We need troops, arms, planes, ships— whatever you feel you can offer in the quest to save the world from Ret."

"What would be the nature of this attack? Air? Land? Sea?"

"Sea," came the quick reply. "The Manor is on an island, right off the mainland but also right on the ocean. Thus, we believe it would be in our best interest to launch a naval attack."

"Do you expect the Manor will fight back?" Serge interrogated. "Are they capable of retaliation?" To be honest, he was wary of the whole idea and was searching for an excuse to stay out of it.

"Doubtful. The only problem I foresee is if Ret resorts to using his powers. Even then, he does not have power over water yet, which is another reason why a naval attack is so advantageous as opposed to land or air, both of which Ret can control. But if I know Ret, he's not a fighter. He never uses his abilities to harm people."

"How does the American cabinet feel about instigating a battle on their own soil?" Serge continued to probe.

"They're not exactly fond of the idea," Lionel admitted, "but they know the UN and many of its member nations are supportive of it, so I'm sure they'll come around."

Serge had run out of questions, all of which had been expertly fielded by his guest. It was time to make a decision.

After a brief pause, he sighed and said, "I'm sorry, Dr. Zarbock, but I cannot pledge my support to such a campaign as of yet. Let me discuss it with my colleagues, and then I'll get back to you."

With disappointment, Lionel put his hand on the politician's shoulder and said, "I understand." They both made for the car.

The journey back to the airstrip started out in total silence. Both men tried to appear dejected—the president because his excavation efforts had been spurned, the physicist because his invitation had been declined. But both of them were merely faking it, for Serge had tried to use the tree as leverage in order to mask the real reason why he was digging it up, and Lionel had a backup plan that he was sure would work.

After a few more minutes, Lionel, who always got his way, pounced.

"You don't happen to have a brother named Ivan, do you, Serge?" Lionel asked, suppressing his sly grin.

Greatly surprised, Serge replied, "Actually, I do."

"Does he have a speech impediment, by chance?" Lionel continued to wiggle the bait.

As if it touched on a sensitive subject, Serge nodded, "Yes."

"A lisp?"

"How do you know my brother?" Serge earnestly queried.

"I met him a few years ago," Lionel retold.

"Where?" Serge pressed. "I haven't heard anything from Ivan in many years."

"We met at Sunken Earth, that civilization underneath the Atlantic Ocean—you know, the one that Ret completely wiped out when he stole the earth element from them."

"What was my brother doing *there?*"

"Cooper and Coy took him there to help them with their scheme," Lionel beguiled. "Apparently, Coy had picked up Ivan a few years back and enlisted him as his personal servant."

"Where is Ivan now?" Serge wondered, as if eager for a reunion.

"I regret to inform you," Lionel said, looking Serge in the eye, "your brother is dead. Cooper and Coy abandoned him at Sunken Earth."

Despite his stone-faced demeanor, Serge's eyes welled up with tears. Lionel hoped his listener's clenched fists were evidence of a desire to avenge his late brother, and, as it turned out, they were.

By the time they arrived back at the helipad, the Russian president had pledged his country's full military arsenal in the cause to destroy Coy Manor.

THE KEEP'S SAKE

Mr. Coy had just finished visiting with a group of students in the Manor's auto shop when a member of his staff came rushing up to him.

"Hello, Lucy," Coy greeted her.

"Sir, there's a man swimming across the creek!" she urgently announced.

Concerned, Coy replied, "I tell you those protestors are getting bolder by the minute." He followed her to the nearest surveillance kiosk, where a series of screens showed continuous footage from many of the cameras that were hidden throughout the property.

"That's no protestor," Coy observed, finding the corresponding screen and zooming in on the man. "That's Stone!" Then, turning to Lucy, he instructed, "Quick, find Ret and tell him to meet me there right away." The two promptly departed.

Stone had already come ashore and trekked several yards toward the Manor when Mr. Coy confronted him.

"Afternoon, Stone," came his stiff greeting. Even though Ret insisted the former principal was a changed man, Coy still had his doubts.

A bit out of breath, Lester said soberly, "Ben, there's something I need to show you."

"Go right ahead," Coy returned, still untrusting. "Show me."

"Not here," Stone told him. "I don't have it with me."

Just then Ret arrived.

"Mr. Stone!" Ret rejoiced. "I've been wondering where you've been." Then, upon realizing his former foe was soaking wet, he asked, "Did you swim here?"

"I did," Stone answered, happy to see Ret. He turned back to Coy and said, "I need you to come to my house—to the Keep."

Wary, Coy glanced at Ret and stated, "Only if Ret comes with me." Ret looked confused, unsure of what was going on.

"By all means," Stone agreed.

"But I'm *not* swimming there," Coy added emphatically.

Unwilling to let Stone into his home, Coy set out to find a hardly known and little used entrance into the Manor's underground hangar. The first task was to locate a good-sized and half-buried rock that was not too far away. With both feet planted against the natural marker, he turned to his left and walked five paces, then turned left again and went ten paces, and finally turned left one more time and finished with another five paces. His path in the long grass created a large letter C. Next, he jumped in place a time or two, as if to make sure he had arrived at the right spot. The ground beneath his feet sounded hollow. Satisfied, he dug his fingers an inch or two into the sandy soil until he found a large circular handle and, pulling it, revealed a hidden trap door.

"After you," Coy called out to the two onlookers, inviting them to climb down the spiral staircase that led into the hangar.

"You're amazing," Ret remarked as he passed by Mr. Coy.

"I know," Coy boasted.

The staircase led them to the suspended driveway that hung above the rest of the hangar. There was a simple car there, the one Missy drove to take the youth to school and back each day. The trio piled in.

"Would you mind firing her up?" Coy requested of Ret. "I don't have the key on me." Ret used his power over metal to turn the ignition.

"You're amazing," Coy told him as the car roared to life.

"I know," Ret joked.

Flooring the gas pedal, Coy sent the sedan speeding toward the hangar's wall. Stone, who was expecting an impending crash (as would any normal passenger), gripped the backseat and held on for dear life, but, as always, a wall parted where you'd never expect it to, and the car safely passed through to the other side. The submerged bridge emerged from the waters of the creek, and the car began to make its way to the mainland.

Unfortunately, the appearance of the passageway aroused the mob that was still encamped on the other shore. They rushed to their feet, grabbing whatever ammo they could find. As Coy's vehicle rolled onto Alley Street, it was assailed by all kinds of objects: empty cans, seaweed, large eggs, soft fruit, even a roll of toilet tissue. When a small rock created a nice nick in the windshield, Ret repaired the glass subconsciously.

"I see you're not too popular these days," Stone pointed out.

"They'll thank us later," the driver asserted.

Mr. Coy didn't need directions to their destination on Skidaway Island. As they approached the house, Coy solicited Ret's services yet again.

"Do you see a force field around the property, Ret?" he asked.

"Yeah, how could anyone miss it?" Ret responded. Coy rolled his eyes. With his power over energy, Ret could see the otherwise invisible dome that protected the entire lot, electrical currents zigzagging across it in all directions.

"Would you mind parting it?" Coy besought. With ease, Ret not only created a gap in the fatal barrier but also pushed opened the metal gate.

"You two are quite a team," Stone commented as they arrived in the driveway.

"If you think that's cool," Ret replied, "watch this." Without making a sound, Ret influenced the energy in the air immediately around himself to create a force field of his own. Though mostly invisible, Stone could see the empty space around Ret's body rippling like waves of heat rising above hot asphalt. Mr. Coy cautiously reached to test the protective barrier's strength.

"Yikes!" Coy shouted, quickly pulling his hand back. It felt like he had just inserted his finger into an electrical socket.

"Just something I've been working on lately," Ret stated with a coy grin as he relinquished his control on the air.

The Stone residence was in a state of ill repair these days. The hedges needed trimming and the grass mowing. The plants in the porch's hanging baskets had turned to powder, and the rocking chairs were too entangled in cobwebs to even sway in the light breeze.

"I know what I'm going to buy you for Christmas, Lester," Coy jabbed as they all helped to brush away a large pile of leaves just to get to the front door. "A rake."

"I never come in this way," Stone explained.

"Have you been here at all since we got back from Canada?" Ret wondered.

"Oh yes, I came that very same day," Stone said. "I figured Lye had already seized control of the Keep, but to my surprise he hadn't. In fact, there were no signs that he or any of his cronies had even been here since I left, which makes me wonder if he's up to something. He would stop at nothing to prevent the Keep from falling out of his hands. But now that I'm in possession of it again, it would be nigh impossible for him to regain it. That's why I returned immediately—for the sake of keeping the Keep."

The front door creaked open with all the creepiness of a haunted house. The late afternoon sun cast eerie shadows on the living room's dark walls. The men's footsteps left prints in the soft, underused carpet, and the smell of dust filled their nostrils. Ret's heart churned when he saw a picture of the late Virginia Stone on the bookcase. He felt to stand in front of it so that her surviving spouse wouldn't see, as if Lester didn't already know it was there, but of course the widower glanced at it as he strode by. Old habits die hard, but, unfortunately, this one never would.

Lester marched directly to the large grandfather clock against the wall. He gently pulled open the glass door and pushed the pendulum aside, then stepped inside and disappeared from view. Mr. Coy, having been a guest (albeit an uninvited one) in the Stone's home once before, followed after Lester, turning back to beckon Ret who was slightly puzzled to see his two associates climbing into a clock.

Once inside, Ret watched as Stone fiddled with the controls, which were not an array of push buttons but the face of a small clock. Stone's manipulation of the hour, minute, and second hands meant nothing to Ret, but it set the people-mover in motion. Down they went, through darkness for a few moments, until they arrived at the first floor.

Ret stepped out into a very vast and entirely empty room. It was in the shape of a decagon, with a long corridor beginning where each of the ten walls met. One of the walls had the number 2000 painted on it in big, black characters, and the wall to the right of it said 2010. The rest of the room looked largely unfinished. Without saying a word, Stone set off toward the corridor between the two numbered walls. His two companions followed.

Ret's insatiable thirst for knowledge slowed him down as he entered the corridor. To his left was the start of a long hallway, lined on both sides with nothing but doors—a couple hundred of them. The first door on the left had a date etched into its surface: January 1, 2000. Then Ret glanced at the first door on the right: December 31, 2000. As far as he could see, each door represented one day in the year 2000.

Ret turned around and peered down the hallway that began on the other side of the corridor. It stretched out in the opposite direction, each one of its doors pertaining to the year 2010. He then continued down the center corridor to the next two hallways: on the left was 2001, to the right was 2011.

Ret was becoming suspicious, even a bit uneasy. For one thing, the labyrinth was as silent as a tomb, and it didn't help that everything was white—from the ceiling to the floor and even every door—giving the whole place the look and feel of some sort of asylum from the after-life. Both curious and nervous, Ret resisted the urge to open any doors and instead set out to rejoin his friends. He took a few more steps forward and saw the pair off to his left. Stone had stopped and was standing in front of a door near the other end of the hallway, with Coy not far behind. Ret followed after them.

"Are you sure you have the right year, Stone?" Mr. Coy asked. There was noticeable anxiety in his voice, as if he was approaching something unpleasant from the past. The further his feet took him into that year, the more unwilling his heart became.

His speed already reduced to a snail's pace, Coy stopped several feet before he got to Stone, reluctant to go any further.

"Come here, Ben," Stone softly called, still staring at the door in front of him.

At a rate of what seemed like one step per hour, Mr. Coy arrived at Stone's side and joined him in glaring at the door before them.

"Why have you brought me here?" Coy stated more than he asked, well aware of the date on the door. "This was the day—"

"I know," Stone interrupted. "I need to show you something."

Stone reached toward the door, turning back the clock while simultaneously turning the knob, every click of whose gears could be heard throughout the entire year. He pushed the door open and waited for Mr. Coy to enter first, which took a few moments. After standing in the darkness for a time, Coy pulled the ripcord to turn on the fluorescent bulb that he knew would illuminate the past.

It was like standing in a life-sized scrapbook, its decorated pages plastered like wallpaper and completely covering every square inch of all four walls. There were newspaper articles about cleanup efforts after a tornado in Oklahoma City, the rising death toll from a bombing in Chechnya, and counter-terrorism victories in the Middle East. A medical mask hung next to a map that pinpointed each location of the day's confirmed cases of SARS. There was a running list of nations that had joined the European Union, with Lithuania as the most recent. Enlarged versions of the United States Treasury's newly released $20 bill had been well-examined for flaws in its new anti-counterfeit features. Talk of tax cuts and anthrax could be found in magazine cutouts along the baseboards. Someone had become a member of the 500 home-run club. Pictures of the phases of a lunar eclipse were pinned next to a study about the overfishing of the world's oceans.

Ready to return to the present, Mr. Coy began to turn toward the door until he felt Stone's hand on his shoulder. The previous principal pointed to a small filing cabinet in the far corner of the small room. Coy dismally looked at Stone who only nodded encouragingly. Coy trudged to the cabinet and opened the top drawer.

A collection of hanging files filled the drawer, each one devoted to a certain subject: marriages, patents, arrests, inventions, lawsuits, awards, births, and—

—deaths.

Mr. Coy moved to shut the drawer. Stone stopped him.

"Why are you doing this to me?" Coy asked, understandably annoyed. "I've moved on."

"Trust me," Stone importuned. Coy glared wide-eyed at such a request from his former foe.

Against his wishes, Coy reopened the drawer, pulled out the contents of the folder labeled "Deaths," and began to sift through the alphabetized pages. After the death certificate of one Michael Clements and following the obituary of a Suzanne Copeland, there it was: the news story announcing the passing of Helen Coy.

Ben couldn't help but smile a little when he saw the image of his deceased wife. It was his favorite picture of her, wearing that striped blouse he had given to her for her birthday the year before. She had her hair up, which was not how she preferred to wear it but did so anyway because she knew he liked it. Ben could even see the lines in her forehead that she loathed but he loved because he thought of them as wrinkles in time, reminders of the years they had spent growing older together.

But his smile turned to a frown as his eyes moved from photo to text. He knew it all too well, so he just skimmed it, picking up bits and pieces: summa cum laude, world renowned, humanitarian efforts, adored by all, loving wife, caring mother, fell ill, unknown causes.

Coy closed the folder, but Stone quickly inserted his hand to save the place. He pulled out Helen's story and flipped it over. There was a small envelope stapled to the back.

Coy squinted at Stone with curiosity, then took the page and opened the envelope. He found a small slip of paper inside, one he had met before. He took it out and read the phrase that had haunted him for so many years:

How could you do this to me?

With familiar sorrow, Coy looked down and said submissively to Stone, "Can I go now?"

"Look inside again," Lester bade him, referring to the envelope.

Coy sighed and looked once more. This time, he found a second slip of paper, on which was written the following message in Helen's ill-stricken handwriting:

To the love of my life:
Please use this to cure the world.
Yours forever and always,
H

The message was followed by a brief but complex scientific formula containing the alphabetic symbols of certain elements with their corresponding coefficients and subscripts, which Mr. Coy knew constituted the molecular structure of the mysterious liquid that they had encountered at the uncharted island now known as Waters Deep.

Baffled, Coy gaped at Stone. "What *is* this?" he pressed with great interest, holding out the second slip of paper.

"It's the real message she was going to give to you that day," Stone answered, "but Dr. Cross stole it and replaced it with one he had forged." He pointed at the first slip of paper. "Cross is a fraud. Lye told him to poison Helen once she decoded the formula, to steal it so he'd have it, and then do something terrible to keep you away from the Deep." Shaken up by retelling the tragic tale, Stone finished his plea for forgiveness by tearfully saying, "It wasn't your fault, Ben. I'm sorry you thought it was all this time."

Mr. Coy's head fell as far as it could go. It didn't take long until his body began to convulse from the shedding of heavy tears. The restrained whimpers of a grown man broke the silence in the little room. His arms fell to his sides, and he wept openly.

When a third tear fell from Coy's fallen face, Stone began to produce more of his own. For all their differences, the two of them had something painfully in common: each man's wife had been murdered by Lye. Though initially goaded by guilt, the sorrow that Stone felt toward Coy these days was fueled by empathy, now that he knew what it was like to lose his own wife. He had gained compassion by the things which he had suffered. After a few moments, Lester grasped Ben's shoulder to console him as they cried together, one weeping widower to another.

But Mr. Coy was not shedding tears of sadness.

No, his were tears of joy. When he at last looked up, a wonderful smile filled his flushed face. His bright countenance was awash with confident confirmation that what he had known in his heart had been right all along. There was no anger in his appearance—no malice in his mien—but instead, true love and immense relief. Not an ounce more of happiness could have been squeezed into his bright-eyed and tear-streaked expression.

"Thank you," Coy whispered as he embraced Stone. "Thank you." He set the folder on top of the filing cabinet and left the drawer ajar. Then he walked out of the room shoulder-to-shoulder with Stone and shut the door. Ret was standing close by with a broad smile on his face, having overheard the dialogue and seen the documents with his ears and eyes of airwaves.

"So," a jubilant Coy clapped, "what else do you have to show us, Stone?"

"Actually, I—"

Suddenly, the piercing sound of a loud siren filled the confines of the Keep. Stone's eyes furrowed in dreadful disbelief, well aware of what the alarm meant.

"What is it?" Coy inquired of the perplexed ex-principal. "What's wrong? Are we in danger?"

"Follow me!" Stone shouted over the noise.

In a dash, they ran back to the main room and boarded the elevator. Stone placed his index finger on the face of the control clock and began to rapidly spin all three of its hands counterclockwise. The elevator instantly descended. Revolution after revolution, Stone's finger was working around the clock, as if he was rewinding it. Wherever they were headed, it was obviously going to be the end of the road.

Ret kept his sights set on the scene in front of him. Every second, the elevator was plunging deeper and deeper into the Keep. Each level they passed by took them yet another century further into the past. There was only enough time to catch a glimpse of the years on the walls: 1970, 1870, 1770. He blinked and missed the 1600s. The ringing of the alarm refused to be diminished with the passage of time. Very soon, they had plummeted past a full millennium. Yet their fall continued.

A few moments later, the scene went dark. The elevator slowed, then finally stopped and opened. Stone rushed forward and burst through a set of double doors, entering a room that was small in size but big on electronics. In the middle of the main instrument panel, a red button was blinking to the rhythm of the still-audible alarm. Stone immediately smashed the flashing button, which shut off the siren and turned on a video. The three men focused their attention on what seemed to be streaming footage from a live broadcast, which began playing on the large, glass screen on the far wall. Ret was about to get his first glimpse into Waters Deep.

CHAPTER 4

DEEP TROUBLE

It was a cold, dark room. Obviously underground, the walls had been crudely carved out of sheer rock, the ceiling left unfinished like a cave. A heavy wetness hung in the air, making everything moist and damp. In the center of the room sat a large table, much longer than it was wide, its metal surface perpetually plagued by a layer of condensation. A floral arrangement served as centerpiece, consisting solely of black Venus flytraps, whose red-colored veins and violent-looking teeth were a perfect match for the dismal décor of Waters Deep.

There was one chair at the table that was bigger and better than all the others, rivaling a throne with its high back and oversized armrests. It came as no surprise to find it positioned at the head and occupied by Lye. Seated in the first chair on his right was Dr. Victor

Cross, his thin lips too scared to smile on account of his austere demeanor. Across from Cross sat Commander Jaret, doing his best to still appear allegiant to Lye. Three other people were in attendance: a heavily-decorated military general, a high-powered business-woman, and an Oriental man who looked very old and just as wise. A fourth individual was there, not in person but as a hologram.

Cross cordially began, "We thank you all for coming to this very—"

"Enough with the pleasantries," Lye sneered. "Don't make me gag."

"Very well," Cross respectfully submitted. "I turn the time over to you, Lord Lye."

"Status reports!" Lye ordered. "Ladies first."

The businesswoman immediately responded, "Ret has not traveled outside the Tybee area since he returned from Antarctica. As far as we know, neither has Coy, though we all know he's harder to keep track of."

"Excuses," Jaret muttered, trying to sound critical.

"Any new scars?" Lye pressed unappreciatively.

"Yes," the woman was pleased to report. "My sources at the school tell me a new scar has indeed appeared."

"Was it the Deep?!" Lye asked emphatically. "Was it the scar for the Deep?!"

"No," she was happy to tell him, as if her life

depended on it. Lye seemed extremely relieved.

"Still," Cross mumbled to Lye, "that means the clock is ticking with the tree. Now it's only a matter of time before Ret discovers it."

"Indeed," Lye grumbled. Suddenly eager to learn the progress of the excavation of said tree, Lye moved on. "President Topramenov," he called out to the hologram across the table, "how was the inspection visit from Zarbock?" Under his breath, Lye added just loudly enough for Jaret to hear, "Lionel *used* to be my prisoner, you know." Jaret looked down in shame.

"It went precisely as we had hoped," said the image of Serge, who was being televised from his private office in Russia. "I showed him the excavation site, told him the phony explanation for it, and he bought it."

"Did he tell you to stop the operation?" Cross wondered.

"No, quite the opposite," Serge reported.

"Then it's full steam ahead," Lye mandated. "Now that the scar has appeared, we must get inside before Ret does. I've been trying to penetrate that blasted tree for centuries, and this is the closest I've ever been to doing so. Tell your men to work day and night. Increase the workforce. No breaks. Double shifts."

"It shall be done," Serge obeyed.

Next, Lye glared at the military general, who

understood it was his turn to report.

"Since we last met," the military man spoke up, "nine more nations have pledged their support in the cause to attack Coy Manor, which brings the total to 34."

"A decent number," Lye said, unimpressed.

"The nation of Cuba has allowed us to begin stock-piling supplies within their borders," the general continued. "We already have a sizeable naval fleet moored off their shores, with more ships arriving every day." Then, with hesitation, he asked, "Any idea when exactly the attack will take place, my lord?"

"*I* am the one who asks the questions—not you!" Lye growled. "Like I told you before, you are to have everything in place as if the attack were to be carried out tomorrow."

"As you wish," the general replied.

Now annoyed, Lye progressed to the final report, addressing the Oriental man by asking, "And what of Stone's whereabouts?"

The sagacious elder methodically closed his eyes, as if communicating with some unseen realm, before slowly answering, "He is at the Keep." The military general glanced absurdly at the old man as if he was some sort of soothsaying crackpot.

"Just as I thought," Lye said with some displeasure. "Stone must be eliminated. He knows too much."

"Perhaps we should attack the Manor and the Keep

simultaneously?" Jaret figured he should say.

"Of course not!" Lye shot back, pounding his cane on the hard floor, creating a small spark. "The Keep must be kept intact at all costs. It is far too valuable." Then, with a concluding sigh, Lye said to all of them in his typical, disgruntled tone, "There is no room for error in the tasks that I have given each of you. I expect perfection. Meeting adjourned!" In a huff, he rose from his seat and strode out of the chamber.

There was silence in the room for a few moments. The businesswoman watched one of the Venus flytraps close its fangs on a large moth. The general got up to leave after looking over at the Oriental man and finding him with his eyes closed, arms outstretched, and fingers pinched, presumably in some sort of trance. Before exiting, Cross terminated the Russian president's hologram. When everyone else had filed out of the meeting room, Jaret casually walked around the table, unhurriedly pushing in each chair. Then he discreetly waved at his friends through the hidden camera he had set up and shut it off.

O   O   O

Back at the Keep, the screen went blank. Sitting at the control panel, Stone waited until he was sure the audio connection had been broken before saying, "So that explains why communication from the Deep was reengaged—it was Jaret who did it." Then, speaking from experience, Stone observed, "Dangerous move."

When no one replied, Stone turned around in his chair to make sure Ret and Coy were still there. They were: while Ret was staring at Coy, Coy was staring into space, stunned to have learned of Lye's plan to attack the Manor—and at any given moment, too. He was beyond belief, to say the least.

Knowing what was troubling him, Ret sheepishly asked, "The defense system that you and Thorne installed should be enough to counter an attack—right, Mr. Coy?"

In all seriousness, Coy glanced at Ret and shook his head in a most hopeless manner. "Not an attack of this scale," he said.

"What should we do?" Stone wondered.

After a brief moment of contemplation, Coy made up his mind and made for the door. "Come on!" he instructed.

"Where are we going?" Ret asked as he and Stone quickly followed.

"We've got to evacuate the Manor," Coy explained, "immediately." He pried open the elevator doors and began to spin the hour, minute, and second hands in a clockwise direction, causing them to fast-forward through time.

"Where will we all go?" Ret inquired.

"Here, to the Keep," Coy expounded. Although he had suddenly become very anxious, it seemed Mr. Coy had already accepted the likelihood that he was going to lose the Manor and that there was nothing he could do about it. "The Keep will be our home now." Despite the gravity of the situation, Mr. Coy seemed to be holding himself together quite well—until...

"Ben," Stone rebutted, "I'm not so sure relocating to the Keep is the best—"

"Then what do you suggest we do?!" Coy snapped, glaring Stone square in the face. "Live on the streets? Rent out a hotel? Be fugitives for the rest of our lives?" Stone swallowed hard. "We'd be in danger wherever we went. The Keep is the safest place for us now. Lye said it himself: he would never attack it."

"I see your point," Stone said.

No matter how quickly Mr. Coy spun the control clock, the elevator ascended at the same speed. With the centuries flashing by, Ret kept an eye on Mr. Coy. He knew the man must be panicking inside, yet it wasn't until they passed the sixth century A.D. when Ret saw a teardrop cascade down Mr. Coy's cheek. It reminded him of the time in Sunken Earth when his late butler Ivan was killed and Mr. Coy refused to turn back despite Ret's yearning to do so.

As soon as the elevator arrived at present day, Mr.

Coy bolted through the grandfather clock.

"You stay here, Stone," Coy told the homeowner on his way out the front door. "Do whatever you can to make room for us—all of us. My goal is to have everyone sleep here tonight."

"Understood," Stone said, already starting to rearrange furniture.

Just as he was about to fly down the front porch, Mr. Coy abruptly stopped. Following close behind, Ret nearly ran into him. Coy paused, as if he had forgotten to do something, then slowly turned around and walked back through the front door. He located Stone, who was moving a couch, and put his hand on his shoulder. Stone looked up, expecting more orders, but what he heard took him by surprise.

With a voice of tenderness, Coy said, "Thank you, my friend."

It was no small thing to hear Benjamin Coy refer to Lester Stone as his friend. Vindicated at last, all that the forgiven foe could do was smile, too overwhelmed to speak. Ret beamed from the doorway.

Then Coy hurried out the door and down the porch. He and Ret piled into the car and sped out of the driveway.

O   O   O

Soon after the meeting at Waters Deep, Commander Jaret began to make his usual rounds throughout the compound. He checked up on some subordinates, handled a couple of security issues, and barked a few orders. When it appeared things were running smoothly, he nonchalantly slipped away, headed for one place in particular.

The dungeon was the best-kept secret at Waters Deep. Like so many other things under Lye's control, no one really knew much about it even though it was practically right in their midst. Off-limits to virtually everyone, no one knew what it looked like, and only a few of the top-dogs even knew how to get into it. Fortunately, Jaret was one of those few.

He made his way to the north side of the complex, trying to look as natural as possible since he was well aware that every square inch of the facility was under constant surveillance. He was searching for one door in particular, the one he had seen Lye go through whenever he paid a visit to the dungeon (which was often). He strode up to it, pulled from his pocket a miniature stun gun that he kept on his keychain, and applied an electrical shock to the door to prompt it to open. He had seen Lye do the same with his cane on each occasion.

As soon as the door parted, a heavy mist spilled into the facility, more like cool steam than thick smoke.

Jaret tried to waft it away in order to see more clearly in front of him, but it refused to dissipate. Eventually, he took a wary step inside. The door shut behind him.

The commander found himself in a fog—literally. He brought his hand up to his face and could scarcely see it. His surroundings were not dark; in fact, they were much the opposite. But the incessant mist swallowed everything from view.

Jaret began to probe the ground with his foot in order to determine where he could safely go. Both to his left and in front of him, the floor abruptly ended in less than a yard. Such was not the case to his right, however, so he cautiously started in that direction.

The path maintained a very slight decline. Basically blind, he maintained constant contact with the wall at his right to keep his bearings and prevent him from wandering off. After creeping a few steps, he could feel the walkway growing narrower and narrower until he was forced to turn sideways, his back against the wall and the tips of his shoes hanging over the edge.

Shuffling along, Jaret slowly made his way down the ramp. As his eyes had been rendered useless, he relied on his other senses. The wall at his back was wet, the ledge at his feet slippery. He feared a misstep would send him to his death. He wondered if he should turn back, but then he started to hear noises. First it was an occasional moan, then the faint rattle of heavy chains.

He kept descending, dragging his shaky feet.

Eventually, his leading hand came to a vertical, iron bar. He instinctively wrapped his hand around it, relieved to have something to latch on to. He groped further and found more bars, at least a dozen of them, which stretched down to his feet but only about halfway up his chest. He figured he had arrived at the first prison cell. He turned around and crouched down as best he could, firmly gripping a bar with each hand.

"Hello?" Jaret softly called into the cell. When there was no answer, he gently tapped on one of the bars, creating a deep but minor echo.

A moment later, something moved within the chamber. Whatever it was—man or beast—it seemed to be in no rush as it made its way toward the front of the cell, pulling its chains behind it. Unsure of what to expect, Jaret gripped the bars more tightly. It sounded like the creature was dragging itself along the ground. Finally, a man's hand appeared a few inches above the floor, his fingers reaching for the bars and then grasping one. When he had done so, he breathed a tired sigh and let go of the bar, as if it had required all of his strength. His curled hand flopped to the ground, his arm falling outside the cell, a little before the elbow.

Jaret leaned forward as far as possible, pressing his face against the slick, wet bars. Whoever this person was, he was extremely old and frail. His skin was pasty white and somewhat soggy. He was breathing, but it was exceptionally slow, as if he might die at any moment.

"What do you want, Lye?" the man asked with scorn, his voice slow and raspy.

"Oh no, I'm not Lye," Jaret politely informed him.

After a brief pause, "Then who are you?"

"Jaret."

"Are you the same Jaret who works for Lye?"

The commander thought for a moment, then figured there might be cameras watching, and responded, "Yes."

"Oh," the man replied with disgust. "We've heard about *you*."

"I've come because I need your help," Jaret pled.

"I don't help my enemies," said the man coldly.

"It's not for me," Jaret petitioned. "It's for Ret."

The prisoner said nothing for a few seconds, but Jaret thought he saw a flicker of strength come into his emaciated hand, the fingers forming a soft fist.

"Ret Cooper?" the man asked.

"Yes," Jaret affirmed. "Have you heard of him?"

"Oh yes," the man said. "Say his name again."

Somewhat confused, Jaret stated, "Ret Cooper."

"Louder," the man urged with growing vitality.

Jaret did so.

"Louder!"

With all the force his voice box could summon,

Jaret yelled, "Ret Cooper!"

The name of Ret Cooper seemed to swirl the fog as it reverberated off the unseen walls of the dungeon. When the final resonance faded away, however, a new noise stirred the air. It started out small but grew—and grew. It was the sound of cheering—the roar of a crowd, thousands strong, each lending his or her voice to encourage their number-one fan. In that moment, Jaret got a small sense of the immense magnitude of the dungeon.

"How do you know Ret?" Jaret wondered of the man.

"Look at my hand," he said.

Jaret squatted down as far as he could go without falling off the precarious ledge. He raised the man's emaciated hand to his face. There, on the palm, were three scars, barely illuminated but identical to ones on Ret's hand.

Jaret gasped, "You're also one with scars?"

"We all are," the man told him.

"How many of you are there?"

"You're welcome to keep going and count us yourself," the man said, still leery of Jaret's motives.

"I would, but I don't have time right now," Jaret explained. "Ret's in trouble."

"He seems to be doing just fine to me," the man put forth. "He's already found four elements. That's more than I can say for myself."

"Me, too," a voice from the cell next-door chimed in.

"Plus, all of our fifth scars just recently appeared," the man observed.

"Yes, Lye already knows that," Jaret argued. "What can you tell me about this tree in Russia? And what is the sixth element?—where is it? And the relics? What purpose do they serve?"

Silence.

Then, from another neighboring cell, "Don't tell him."

And another, "He can't be trusted."

"Yes, I can!" Jaret affirmed, forgetting about the possible cameras.

"Then prove it," another joined in.

"Very well," Jaret dared them. "What do you want me to do?"

The man closest to him thought for a moment and then stated, "Bring us Lye's cane."

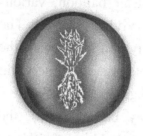

CHAPTER 5

SCARRED HEALTH

In a matter of a few days, Mr. Coy had turned the Manor into a ghost town. Once every student, staff member, plant, animal, and insect had been safely evacuated to the Keep, he focused on relocating as much of the nonliving capital as possible: dishes, furniture, electronics, linens, tools—and, of course, the hidden bust of his mother in the semicircular foyer. It was a tremendously tedious and time-consuming process (especially the dismantling of the carillon), but Mr. Coy considered it a blessing whenever he had at least one more day to save at least one more thing. Although he knew he couldn't take it all, he was certainly going to try.

The Keep was probably the only place on earth that could handle all that the Manor was throwing at it. The spacious grounds that surrounded Stone's mansion

house provided more than enough room to accommo-
date Coy's plane, helicopter, hot-air balloon, various
automobiles, and even the surviving CAVE. The
backyard lagoon, which eventually connected with the
ocean, proved to be a suitable spot for storing the yacht
and *USS Shamu,* among other things.

Elsewhere (which is to say underground), the
twenty-first century had been put on hold indefinitely to
make room for the present. The top-most level of the
Keep's archival labyrinth had been selected as the ideal
location for housing everyone since that floor was
largely unfinished. It was a task that Stone thought was
going to be impossible until he saw the Manor's staff
and students get right to work. The architects drew up
blueprints while the construction crew dug up dirt.
Carpenters labored alongside electricians, plumbers
among painters. Drapes were hung, rooms furnished,
and kitchens stocked. Everyone had a job to do,
according to his or her own talent, and no one
complained.

This was eye-opening to Stone, who served as the
unofficial supervisor of the relocation effort. When it
came to Coy Manor, he had always thought it was the
brick and mortar that were the nuts and bolts of the
whole operation—that the amazing facilities and
eccentric equipment were what produced such incredible results. But now he was realizing the real genius of

the Manor wasn't in a place but in its people—people who had been written-off by society but taken-on by Coy. It was precisely due to this second chance that they had been given why they so willingly took broken things and fixed them, found ugly sights and beautified them, sought out unproductive areas and reversed them— because, at one point, someone had done the same with them. And it warmed Stone's heart to find them so determined to keep that manner as they Manor-ed that Keep.

Still, Mr. Coy's preoccupation with salvaging his house left little time for other things: such as the fifth scar and some strange tree in Russia. When the scar first appeared, Ret had little idea what it meant (surprise, surprise). The closest thing he could compare it to was an ice-cream cone. However, based on what he learned from the meeting at Waters Deep, Ret was now all but certain the scar was a tree. He wished he could see it again, for the scar had since faded, and, as maddening as it was for him, he knew he had pretty much no control over when it would show itself once more.

It took a tragedy for the fifth scar to make its second appearance, namely the sudden and unexpected death of Peggy Sue, the longtime and much-loved director of the Center Street Orphanage. Although the 52-year-old woman had a few extra pounds to lose, she tried to live by the health advice of the day, which made her fatal heart attack all the more surprising. Word of her passing spread quickly throughout the small community, which offered its support to the overwhelmed assistant director. The orphans were understandably crushed, but no one took it harder than Leonard Swain. Peggy Sue had been like a mother to Leo, she being the one who had brought him home from the hospital after he was born. He knew, better than most, that death was a part of life, but the fact that this one had come so quickly made it all the more devastating.

Despite the rain, nearly every citizen of Tybee Island attended the funeral, which was preceded by a viewing. Ret watched as Leo approached the open casket. His forlorn face hadn't known a smile for days, and his eyes were still bloodshot from tear-filled nights. Ana stood next to him. He reached inside the coffin to hold the cold hand of his matriarchal figure one last time. When they moved on, the line of mourners resumed. Pauline paid her respects, followed by Mr. Coy and Paige.

Then it was Ret's turn. As soon as he saw Peggy Sue's dead body, his fifth scar came to life. His eyes widened, not from the sight of a creepy corpse but from the power pulsing in his pocketed palm. Given the terrible timing, he resisted the urge to inspect his hand. Still, the longer he stood at the casket, the more the scar throbbed. It was all he could do not to look at it right then and there. When his turn was finally over, he stepped away, eager to engage in a different viewing.

Unfortunately, the throbbing immediately ceased, and the scar became indiscernible once again. It went as quickly as it had come.

Ret and his scars were in a love-hate relationship. Although they had been together for years, Ret still had no say as to when they came around or how long they stuck around (until he collected that scar's element, of course). This was incredibly maddening for a go-getter such as himself. It was as if the scars were playing a game, the one called patience. But, as with any relationship, he had to trust them.

As usual when death comes around, Peggy Sue's passing spurred honest reflection among some of those who knew her, especially Ana. She became concerned for Pauline who, in many respects, was very similar to the late director: both women were the same age and ethnicity, and both had similar body types, backgrounds, and lifestyles—not to mention a slight addiction to sweet tea and all things fried. The thought of suddenly losing her mother prompted Ana to become seriously concerned about the topic of health.

She quickly realized, however, that there was no shortage of information on the subject. She read all kinds of studies and blogs—journals and papers— written by everyone from the most intelligent college grad to the most shredded gym rat, but she found they agreed on very little and usually just contradicted each other. She marveled how every food could be both good and bad depending on who you asked, and if she wanted a food to be healthy or unhealthy, she could find so-called evidence to support it either way. Just when she thought she was starting to get a good grasp of things, she would come across something else that would throw it all into question: good fats versus bad fats, clean carbs versus dirty carbs, organic or not organic, vegan or vegetarian. She was more confused by what GMO meant than what HMO was, she could hardly pronounce the names of artificial sweeteners, and she was still unsure of her stance on high-fructose corn syrup. What's more, the ever-increasing dos and don'ts of ingredient lists were making eating a nightmare.

In the midst of this war of words and tumult of opinions, Ana was certain of only one thing: when asked what was healthy, her answer was, "No one really knows." Sure, everyone and their dog claimed to have the answer, but each self-defined description differed from the next. Tenets were influenced by what sold the most products, and principles were swayed by so-and-so celebrity's diet. The only fact in the folly of fitness was that the truth of what was healthy had become a mystery. And so, Ana resigned to let the scientists and meatheads keep battling it out.

In the meantime, Ana asked Pauline to at least go and see a doctor.

"Just for a checkup," Ana told her.

"Ana, my dear, I'm very healthy," Pauline reassured her.

"Yeah, probably, but isn't that what we all thought about Peggy Sue?" Ana asked gravely.

"Okay," Pauline obliged, unable to refute her daughter's point. "What could it hurt?"

The next time a doctor came as a guest speaker to instruct Coy's medical students, Ana asked him if he wouldn't mind examining her mother, which he was happy to do. The doc's recommendation was clear: although Pauline didn't appear to have any major health issues, she could benefit from going on a diet and getting more exercise.

"I think I'll get a second opinion," Pauline said later, her ego a bit bruised.

The next day, she went into town, got that second opinion, and the diagnosis came back even harsher than the first: improving her eating and exercise habits wasn't just a good idea, it was essential.

"I guess I *do* need to start going to the gym again," Pauline admitted to Ana after sharing the news with her.

"There you go, Mom!" Ana cheered her on. "Go pump some iron!"

"Maybe," Pauline chuckled, "but I mainly just like to swim."

One fall day, Mr. Coy took a break from "Operation: Move the Manor" to resolve a few pressing matters. First and foremost, he was worried about Leo, who wasn't coming around much these days. The obvious reason was distance since the Keep was even harder for the boy to get to than the Manor, but Mr. Coy wondered if a less-obvious reason might be depression, brought on by Peggy Sue's passing and kept on by the plight of an orphan. The other concern, which was always on his mind, pertained to the fifth element, whose procurement he still wished to somehow make a priority despite being tied down in relocating the Manor. Fortunately, he had an idea that he hoped would solve both issues simultaneously.

That afternoon, Mr. Coy paid a visit to Tybee Island's orphanage. He climbed the stone steps that led into the old building, presented a bouquet of flowers to the beleaguered assistant director, and then asked to speak with Leonard Swain.

"Hello, sir," Leo said in a melancholy tone.

"Hello, son," Coy greeted him warmly. Leo always liked when Mr. Coy called him 'son.' It never failed to cheer up the fatherless lad. "I haven't seen you very much lately. You doing okay?"

"Been better," came the reply.

Mr. Coy put his hand on Leo's shoulder and told him tenderly, "I know it's hard when someone you love dies. Want to know something that has helped me?" Leo nodded. "Staying busy, which is why I've come here today: I have an invitation to extend to you." Leo looked intrigued. "How would you like to come and live with all of us at the Keep?" Leo's face brightened up a bit. "There's something I need you to do there."

"What's that, sir?" Leo asked.

"I'm a little strapped for time right now," Coy explained, "so I need you to help me do some research. Ret and I recently learned there is a tree in Russia that is somehow linked to the fifth element. Lye has known about it for a while and has been trying to get inside. What I need you to do is search every room in the Keep for information about this tree and why Lye is so interested in it. Start from present day and work backwards in time, then let me know as soon as you find anything. Deal?"

"Deal!" Leo agreed, excited about the assignment.

"Great," said Coy. "Now, go pack your things. I'll take care of the paperwork."

Leo ran off but then abruptly stopped, as if he remembered something. He slowly turned around and asked, "But what about my friends? The other orphans are like my family."

"You can come back and visit whenever you'd

like," Coy smiled. "And tell them they are welcome at the Keep any time."

Pleased, Leo took a few hurried steps away before suddenly realizing something else and stopping again. He ran back to Mr. Coy and embraced him.

"Thank you, Mr. Coy," Leo whispered.

Tearfully, Mr. Coy replied, "You're welcome, son."

O   O   O

With so many other things going on in life, Ret couldn't help but feel a little foolish being at school these days. Given his thoughts of drifting continents and global protests, he was struggling to concentrate on the current lecture in class:

"There are three main nutrients in nature," the teacher began. "Proteins, carbohydrates, and fats." Ret wondered if he should be writing any of this down. He glanced at Paige, who was feverishly taking notes, and figured he could just borrow hers if he needed to.

"Proteins are made up of things called amino acids," the teacher continued. "They help with many bodily functions, including the building and repairing of muscle tissue. Some amino acids cannot be made by the body and must be obtained from food; these are called essential amino acids. Good sources of protein include meat, cheese, and eggs." Ret watched as Paige captured every word.

"Carbohydrates are sugars. Some are simple (like candy and soda) while others are more complex (like potatoes and whole grains). The body uses carbs as a source of energy." Ret yawned and put his elbow on his desk to hold up his head.

"Fats are also a source of energy and come in different kinds: saturated fats can be found in dairy products and red meat, while *un*saturated fats can be found in nuts and oils. Fats are composed of fatty acids, some of which have been classified as essential fatty acids because they, like essential amino acids from proteins, must be obtained from food."

The teacher then displayed a graphic: "This is the Food Guide Pyramid, introduced by the United States government in 1992." Ret liked pictures. He picked up his pencil and started drawing what he saw on the screen.

"As you can see," the teacher explained, "the pyramid tells us our daily diet should consist of six main food groups. On the bottom is the bread, cereal, rice, and pasta group. It is the largest group, and it is recommended that we consume six to eleven servings per day." Ret drew a big loaf of bread in the bottom of his pyramid, followed by the numbers 6-11. "Next is the vegetable group at three to five servings per day." Ret drew a carrot, 3-5. "Close behind is the fruit group, two to four servings." Apple, 2-4. "Moving up the pyramid, we come to two smaller groups. There's the milk, yogurt, and cheese group at two to three servings, and then there's the meat, poultry, fish, dry beans, eggs, and nuts group, also at two to three servings." Ret was getting hungry. "And finally, in this little part at the very top of the pyramid, we find the fats, oils, and sweets group, which we are told to eat sparingly." Ret didn't know what to draw for fats, and he figured he'd spare himself from writing out the long word *sparingly*.

The teacher advanced to a new graphic: "Then in 2005, the government came out with MyPyramid." The image still featured a pyramid shape, but the food groups were more vertical wedges than horizontal quadrants, and a stick-figure man was seen climbing the left-hand steps of the pyramid. "The food groups are listed along the bottom, and each is color-coordinated in the pyramid." Ret scanned the food groups along the bottom: the grains group was still the largest, colored in orange; vegetables in green and milk in blue were next in size, both smaller than grains but about equal to each other; the fruit group, in red, came next, followed by the even smaller purple group of meat and beans.

A student at the very front of the room raised his hand and asked, "What does the yellow wedge represent?"

Ret hadn't seen a yellow wedge. He looked harder. There, squished between the fruit and milk wedges, was a tiny sliver of yellow. It was difficult to see and wasn't even labeled. The teacher quickly said it represented fats and oils, then moved on.

"Then, most recently in 2011," the teacher resumed, "the government unveiled yet another concept on the subject of health. They call it MyPlate." A third picture appeared on the screen, this time of a cute little place-setting with a fork on the left. The main plate was divided into four sections that were all roughly equal in size: grains and vegetables vying for first, and fruits and protein tying for second. Then, at the top right of the main plate, there was a small side dish that was for dairy.

Wait. That only made five food groups when there should have been six. Ret counted again. Something was missing. Where was the sixth food group?

Ret searched the MyPlate graphic for the sixth food group, assuming it had been squeezed into a small and inconspicuous crevice again. But the fats and oils food group was nowhere to be found. It was missing.

Without any warning, a surge of energy rushed into Ret's right hand, enough that he broke his pencil into three pieces. A few of his classmates glared at him. Once they had turned away, Ret stole a glance at his palm, with Paige and Ana leaning over to have a look. The fifth scar had come alive again.

If the scar was indeed a tree, then it was a very peculiar looking tree. It had the general shape of a figure-8—either that or the mathematical symbol for infinity, though standing upright rather than on its side. The top half was bushy—not so much with leaves but with needles—and was more pointed at the tip before it fanned out in its midsection and became more slender again as it neared the trunk. The trunk seemed to twist as it plunged underground. The tree's roots made up the bottom half of the scar. Like the top, they swelled in the middle before narrowing until they eventually came together at the bottom.

All in all, the symbol was easily the most detailed scar so far, hands down. Somewhat of an artistic master-piece, it had many features, almost like it was a living system, yet every single component seemed connected to one another in a most continuous and harmonious manner. In a word, it was striking.

Ret's attention returned to MyPlate. He counted the food groups again: one, two, three, four, five—the sixth was nowhere to be found. The scar pulsed again. By this point, his befuddlement was so profound that it prompted him to do something he almost never did in class: he raised his hand (his left one).

Suddenly, the teacher went mute. She saw a student in her class, raising his hand, but she didn't want to call on him—no, not *that* student. She pretended not to notice.

"I have a question," Ret put forth. Most of the class looked back at him.

Annoyed, the teacher sighed and said, "Yes?"

"What happened to the fats food group?" Ret asked.

Confused, the teacher replied, "What do you mean?"

"The Food Guide Pyramid had six food groups, with fats as the smallest," Ret explained himself. "The MyPyramid thing still included fats, though just barely. But now, with MyPlate, fats aren't even on the table. Why is that?"

The teacher was at a loss for words.

Fortunately for her, one of the students said, "Maybe it's assumed we'll consume some fats from protein and dairy."

"Actually," an astute classmate butted in, "according to MyPlate's guidelines, we should eat lean protein and fat-free dairy."

"So apparently," Ret rejoined, "we are being told not to make any room on our plates for fats."

No one could respond.

So Ret added, "I wonder why?"

"Well, *everyone* knows fats make you fat," the teacher said matter-of-factly, eager to regain control of the conversation. Paige stopped taking notes, unsure if she agreed with that statement.

"Why?" Ret questioned.

"They just do," was the teacher's most educated reason. "It's in their very name: fat. And saturated fats are particularly bad. It's a universally known fact."

"Prove it," Ret sincerely desired.

"Excuse me?" the teacher balked.

"How do you *know* that?" Ret interrogated.

"Because," the peeved instructor hissed, subconsciously putting her hand on her hip, "according to the American Heart Association, diets that are low in saturated fat and cholesterol may reduce the risk of heart disease."

"'May'?" Ret politely pointed out. "That doesn't sound too convincing."

With a snort, the teacher embellished, "You see, y'all are just too young to understand this yet. Quite a few decades ago, researchers set out to learn why rates of heart disease, diabetes, and obesity were climbing. Several studies linked these problems to diets that were high in saturated fat, things like butter, burgers, bacon—you know, the good stuff." She chuckled to herself. "But now we know we should eat more grains, fruits and vegetables, lean meats, and fat-free dairy—just like MyPlate says."

Suddenly, Ana joined the conversation: "Wait a minute." Given her ongoing crusade to find out the truth about what's really healthy, she had been listening intently to the lecture, hoping it would provide some insight. Suspecting some inconsistencies, however, she flipped back in her notebook to a lecture the teacher had given on this very subject. It was true that Ana wasn't exactly the brightest bulb in the box, but when it came to common sense, she was no dummy.

"So why is it that according to the Centers for Disease Control and Prevention," Ana started reading some of her notes, "heart disease, which is almost entirely preventable, is currently the leading cause of death in the United States—or one in every four deaths?" That was how Peggy Sue died, Ret recalled.

"Why, since 1980," Ana continued, "has the number of Americans with diagnosed diabetes more than tripled? And why, since the 1970s, have obesity rates more than doubled among adults and children, with two-thirds of adults and one-third of children either obese or overweight? If fats are unhealthy," Ana concluded, "and society has been moving away from them, then why are we becoming more and more unhealthy?"

The teacher was speechless. The facts were staring her in the face. Lucky for her, the bell rang, signaling the end of the school day. Ret, Paige, and Ana stared at each other with suspicion, like detectives unraveling a mystery, while the rest of the class scurried out of the room.

With an offended air, the teacher strode up to their desks. "I don't know the answers to all of your questions," she sneered at the three of them, "but if you're so smart, why don't *you* tell us?" Then she spun on her heels and walked away.

Ret glanced at his scar and clenched his fist. It was time to go to Russia.

CHAPTER 6

MIST SECRETS

Stealing Lye's cane was going to be no easy task. For starters, Jaret had never seen the evil lord without it, always clutching it as if it was glued to his hideous hand. Like a child and its favorite toy, Lye took his cane everywhere, so much so that Jaret wouldn't be surprised if he even slept with it. Of course, it wasn't *his* cane—Lye had stolen it from the First Father a long time ago. So Jaret felt perfectly justified in trying to get it back.

As difficult as it seemed, however, the real worry was in the consequences. Whether or not the mission was a success, it would be considered an act of treason, punishable by death—or worse: becoming one of Lye's prisoners. Yes, in Lye's sinister mind, death was a blessing; to put someone out of their misery was an act of mercy. That's why he usually kept his most despised enemies alive indefinitely. In fact, rumor had it there were some prisoners in the dungeon at Waters Deep who had been there for centuries, even though no one knew how Lye was able to postpone death among his captives or even himself.

In the course of devising a game plan, Jaret had the idea to inform Mr. Coy of his intentions just in case something were to go wrong. Coy was surprised by the proposition, of course, and tried to talk Jaret out of it, saying it was too dangerous and not worth the risk. But Jaret had already made up his mind. After years of serving the bad guy, he yearned to do something to help the hero. He didn't know *why* the cane was so important, just that it was, and he hoped, by gaining possession of it, that he could use it as collateral to buy time, save a life, or even preserve Coy Manor.

What's more, Jaret missed his wife and daughter, and he figured this would be a great way to officially cut ties with Lye and go out with a bang so he could finally go home once and for all. It was a sentiment to which Mr. Coy could easily relate. And so, although he still disapproved of the plan, Coy gave the brave man his blessing and asked him to touch base immediately afterward.

"If I don't hear from you, captain," Mr. Coy told him, "I will assume you are in trouble."

"Understood," Jaret replied.

"I guess that leaves only one question," Coy said.

"Yes?" asked Jaret.

"Have you ever—*Ben Coy?*"

It was a piece of advice that Jaret knew he would need. He figured the best place to steal the cane would be in the dungeon, whose thick mists might provide enough cover to allow him to sneak up on Lye and then make a run for it. As his cell phone was synced with the Deep's surveillance system, Jaret kept an eye on Lye's location as best he could, waiting for that moment when he seemed headed to the dungeon. When that moment arrived, Jaret struck up his courage and decided to go for it.

To the north side of the complex he hastened, making sure not to follow Lye too closely. From a distance, he watched his superior stride up to the familiar door and cause it to open by striking it with a slight electrical current from his cane. Lye stepped inside the dungeon and then, to Jaret's astonishment, turned left as the door reclosed. This was absurd to Jaret who, when he had visited the dungeon not too long ago, probed the entryway with his foot and felt the floor abruptly end to his left.

When a moment or two had passed, Jaret made his way to the door and, like before, prompted it to open by using his miniature stun gun. Fog spilled out as he walked in, the door shutting behind him. He was greeted by a familiar sight—a sightless one, that is. Enveloped in vapor, his vision had become all but useless, so his other senses took over like before. This time, however, his ears picked up something that he hadn't heard during his first visit: a very faint squeaking sound, like the noise a rusty wheel makes when it needs grease. It was coming from below him and seemed to be growing more distant by the second.

Still standing by the door, Jaret cautiously crouched down and got on his knees. He turned left and crawled until he arrived at the edge. Extending one hand, he slowly reached out to see if he could find anything to help him understand where Lye had gone. Reaching as far as he could, he almost lost his balance when he caught hold of something. It was a cable of sorts, strong and tense as if it was supporting something heavy.

Jaret had discovered an elevator, the unenclosed kind that you'd expect to find in a primitive mine shaft. He could feel the cable vibrating and still hear the pulley squeaking, leading him to believe Lye was onboard and already well on his way down the line.

Jaret knew he needed to catch up somehow. He grabbed the cable with both hands and leapt from the ledge, then immediately wrapped his legs around the line, holding on for dear life. On account of the ubiquitous mists, the cable was extremely slippery. To keep from sliding too fast, Jaret gathered the bottom of his shirt around the cable to aid his grip, then angled the thick soles of his heavy boots to give him more traction.

Slowly but surely, the resigning commander slid his way down the line, straining his ears to gauge how far he was from the elevator. When it seemed he wasn't gaining on Lye, he loosened the grip of his hands and feet in order to hasten his descent. Soon, the squeaking grew louder. He loosened his grip even more.

Suddenly, there was a loud clang as the metal elevator made contact with the ground. Startled, Jaret immediately stopped. The cable had ceased vibrating. He glanced around, hoping to see something — anything — but nothing. So he listened.

Shuffle, click. Shuffle, click. Shuffle, click.

It was the sound of a feeble, old man hobbling along with the help of a cane. Fortunately for Jaret, it seemed like Lye wasn't moving too fast.

Quietly, Jaret resumed his fall. Sensing himself nearing the ground, he relaxed his legs in preparation for making a smooth landing on top of the elevator, then gradually slowed and gently touched down. With ever increasing caution, he laid down on his stomach and slowly slid feet-first off the elevator until his boots met the floor. He knew the slightest noise might cost him his life.

Jaret was relieved to find the view on ground-level to be considerably less obscured than the one in the air.

Although the area was still plagued by the pervasive mists, they weren't quite as dense down here, as if this was where they originated and had not yet expanded to fill the empty space above, like how steam escaping from the top of a train starts out small and contained but quickly disperses. Though a boon to his vision, this was also a bane to his stealth, meaning he had to be extra careful not to be spotted.

The ground was rocky and uneven, not to mention wet and slippery. Jaret hid behind the first boulder he came to, anxious to conceal himself until he learned Lye's location.

Shuffle, click. Shuffle, click. Shuffle, click.

Jaret looked in the direction from whence the sound was coming. He could see a figure moving away from him. Although it was no more than an outline, he knew the hunched silhouette belonged to his boss.

Jaret pursued, watching his every step and making sure not to dislodge even the smallest pebble. Keeping his balance proved a challenge on the wet and sometimes mossy rocks.

Shuffle, click. Shuffle, click.

Although Jaret had no idea where he was going, Lye most certainly did. The should-be-dead but oh-so-determined senior carried on without abatement, uttering the occasional grunt whenever he lost his footing or his cloak got snagged. It appeared he was desperate to reach a certain point, almost like his very life depended on it.

Wherever they were headed, it was a place with lots of water. The landscape was changing by the minute, this time becoming more and more saturated not from the water in the air but on the ground. Puddles and ponds were popping up all over the place, fed by underground hot springs whose heat had turned the air warm and exceptionally humid. Great pools— some shallow, others deep—were filled with crystal clear water, their lower reaches sporting rich shades of blue and green. Some spots were inundated, spilling over and running down the rocks, creating waterfalls and streams, with every body of water giving off its share of steam. It was beautiful, paradisiacal even— the kind of place that people pay to go to for a tropical vacation.

There was a certain kind of hot spring that Jaret liked best of all, however. The biggest and brightest, these favorites were like full-circle rainbows, painted on the ground: a rich, dark blue filled most of the center, while the fringe changed from turquoise to yellow to orange to red—each color the purest of its kind. The lighter hues along the outermost edges dribbled away, sweeping and swirling like flames of a fireball. From a bird's-eye view, these springs resembled miniature suns, stunning in every sense of the word.

Jaret was very familiar with these colorful springs; they could be found in great numbers aboveground throughout the island of Waters Deep. In fact, the first time he saw one, the sight seemed to ring a bell in his brainwashed mind, reminding him of a time years before when he had been sent out West for training as a member of the U.S. Coast Guard. He had gone to a national park one weekend—"What was it called, Purplerock?...no, Purple*stone?* Oh I remember, Yellowstone!"—and seen one of its main attractions: the Grand Prismatic Spring, the largest hot spring in America whose vibrant colors are created by pigmented bacteria in the microbial mats that grow along the edges of the mineral-rich water. The same phenomenon was present on Waters Deep many times over (which is what originally led Ben and Helen Coy to the island years ago and, more recently, drew the Coopers' and Coys' attention when they were unknowingly heading toward the island while fleeing Fire Island in the hot-air balloon).

But Lye cared little for this marvelous display of nature's wonder, bypassing the vibrant springs altogether in his undaunted march to his unknown destination. Every time Jaret heard the *click* after each *shuffle,* he was reminded of his own quest to filch the cane.

For several minutes, the chase continued. Based on the size of its floor, Jaret assumed the room they were in had to be enormous. More than once, he thought he heard the echo of heavy chains being rattled against iron bars, followed by the blood-curdling cry of an eternally incarcerated soul. It caused Jaret to halt for a moment and wonder if this gigantic room constituted Lye's dungeon, which he knew was large but "surely not this large?" He tried not to think about it.

With so much else to look at, Jaret's gaze was shifting more and more away from his steps, causing him to slip more often. One time, he tripped and put his hands down to break his fall, but one of his palms got cut on the jagged edge of one of the rocks. He applied pressure until it stopped bleeding, then ripped off the hem of his shirt and dipped it in a nearby pool of water to clean the cut as best he could. He began to wipe the wound when, to his amazement, it started to heal right before his very eyes. In a matter of seconds, it was gone, with no sign of a scar. Jaret was awe-struck. He had figured the pure water contained some minerals that would aid the healing process, but he hadn't been expecting to be healed almost instantly.

The miracle got him thinking. As arduous as the journey had been thus far, he didn't feel very tired or sore—actually, not at all. In fact, the farther he went, the better he felt. New life seemed to enter his body with every breath. He walked over to the nearest pool and stared at its surface, so clear and still that he could see his own reflection. He looked much the same, but younger—a little less gray in his hair, a few less wrinkles in his forehead. He was beginning to suspect Lye knew something that he didn't know. He kept following.

Not much later, Jaret saw Lye finally come to a stop, and he knew they had arrived. Before them was a great fountain, shooting up from the ground like a geyser. It was in a state of constant eruption, at least a hundred feet tall and surrounded by several other fountains, all of which were smaller but some still quite large. The ground was slightly rounded, like the top of a giant basketball, and as the fountains fell to the floor, the water rippled away in all directions, infiltrating the entire room's water supply. Like so much else in the vicinity, it was a breathtaking display of raw power, and it looked like a good candidate for the source of all water.

Jaret hid in the cleft of a rock and waited for Lye's next move. The villain didn't look so good, trembling as he shuffled toward the fountain. As the rippling water began to lap at his feet, he fell on his face and started to slurp it up. Jaret thought that was rather odd. Was Lye dying of thirst? He kept watching.

A few moments later, Lye rose to his knees, looking much refreshed. He pulled a flask from his robe's inside chest pocket and shook it. It was empty. He needed two hands to unscrew the top, so he set down his cane.

Jaret rubbed his eyes to make sure he had seen correctly. Yes, Lye had set down his cane. Now was his chance.

Like a hungry crocodile sneaking up on a drinking wildebeest, Captain Cooper set out on his mission to humble the great Lord Lye. Jaret kept a constant eye on him as he crept closer and closer. When Lye finished filling his flask, Jaret thought his opportunity had ended, but thankfully Lye pulled out a second empty flask and began refilling it, too. The cane stood alone, still laid aside.

The fountain was an ideal place for snooping, as the noise of falling water muffled the sound of Jaret's footsteps. Knowing this time was precious, he tried to hurry, struggling to do so in a quiet manner, especially as the water began to get deeper. He breathed a sigh of relief when Lye brought out a third empty flask. Jaret was getting lucky.

His heart pounding in his chest, Jaret extended his shaky arm and prepared to slide the cane away from Lye's side. He was just a few feet away, however, when Lye did something different. After filling his third flask, he apparently couldn't help himself and began guzzling its contents. With Lye's head cocked upward, this was the perfect opportunity to seize the cane, but the commander was distracted by what was happening to Lye. The long, white hair of his head and beard was shrinking and returning to its original, darker color. His sharp, elongated fingernails were receding. His wrinkly, saggy skin was becoming firmer. His bones were sticking out less and less.

It was true: Lye was becoming younger. Before Jaret's very eyes, the evil lord was shedding years by the second, turning back the clock on his frail body. By the time he had drunk the flask dry, Lye had returned to an age in his thirties, his hair short and black, his hands young and strong.

Still staring from behind, Jaret was mesmerized by what he had just witnessed. When Lye returned the flask to the miraculous water to refill it again, Jaret shook off his amazement and reached for the cane. It was now or never.

His hand sweaty, Jaret slid his quivering fingertips into the rippling water. As soon as he made contact with the cane, however, it did something that he was not prepared for. It released a powerful current that sizzled in the water, emitting the flash of a spark and the sound of a pop.

Jaret knew he was in trouble.

Before Lye could even turn around, Jaret shoved him face-first into the water and threw his wet robes on top of him. Then he grabbed the cane despite the slight shock and ran for his life. He charged through the shallow water, throwing stealth to the wind. All that mattered now was to get back to the elevator before Lye.

Jaret sprinted out of the fountain area and dove into the safety of the rocks. He scrambled from boulder to boulder, trying to keep low without sacrificing speed. His own adrenaline was carrying him now, still in disbelief that he had stolen the cane.

Jaret's spirits were soaring high when suddenly his left leg went completely dead. He crashed onto the ground, making sure to keep a firm grip on the cane. He tried to get back on his feet, but his left leg refused. He shifted all his weight to his right leg and began to hop along, when, a moment later, that leg also fell limp. With his left hand still clutching the cane, he used his right arm to drag himself along the ground, but he quickly lost control there, too. He refused to relinquish the cane, resorting to his left arm's elbow to inch further until he at last became immobile. He cried out in frustration, well aware this was no coincidence. He had seen Lye restrain his enemies numerous times by commanding the water molecules in their own bodies. The evil lord was nearby.

Jaret was shaking from trying with all his might to override the power that had seized control of his body. Then he heard footsteps. They were unhurried footsteps. The image of a man appeared several yards in front of him. Against his will, Jaret's fingers began to be peeled away from the cane until it rolled out of his grasp.

"Curse you, Lye!" Jaret shouted, his face in the dirt, frustrated beyond all reason to not be able to move.

"You foiled my plans once before," Lye sneered, his younger voice sounding oddly familiar. "I will not let you do so again."

"What are you talking about?" Jaret angrily asked.

Just then, Lye borrowed a scoopful of water from a nearby pool and formed it into a life-sized raindrop. He lifted Jaret off the ground and enclosed him in it, just as he had done a few years earlier, this time keeping his head out to allow conversation.

"Look familiar?" Lye cackled, keeping Jaret's back turned away from him.

A scene flashed before Jaret's eyes. He had been in this situation before, stuck in a watery cage, but previously it had been on a burning ship during a hurricane in the middle of the ocean. And he had been clutching a curious sphere.

"You brainwashed me!" Jaret yelled.

"Yes," Lye grinned. "And it looks like I might have to do it again."

"And why is that?" Jaret wondered.

To answer his question, Lye slowly began to spin Jaret around until the friends-turned-foes were face-to-face. Then, for the first time, Jaret saw who Lye was in his younger days.

Shocked beyond all reason, Jaret gasped and stuttered, "You're…you're…"

But before Jaret could speak the name, Lye forced his newest prisoner's head into the water and laughed maniacally.

CHAPTER 7

GOING OUT ON A LIMB

"Has anyone seen Mr. Coy?" Ret asked as he roamed the Keep.

"I think he's out back," someone shouted in reply, "in the aviary."

"Okay, I'll check there," Ret said on his way out the backdoor.

Whether Mr. Coy was there or not, something was definitely going on in the aviary. Even from across the yard, Ret could hear the birds chirping wildly. Feathers were flying out the door, and cages were crashing to the floor. When Ret cautiously peeked inside, he saw Mr. Coy scrambling on his hands and knees, frantically trying to catch a cat.

Ret stood just outside the door and laughed to himself. Then, with a screeching yowl, the cat came flying past him through the air.

"And stay out, you lousy fur ball!" Mr. Coy scolded the feline. The meddlesome cat glanced back, licked its paw a few times, and then trotted away.

"Oh, hello, Ret," Coy came to the door. "I didn't see you there."

"Sir, you're covered in cat hair," Ret pointed out.

"And feathers," he added, blowing one off his forehead.

"Did someone leave the door open again?" Ret guessed.

"I'm afraid so," Coy responded, then whispered, "Don't tell Stone."

"Any word from Jaret?" Ret wondered. It was a question that had been on everyone's mind ever since Mr. Coy informed Pauline of her husband's desire to steal Lye's cane.

"Still nothing," Coy said heavily as he shut the door to the aviary. "I think it's safe to assume he's in trouble."

"Should we go and rescue him?" Ret asked as they headed across the lawn.

Coy considered the idea for a moment before concluding, somewhat unwillingly, "No, it's just too uncertain."

"But you went to Waters Deep not too long ago specifically to *find* Jaret..." Ret tried to persuade him.

"True, but that was when Jaret was on Lye's good

side," Coy said.

"So you don't want to help him?"

"Of course I want to help him, Ret," Coy returned, "but I'm unsure of the best way to do so at the moment. Let me think about it some more. Besides, who knows if Jaret is even still alive?"

Though valid, the possibility of Jaret being dead didn't sit well with Ret. In fact, he didn't even want to entertain the idea, so he changed the subject: "Are you almost done clearing out the Manor?"

"Getting there," said Coy with a tired sigh.

Ret decided to ask the question that he had been wanting to ask Mr. Coy all along: "How would you like to take a break and come with me to Russia?"

"Oh, you're going to Russia, are you?" Coy chuckled. "And how are you going to get there, I wonder?"

"Well, if *you* won't take me, then I was thinking of asking Lionel..."

Coy stopped in his tracks. "Lionel?" he repeated with disgust.

Ret shook his head, knowing he had said the magic word.

"Well played," Coy capitulated. Then with a defeated smile, "When do we leave?"

Ret grinned to know the dynamic duo would soon be off on another adventure.

There was at least one disadvantage to bypassing Lionel for their travel needs: it meant they would have to run the risk of getting stopped or detained (or arrested) as they moved about the globe. Of course, it was a risk that Mr. Coy was more than willing to take if it meant they didn't have to rely on Lionel. Besides, Mr. Coy had an idea.

The plan was to sneak aboard a cargo plane that was headed to Moscow. Mr. Coy asked one of his students—"Jessica will do fine"—to play the role of an innocent traveler who was heading to—"oh, I don't know, Chattanooga." That destination wasn't important; what mattered was that Jessica got her two suitcases (in which Mr. Coy and Ret were hiding) onto the conveyor belt and into the behind-the-scenes realm of airport baggage. Although it took every last ounce of strength to lift her way-over-the-weight-limit luggage onto the platform, she paid the extra fee and watched until each suitcase had been successfully conveyed away. Then she tore up her boarding pass and went home.

After a few moments, Ret unzipped his suitcase from the inside just enough to take a look around. They were in the belly of the airport now, still undetected as their causeway joined the general body of tagged bags, which was a literal sea of suitcases. Ret glanced ahead to make sure Mr. Coy was still in front of him, and although all of the luggage was starting to look the same, he knew Mr. Coy's had a distinguishing feature: a large sticker slapped on the side that read *Have you ever—Ben Coy?* Yep, they were still side by side.

Ret knew it was his job to make sure they got through the security screening without any trouble. Through the unzipped crack in his suitcase, he kept an eye out for the computer tomography scanner, the hollow tube through which the bags were flowing. Switching his vision into energy mode, he watched as each bag was bombarded by X-rays that the computer then used to create a tomogram, which detailed the mass and density of certain objects within each bag. While most bags passed without a problem, Ret saw one throw up a red flag, though when it was examined, the object in question was nothing but a tennis racket.

When it was Mr. Coy's turn to be inspected, Ret concentrated on the X-rays that were being emitted from the CT scanner. He bent them around Mr. Coy's body, partly so that they wouldn't harm him but mostly so that they wouldn't be slowed down by his mass and density, which were much higher than, say, a pair of pants. When the X-rays were processed, Mr. Coy's tomogram passed with flying colors. Ret followed the same procedure when it was his turn, and he safely exited the scanner.

Where the conveyor belt ended, a steep chute began, consisting of many horizontal metal rods that spun as baggage slid down them. Ret held on as his suitcase took the plunge, bracing for impact at the end of the ride. As soon as he collided into Mr. Coy's bag, he heard him pass gas.

"Gross!" Ret quietly laughed.

"*You* made me!" came Coy's excuse. A few seconds later, Ret heard him say "Whew!" followed by a gasp for fresh air.

The next order of business was for the two stowaways to finagle their way aboard the correct flight. They had already found out ahead of time (and planned accordingly) that a cargo plane would be leaving for Moscow that same afternoon, and its freight proved easy to find since it consisted of mostly crates and boxes.

"Do you see it?" Coy asked from within his suitcase.

"Yeah," Ret told him softly after eying the right load. "Hang on."

Since their suitcases were the durable plastic kind, Ret was able to use his power over earth and all its minerals to gently nudge the two of them off the luggage carousel and onto the ground. Then he stood each of them upright and manipulated their little wheels to carry them in the right direction, praying none of the baggage personnel would interfere with what looked like two runaway suitcases.

As soon as the cargo was loaded and the hatch closed, Ret and Mr. Coy unzipped their suitcases and spilled out.

"Finally," Coy said, stretching his legs.

"You said it," Ret cracked his back.

"I can't believe that actually worked," Coy marveled. "Thanks to you, of course."

It was a long flight to Moscow, one that would have been called a red-eye had it been scheduled for passengers, but it provided ample time for Ret and Mr. Coy to figure out their next move.

"So what's your plan after we arrive in Russia?" Mr. Coy asked.

"I'm not sure yet," Ret admitted, biting into an apple. "I'm hoping my scar will tell us once we get there."

"Where'd you get the apple?" Mr. Coy asked, suddenly hungry.

"There's a bunch in this crate over here," said Ret. "Want one?"

"Sure." Coy caught the fruit and, after taking a bite, said, "Well, if we have any time to spare, there's someone in Moscow I've been meaning to visit."

"Who?" Ret wanted to know.

Coy took another bite and nonchalantly said, "The president."

"What?" Ret choked. "That's crazy!"

"Yes, but what's even crazier is I think he is Ivan's brother," Coy explained.

"What makes you think that?" Ret inquired.

"When Helen and I first met Ivan in the streets of downtown Moscow several years ago," Coy recalled, "he told us his last name was Topramenov. Now, while Romanov is a very common surname in Russia, *Top*ramenov is pretty unusual. To be honest, we figured he made it up because he was a little tipsy and because Helen and I were both eating a cup of Top Ramen noodles at the time. Still, he always insisted that was his name."

"Wait," Ret deduced. "Wasn't Topramenov the name of the president who attended the meeting at Waters Deep as a hologram?"

"Yes, it was. You see, Ivan was a member of the Russian royal family and, as the oldest child, had a promising future ahead of him—that is, until it became clear he had a lisp. His parents tried everything they could think of to fix his speech problems, but nothing helped. They called it an embarrassment. People made fun of him—they called him Ivan the Unintelligible. He was considered a shame to the royal family. Eventually, he ran away and fell into deep despair. Like so many others, he turned to alcohol. He was contemplating suicide when Helen and I found him."

As heartbreaking as Ivan's story was, Ret never

tired of hearing it because, in the end, it was a story of redemption.

"But what if they're not brothers?" Ret imagined. "Or what if the president gets mad at you when you tell him Ivan is dead?"

"It's worth a try," Coy shrugged his shoulders. "If you have a better idea, I'm all ears."

When Mr. Coy ate an apple, he ate the whole thing. All that remained was the stem and a few seeds, which he handed back to Ret while saying, "Here's your apple back." Then he propped his head against his suitcase and tried to get some rest.

Ret placed the stem and seeds on a box beside him, right by the core that remained of his own apple. Although it took a while, he eventually got comfortable enough to doze off.

Not much later, however, Ret was jolted back into consciousness. The flight was experiencing turbulence. At one point, his apple core fell from its place and landed in his lap. Half asleep, Ret picked it up and put it back.

A few moments later, there was another shake, and the apple again rolled into his lap. He retrieved it and was about to return it when he realized he wasn't holding just a core but a whole apple. Confused, he looked around for the core, but it was nowhere to be seen. Then he glanced at Mr. Coy to see if this was another one of his jokes, but he was fast asleep.

Another bout of turbulence dislodged the stem and seeds of Mr. Coy's eaten apple. Ret grabbed the stem and cradled it in the palm of his right hand. The fifth scar gave off a faint pulse. Ret pinched the stem between his thumb and index finger and held it out. He concentrated on the scar and let its energy flow through his fingers and into the stem. Then, as if his arm were a tree branch, the stem began to regrow its fruit. The apple started out small and green, then grew larger until it was fully developed, ripe and ready to eat.

Ever curious, Ret set the apple aside and took up one of the seeds. It hadn't been in his hand very long before it started to sprout. What began as a root and a shoot grew very rapidly into a sapling of a swelling caliper. Soon, Ret was forced to let go as a full-blown tree emerged, its branches knocking over boxes as it stretched toward the ceiling. When one of its roots slithered underneath Mr. Coy, he was aroused from sleep.

Like Jack and his beanstalk, Coy rubbed his bulging eyes and asked, "Is this a dream?"

"No, it's a tree," Ret remarked.

"You—*you* did this?"

"Sure did," Ret said with pride. The tree was now beginning to blossom.

"Well, now we know what the next element is," Coy concluded, admiring the fruit that was fast appearing.

"What, apples?" Ret kidded.

"Something like that," said Coy as a ripe one fell on his head.

Fortunately, Ret figured out how to reverse the growth process before the plane landed in Moscow. By the time the cargo hold burst open, Ret shoved the tree back into its tiny seed, and he and Mr. Coy zipped themselves back into their suitcases. They joined the rest of the load on the journey to the sorting yard, where they easily slipped away unnoticed.

Ret had never been to Moscow before. It seemed a typical capital city, large and in charge with all the sights and sounds of a bustling metropolis. The place reeked of history, overflowed with color, and Ret was grateful Mr. Coy knew where he was going. They seemed to be headed into the heart of the city.

"Here we are," Coy announced as they arrived at a very official-looking building. "The Kremlin Senate." It was a commanding edifice, centuries old but still impressive. Its neoclassical architectural style gave the yellow structure a parliamentary look and feel. In the shape of a triangle, two of its sides met in the middle at a large rotunda, the state flag waving above its green dome.

"Is this where the president lives?" Ret asked as they walked across the square.

"Maybe," Coy answered. "I know it at least houses the presidential administration, so let's hope the president is working today." When they arrived at the entrance, Coy turned to Ret and whispered, "Okay, you wait here. There's a chance they might recognize you." Then, with his characteristic confidence, Mr. Coy turned on his heels, struck up his chest, and waltzed inside.

About ten seconds later, Mr. Coy came back through the door, accompanied by a pair of unhappy officers who escorted him to the top of the stairs and shooed him away.

"Apparently, this place is closed to the public," Coy told Ret. "That's Russia for you."

"Well, now what do we do?" Ret wondered.

"Don't ask me," Coy shrugged. "Ask your scar."

Ret looked down at the tree on his palm. Then he looked up at a tree around the corner. He smiled; it just might work.

Ret led Mr. Coy to one of several large spruce trees that were growing along the backside of the three-story Kremlin Senate building. Ret hid himself among their dense boughs and then instructed Coy to start climbing one of the trees.

"What?!" Coy asked.

"Trust me," Ret pled.

"Alright," Coy warily obliged as he took hold of one of the sturdy lower branches.

When Mr. Coy had climbed to a height that allowed him to see inside one of the windows of the first floor, Ret called out to him, "What do you see?"

"Some guy, talking on the phone."

"Is he Topramenov?"

"No."

"Okay, keep climbing," Ret said, looking around to make sure no one was watching them.

Grumbling, Coy made his way farther up the tree. The spruce's spiky needles weren't exactly kind to his hands, and the higher he went, the more flimsy the branches became.

When Coy arrived at the second floor, Ret asked, "Now what do you see?"

"The kitchen."

"Okay, keep climbing."

"I can't," Coy said. "I'm at the top of the tree."

Ret glanced upward. Sure enough, Mr. Coy had reached the top, looking like an ornament in a Christmas tree as he clung to the trunk.

"Alright, hang on." Knowing he had just recently grown an apple tree from seed, Ret wondered if a living tree might respond in the same way. He pressed his palm into the grass at his feet and directed his energies into the tree's roots. Soon, the spruce began to grow.

"Oh boy," Coy said as the trunk started to extend. "Easy does it."

When the window of the top floor had been reached, Ret relaxed his hand and asked, "Well?"

"It's a storage room."

Despite the third strike, Ret wasn't about to call it quits. It was time to branch out.

Ret planted his hand firmly in the lawn and let his newfound power run wild. He directed the tree to grow out instead of up. The stump swelled as it prepared to support the onslaught of lateral growth. The spruce's limbs began to extend outward, taking Mr. Coy with them.

"Where are you taking me?!" Coy softly yelled at the ground.

"Just tell me what you see."

"Two secretaries," Coy reported as the limb carried him past another window. Then "restrooms," followed by "an empty bedroom" and "a computer lab." Ret bent the branch back down to the second floor, where three consecutive windows belonged to a "ballroom" and two to a "dining hall." Ret was about to give up when he heard Mr. Coy say, "Wait, go back!"

Ret brought the limb back.

"There he is!" Coy proclaimed in hushed tones. "It's Topramenov!"

In his excitement, Ret sent the bough crashing through the window. Mr. Coy rolled into the room amid shattered glass.

"What the Kremlin?!" the alarmed president exclaimed. Then, speaking through the intercom on his desk phone, "Quick, get me security!"

"Please, sir, I mean you no harm," Coy reassured him. "I come in the name of your late brother, Ivan."

As soon as he heard his sibling's name, Serge's animosity melted into curiosity. When security arrived a moment later, he sent them away.

Mr. Coy introduced himself. Then Ret came through the window, flying on a spruce.

"And this is Ret Cooper," Coy said. The president had heard both of their names before.

"Sorry about the window, sir," Ret apologized. "Here, I'll fix it." Before Topramenov could tell him not to worry about it, Ret had already repaired the glass.

"Remarkable," Serge said in awe. "So everything they say about you really *is* true."

"Well, not everything," Coy inserted.

Over the course of the next hour, Mr. Coy fed Serge the true story. He told of how he met Ivan — rescued him, brought purpose to his life; how Ivan became part of their family; how his martyr's death at Sunken Earth had been a tragic accident for the sake of a good cause. He spoke of Ret — a hero, not a heretic — and the Oracle — a wondrous sphere, not a wrecking ball — and how their ultimate objective was to cure the world, not take control of it.

Through it all, Ret didn't contribute much to what was said. Instead, he was paying attention to what was unsaid. The dialogue had commenced with the look and feel of a face-off, the president sitting on his side of the desk with skepticism in one hand and uneasiness in the other. But all of that changed when Mr. Coy started talking about Ivan. The simple fact of knowing what had happened to his long-lost sibling seemed to heal a deep wound within Serge's soul. They reminisced about the man they both knew. Among other memories, Mr. Coy fondly recounted the night of the winter formal dance during Ret's freshman year of high school when Ivan was blamed for a bomb scare. They laughed together, they cried together—one his former boss, the other his forever brother—eking out a eulogy that had been much deserved but never given. And, as Mr. Coy had hoped, the simple act of telling the truth had the effect of begetting trust.

"I thank you for all that you have shared with me today," Serge said sincerely. "My brother and I were best friends. Nika and I were crushed when he disappeared."

"Who's Nika?" Coy asked.

"My younger sister," Serge replied. "Surely Ivan told you about her?"

"No," said Coy. "Ivan never talked about his family."

Mr. Coy grasped his shoulder and said, "There's still hope."

"Yes, well, you've done enough for me already," Serge said broadly, wiping his eyes. "Now, what can I do for *you?* I'm sure you'd like to see this tree that you've heard so much about."

"Yes!" Ret rejoiced. "Please!"

"Very well," said Serge. "We'll leave at once in my helicopter."

Traveling with a president was a whole lot better than traveling in a suitcase. Within the hour, Serge and his two VIP's were en route, headed due east to a destination that was pretty much in the dead center of Russia. On the way, Topramenov told Mr. Coy and Ret all about the mystery of the Tunguska Explosion and his elephantine efforts to unearth it. In the process, he mentioned Lionel's recent inspection visit.

"So Lionel has known about this for weeks but never told us?" Mr. Coy stated more than he asked, glancing at Ret.

"And he was the one who pressured me into joining the cause to attack the Manor," Serge added.

"What?!" Coy huffed. "Is he in league with Lye?"

"I doubt it," Serge said. "He told me it was the UN's idea. Plus, Lye speaks of Lionel with great disdain."

"Well then, Lye and I have something in common," Coy said with frustration. "That guy is a thorn in *my* side, too."

"Lionel *did* tell me before we left Antarctica," Ret spoke up in defense of his friend, "that the real challenge going forward would be for him to help us while making it look like he's trying to stop us."

Coy stared at Ret, rolled his eyes, and repeated, "Thorn in my side."

Ret wasn't sure what to say, so he looked out the window. He got a little startled when the seemingly endless forests abruptly ended and the helicopter flew into the airspace above a massive open-pit mine. Conversation in the cabin died as all eyes flocked to the windows. The tree was easy to spot, somehow still holding its ground despite the ongoing excavation effort. Ret's scar was throbbing in his hand.

The helicopter lowered into the mine. Serge radioed the project's superintendent, instructing him to call it a day and send the workers home. Though surprised, they gladly obliged.

As Ret climbed down from the helicopter, he felt as though he had just landed on Mars. The dirt was dry and red, the landscape totally barren all around them. They made their way toward the lowest level of the pit while the last of the laborers were making theirs to the top. By the time the trio reached the bottom, the mine was silent.

Serge looked to Coy. Coy looked to Ret. And Ret looked to the tree. It was high above them, still clinging to its original soil like a birthday candle in a cupcake. Many of its roots had been exposed, jutting out from the dirt like the stakes of a circus tent. Ret couldn't help but feel sad to see such a glorious creation being treated in such an inglorious manner. It looked so unnatural and even a bit abusive.

Ret approached the nearest root, whose massive girth made him feel remarkably small. He placed his hand on its strong and sinewy surface, hoping it could somehow feel his sympathy.

Just then, a noise stirred the silence in the mine. It sounded like the underwater call of a great whale, neither loud nor harsh but still strong and deep.

Ret took his hand off the root, waited a moment, then put it back. The sound was heard again, this time consisting of a few different tones coming from multiple places around the site. It almost seemed as though the roots were communicating with one another.

"What's he doing?" Serge whispered to Coy.

"Shh," Coy replied, straining to hear the sounds.

Ret removed his hand. The noises died. Then, with all his might, he pressed his hand against the root and blasted it with all the power that was pounding in his palm. The entire tree instantly groaned, and a roar rattled the mine. The roots began to vibrate, and the ground started to shake. Serge lost his balance, but Mr. Coy steadied him.

Ret backed away from the root. He had set something in motion. The tree knew there was someone with the scars in its presence.

Suddenly, a crack appeared in the ground, coming towards Ret like a gopher tunneling through the dirt.

"Ret, look out!" Mr. Coy called.

Ret could sense the earth being disturbed all around him. He turned to face the crack that was headed towards him and mentally held the soil together, sealing it like cement. But then another crack appeared, this time from behind him, followed by three more on his right and two more on his left. When he couldn't contain them all, he decided to make a run for it.

Ret ran for cover behind one of the massive roots, but while his back was against it, he felt something being wrapped around his wrists. The main root was sprouting smaller ones, and they were tying him down! Ret wiggled himself free and took off again.

The mine's entire floor was agitated now. Worms, snakes, moles—whatever they were, they were all making their way toward Ret. He wasn't safe anywhere on the ground. Just as they were closing in, Ret pushed off the ground with a gust of wind, narrowly escaping the clutches of whatever was pursuing him.

He soon discovered, however, that the foes at his feet were roots, and they were as clever as weeds. A few of them lunged from the earth and wrapped themselves around Ret's feet. Ret tried to hover higher into the air, but the roots were too strong. Desperate, he hurled great fireballs down at the ground, hoping to burn the roots away, but they proved to be indestructible and refused to be consumed.

More roots joined in, latching onto Ret's legs and pulling him downward. He was powerless against the onslaught as the vine-like cords began to cover his entire body, like a spider wrapping its prey.

From the sidelines, Mr. Coy and Serge watched in helpless horror as the roots dragged their catch beneath the dirt and Ret disappeared underground.

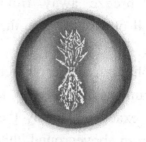

CHAPTER 8

THE UNTIMELY GUARDIAN

Although he couldn't see anything, Ret knew the roots of the great tree were dragging him underground—quickly but safely, and far underground. He could feel the dirt becoming harder and more compact as the seconds passed until, eventually, he broke through it. Like coming to the surface after being underwater, the earth gave way, and his journey came to a stop. The roots unwound themselves around his body and slithered back into the ground, leaving Ret lying on his back.

Ret opened his eyes but quickly shut them, blinded by bright light. He gave his vision time to focus, squinting as he surveyed his new surroundings. He found himself in a vast wilderness, its dry feel and barren look belonging to a desert place. When he stood up, the parched soil crunched beneath his feet, consisting more of coarse gravel than smooth sand. Void of any substantial vegetation, the landscape was dotted with spindly-leafed shrubs, a breeze away from becoming tumbleweeds. The smell of dust hung in the warm air.

Although the scene before him stretched out for untold miles, the view behind him was blocked by a massive root: the taproot, to be exact. Obviously the primary root of the mother tree from aboveground, this bulbous system clung to the earth, sending out dozens of secondary roots that were as tall as buildings and as long as rivers. Resembling the tentacles of a monstrous octopus, these appendages of the main bulb cut into the ground as they snaked out of sight, spawning their own offshoots that further deformed the landscape.

It was about this time when Ret realized he must be standing upside-down. He felt perfectly normal—no blood rushing to his head or anything like that—yet the fact that he was in the presence of the tree's central root system was proof enough that he had been taken into the earth and was now on the flipside of life on ground level. It was an anomaly that left him in a stupor.

"Welcome."

Startled, Ret spun around to locate the speaker. Not far away, in the shade of one of the towering roots, there was an older man sitting peacefully on a wooden bench.

"Who are you?" Ret asked cautiously.

"I am Neo," the man calmly replied with a gentle smile, "Guardian of the Wood Element."

"What?" Ret said in shock. "You're the...the Guardian?"

"Does that disappoint you?" Neo chuckled.

"No, no—this is great," Ret explained, coming closer. "Usually it takes a lot longer for things to come together like this."

"Well, I'm glad I could speed up the process for you," Neo said humorously. Such a statement seemed out of character for an elderly fellow who seemed to have all the time in the world. He was a thin man, his hair gray and clothes plain, who did everything in the most unhurried manner. Even his breathing seemed delayed.

A few awkward moments passed. Ret waited for the Guardian to say something—anything—but the man seemed wholly disinterested in the fact that one with the scars had finally arrived to collect his element. Ret wondered if Neo was all there. Maybe he suffered from narcolepsy.

"So..." Ret said broadly. "Where is the element?"

"It's over there." Without lifting his hand, Neo used just one finger to point toward the giant bulb of the taproot. "Inside the main root there, somewhere." Neo's flippant attitude toward something as important as the element didn't sit well with Ret.

"Okay then," Ret said, groping for words. "Mind if I take a look?"

"By all means."

Confused, Ret asked, "Aren't you going to come with me?"

"Maybe later."

Ret was beside himself. "Okay, well, I'm going to collect the element now..." He was waiting for the Guardian to take control of the situation and commence with the usual protocol. But Neo did no such thing. He just sat there like a bump on a log, staring into space.

Ret took a deep breath and said, "Look, I realize you're very old, and you're probably tired of being a Guardian and all, but there are a couple things that need to happen before I can get the wood element. First off, I need to pass some tests in order to prove to you that I have power over the first four elements. You also need to give me the relic that was given to you by my First Father."

Neo looked over at Ret and said, "I know." Then his gaze returned to the landscape.

With a sigh, Ret threw his hands up and began to walk away, heading toward the great root. "Fine," he muttered to himself. "I'll just do it myself." He stopped a few steps later, however, after checking his pockets and coming to an unfortunate realization: he didn't have the Oracle. It was aboveground, still with Mr. Coy. "Great," he mumbled. "Just great."

Still undaunted, Ret strode over to the nearest root and placed his hand on it, fully expecting a similar series of events to follow that would transport him back to ground level where he could get the Oracle from Coy. He waited for the root to utter its whale-like sound again, but it didn't. He pressed harder but still nothing— no noises in the air, no cracks in the ground, nothing.

His head down and hands on his hips, Ret glanced over at the Guardian. Neo had his legs crossed, still staring into nothing.

Ret approached him and asked, "Will you at least tell me how to get out of here?"

"You're a smart guy," was all Neo said.

After waiting for Neo to say more, Ret bent his head back and rolled his eyes in frustration. "And what does that mean?" His patience was wearing thin.

"It means I'm sure you'll figure it out," he explained.

At his wit's end, Ret exhaled with exasperation and plopped down on the bench next to Neo. He propped his elbow on the narrow armrest and began to massage his forehead with his fingers.

"You know, with all due respect, sir," said Ret, "you are the most unhelpful Guardian I have ever worked with."

"Why thank you," Neo laughed. "I'll take that as a compliment,"

"Of course, Krypto wasn't much help either, but that's because he was already dead," Ret recalled of the Guardian of the Ore Element.

"Oh, Krypto," Neo cooed with fondness, "my old friend. Which element was he given?"

"Ore."

"Perfect fit," Neo smiled. "That man knew what was truly important in life." Then a moment later, "Who else have you met so far?"

"Heliu, Argo, Rado..." Ret rattled off the names without emotion.

"Which elements were they given?" Neo inquired. "And where were they hidden?"

Ret was about to dish out his elemental travelogue when he caught himself. "Neo, sir," trying not to seem disrespectful, "I'm not sure this is the best time to discuss all of this. I mean, I'm already here, you say the element is right over there, and Lye isn't around to get in the way—this never happens. There's got to be a reason why everything has fallen into place so quickly and easily, don't you think?"

As if he had only heard one word, Neo nodded his head and said, "Ah, time." His eyes were closed, and he didn't seem altogether pleased. "So the Oracle has allowed you a bit more time with this element, is that right?"

"Uh, I guess," Ret thought. "Or it's just speeding things up. I know you haven't been aboveground in a long time, but things are pretty crazy up there right now. The continents are coming back together, the whole world is in chaos, and everybody hates me."

"Everybody?" Again, Ret wondered if the Guardian was hearing only a word or two of what he was saying, as some old folks are known to do.

"Just about," Ret iterated.

"Why?" Neo asked.

With a huff, Ret said, "I don't know, ask *them*."

"Why don't *you* ask them?" Neo pressed.

"Because they think I'm strange."

"Have you told them how you feel?"

"I've thought about it," Ret confessed.

"Then why don't you?"

"I don't know," Ret sighed, tired of being interrogated. "Sounds like a lot of work, I guess."

"So you're lazy?" Neo joked.

"No," Ret quickly returned. "I just don't have that kind of time right now. I need to focus on finding the last two elements."

"Ah, time," Neo repeated from earlier, dropping a subtle hint. Then he added, "Well, young man, you might say that's what the wood element is all about: time."

Perplexed, Ret asked, "What do you mean?"

"What does a seed need in order to grow?" Neo put forth.

Ret shrugged and suggested, "Water, sunlight, soil..."

"Those are things that it needs to produce its leaves, roots, and fruits," Neo told him. "But what does it need in order to *grow*—to grow those leaves, roots, and fruits and eventually become the plant it was destined to become?"

Ret shook his head.

"It needs time," Neo answered his own question. "That's what wood is: the evidence of time." The Guardian reached back to touch the colossal root behind them. "Do you have any idea how long it took for this tree to grow?—how much time nature has invested in this tree?" Neo was caressing the root as he would a beloved pet. "Odds are you've had some interactions with plants and seeds recently." Ret nodded in agreement. "Did you supply any water or sunlight or other nutrients to make them grow?"

Ret shook his head; he had not.

"Then what was it, I wonder, that enabled you to do so?" Neo taught. When Ret could not come up with an answer, the Guardian said, "To have power over wood is to have some influence over time."

Perhaps the geriatric's words were true. That night on the cargo plane, Ret had grown a tree from a seed in a matter of minutes, a process that naturally would have taken many years. Then he thought of the day at the Kremlin Senate building, when he had added instant size to the spruce tree, a species known for its very slow growth. Yes, it seemed the wood element *was* a matter of time.

"That makes sense," Ret said, suddenly cheery. "I think I understand now, thanks." He got up to leave.

"Where are you going?" Neo questioned.

"To get the Oracle," Ret told him. "It's just above-ground, I'll be right back. Then I can get this show on the road."

As if Ret had missed an important lesson, Neo closed his eyes and shook his bowed head with an experienced smile. Then he said, "And how do you plan to get back up there?"

"Well, since you won't tell me, I'll just blast through the ground," Ret reasoned. "I have power over earth, remember?"

Just as Ret was about to force his way back to ground level, he heard the Guardian mumble, "Won't work."

Like a meddlesome wart that keeps growing back, Ret glowered at Neo and asked, "And *why* won't it work?"

"Because you're going to try to go up by going down," Neo pointed out.

Shifting his weight to one side, Ret stared at the Guardian with a face that seemed to say, "Would you just go away."

"You're already down," Neo continued. "You need to go up. But you'll never get up by going down. It's all in your head, see. You need to adjust your perception of things."

"So we really *are* upside-down here," Ret stated, trying to add some certainty to what he had already suspected.

"That depends on your point of view," Neo said. "Everything seems right-side-up to me here, but if I were to go to where you just came from, everything would appear upside-down to me. It's all in how you look at things."

Ret had never been so confused in all his life. He finally came right out and said, "Do you want me to collect this element or not?"

"Of course I do," Neo snickered.

"Then why aren't you helping me?"

"I am, you just don't see it," said Neo. "Besides, you're not ready yet."

"Excuse me?" Ret argued, taking some offense.

"You still have much to learn."

"Like what?" Ret debated. "How am I 'not ready yet'?"

His spacey expression looking more and more like a sagacious one, the Guardian taught, "In order to gain mastery over something, you must first become subject to it." Neo was starting to sound a lot like Rado. "This is especially true with the wood element. If you desire to control growth, you must first let it control you."

Ret scrunched up his face and asked, "What does that mean?"

"It means you have more growing to do, son," Neo explained with a fatherly tone. "You shouldn't be trying to get *through* the elements; you should be trying to get the elements through *you*."

"And how do I get the wood element through me?" Ret inquired, feeling put out for being called out.

"Well, for starters, we've been talking for several minutes now, and you still haven't told me your name."

"So?" Ret scoffed. "What does that have to do with the wood element?"

"It has everything to do with it!" Neo countered.

Ret had had enough. The old geezer was messing with his mind—just playing a silly trick that was getting in the way of Ret reaching his objective. For all Ret knew, this annoying man was an impostor, a puppet placed by Lye to hedge up the way.

"I don't have time for this," Ret concluded as he turned to leave. He was too annoyed to hear the Guardian reply, with some disappointment, "Exactly."

"Thanks anyway," Ret said sarcastically as he started pacing away.

"Where are you going?" Neo called from his bench.

"For a walk," Ret informed him, choosing to leave unsaid the real reason of "to get away from you."

"Good idea, always helps me," Neo returned. "Make sure to take your time."

Still marching off, Ret said, "How did I know you were going to say that?"

Then Neo added one final caution, "Don't let the game distract you from the goal, Ret."

Ret froze. His feet slid a bit from such an abrupt stop in the loose dirt, creating a small cloud of dust. Not only was Neo's warning one of Ret's own recent laments, but how did he know Ret's name? Ret spun around to investigate.

But the Guardian was gone. Not even the wooden bench was to be found. Ret was now downright perplexed. Had it all been a product of his imagination—a desert mirage, perhaps?

This could not have come at a worse time. Just a few minutes ago, Ret was on track to collect the element in record speed, but his efforts had been completely derailed—by the Guardian himself, no less! Their conversation left Ret in an unpleasant mood, a mixture of offense and sadness with an overall feeling of vexation. On one hand, he felt quite a bit insulted to have been told he wasn't ready to collect the element ("What more do I need to learn?"), while on the other hand, he was displeased to have been censured by his own critique ("Did I actually let the game distract me from the goal?"). More than anything, however, Ret was dumbfounded to have just been turned away by a Guardian, of all people ("And how did Neo know my name?").

Hoping to clear his clouded mind, Ret trekked deeper into the desert, blazing a trail through the brush. He knew neither where he was going nor what he should be doing, so he wandered and, as Neo had recommended, took his time.

This was one of the strangest lands Ret had ever seen. For the most part, it was remarkably flat. But now, close at hand and in the distance, he could see giant rock formations of the most peculiar shapes. These were not mountains but mesas—great slabs of pure rock with flat tops instead of pointed peaks—and neither were their sides sloped but vertical. In some incredible way, these mega massifs rose right out of the desert plains, like a giant's set of building blocks.

It was clear that the culprit was the extensive root system that meandered throughout the entire area. Over the centuries, as these roots pushed through the earth, they deformed the landscape, forcing sections of rock up here and causing other areas to break away there. Ret likened it to sidewalks back home, displaced by the roots of mighty oak trees growing in narrow parkways. A similar thing had taken place in this lost land, though on a much grander scale.

The scenery took on a sense of fascination when Ret considered the time it took to create it. Much like how a little water can, over time, carve a grand canyon out of sheer rock, these roots had found a way when there wasn't one, cutting a slice and then growing it over a span of years and years. In the process, they split bedrock, leaving behind ravines and gullies that only nature could design, for truly these were amazing sights to behold.

Ret's favorite formations, however, were the buttes—those stand-alone structures that seemed but break-offs of larger mesas, though more impressive because their height exceeded their width. They were so unreal that they almost looked built by man rather than forged by nature. Like isolated skyscrapers, they rose sharply out of the ground, their walls impeccably smooth and straight. Their tops staggered upwards like a tiered and tiled roof, resembling a cake with a topping of large chocolate shavings. Many of the buttes were half-buried in dirt, giving them the appearance of unfinished sculptures, expertly chiseled by a skilled hand.

All in all, it was a land of enchantment, and Ret couldn't get enough of it. He felt like an ant strolling among sand castles. Every mesa and butte—each plateau and hoodoo—was an architectural feat that deserved a lifetime of study. Ranging in color from reds and yellows to every shade of brown, there were curves so smooth and angles so straight that some formations looked like the remnants of medieval fortresses, constructed right out of the cliff sides. Truly, this was a land lost in time, one whose wonder Ret had initially overlooked. Who knew there could be so much beauty in ugliness—so much goodness in badlands?

Just then, Ret saw something out of the corner of his eye. It was a woman, sneaking from boulder to boulder along the base of one of the large mesas. Ret set off in that direction, hoping the individual knew how to return aboveground.

As soon as the person caught sight of Ret, however, she took off running.

"Hey!" Ret called out after her. "Wait!"

The stranger seemed panicked, frantically sprinting toward a dark hole at the base of the large mesa. Ret knew he wouldn't catch her in time, so he rolled one of the free boulders in front of the entrance and blocked it.

Desperate, the woman turned down a cleft in the rock face, but it turned out to be a dead end. When Ret arrived, he saw the terrified soul huddled in the farthest corner, curled up and shaking.

"I'm sorry if I scared you," Ret said delicately, slowly stepping closer. "I'm wondering if you might be able to help me."

Ret's plea for help seemed to calm the poor lady. She slowly retreated from the corner, her hand covering most of her face. She was fully clothed, which Ret thought was odd considering the hot and arid climate.

"My name is Ret," he told her. "What's yours?"

"Nika," she replied.

Ret had found Serge's sister.

CHAPTER 9

CHRISTMAS GUARDIAN ANGEL

Life at the Keep could be summed up in one word: depressing. After all, the very reason for their relocation had been to avert death, which had cast a pall on the entire event from day one. These days, however, the permanency of the situation was beginning to sink in. As grateful as the staff and students were for the safety and security that their new residence afforded, they felt somewhat like refugees escaping persecution. Granted, the Keep *was* just a few miles down the road from the Manor, but at the end of the day the place was still just a house to them—one that didn't quite feel like home.

No, what the Keep really felt like was something of a cross between a hospital and a prison, thanks in part to its white walls, eerie halls, and complete lack of windows. Of course, there *were* windows in the mansion house up on the ground level, but no one lived in it, not only because it reminded Stone too much of Virginia but also because no one else felt comfortable moving in.

As such, everyone lived underground, a dismal situation in itself that made it seem as though they were in hiding (which wasn't far from the truth). They attempted to add some fresh paint here and build a new wing there, but, try as they might, things just lacked a certain Coy factor: there was no savanna for the rhinos to roam in, no aquarium for the sharks to swim in, no bell tower for the hours to chime in. Everywhere you looked, there were reminders that the Manor was a thing of the past: the planetarium's nine magnetic spheres sat in a jumbled mess, the Studatory had been crammed into three metal cargo containers, the life-sized pool table lay dismantled. Perhaps the best symbol of the relocation was on the south lawn, where a veritable nursery had been created from all of the Manor's plants and trees, uprooted and shoved into pots for the time being. Every aspect of daily life had been altered—even the route to school, which no longer started on a suspended platform and crossed a submersible bridge but now began in the most bland and boring way possible: on a driveway.

Yes, one thing was very clear: the Keep was no Coy Manor.

True, the Keep was still impressive in its own right. Its square footage likely rivaled, if not surpassed, the Manor's, and no one had even dared to explore its furthest reaches yet. Not to mention it was also full of unique and valuable (and at times weird) stuff. It even boasted a few features that the Manor did not have, like a force field around the entire property and a direct communication link to Waters Deep.

The main difference between the two properties, then, could be found in their purposes. The Manor strove to help people, but the Keep sought to hurt them; one had all sorts of doodads to teach and instruct, but the other kept all kinds of knick-knacks to spy and exploit. And when it came to what each had to offer the world, they were polar opposites: the Keep a curse, the Manor a cure.

Little wonder their new dwelling was so dismal. Gloom hung in the air, misery lurked around every corner, and the whole kit and caboodle was awash with Lye. Could the Keep ever be turned from an instrument of evil to a vehicle for good?

Maybe. But until then, Christmas was coming, and there was absolutely no evidence of it throughout the Keep. It gave Pauline an idea one afternoon that she hoped would help shake off everyone's blues, especially her own.

"Haul out the holly!" she cried as she entered the small living room of the apartment-like chamber where the Coopers lived, carved out of the unfinished portion of the Keep's top floor. "Only two weeks until Christmas and not a single decoration to be found—no wreaths, no tinsel, not even a tree." She was trying to stay positive in the face of so much dreariness. "I will not rest today until I've found at least one decoration. Who's with me?"

Sitting on the couch, Paige and Ana just stared at her glumly.

"There's some mistletoe growing on one of the trees out back," Paige informed her.

Eager to avoid the task, Ana cheered, "Done!" She nodded gratefully at her friend. "That was easy."

"Not so fast!" Pauline said merrily, helping the girls up off the couch. "We need something in *here*"—sweeping the room with her arms—"something festive to lift our spirits: a snow globe, an ornament, some lights—anything. It's Christmas, go wild! Come on, let's see what we can find in some of these boxes."

Boxes, boxes, boxes. There were boxes everywhere. Any and all of the Manor's belongings that could fit in a box had been put in a box and hauled to the Keep. There were boxes big and small, there were boxes short and tall. There was no end to the boxes, and the last thing anyone wanted to do was go through more—boxes.

"Is this one of those sneaky, motherly ways of getting us to do chores?" Ana complained as she started shuffling through things in the kitchen.

From one of the bedrooms, Pauline sang her reply, "Dashing through the snow, in a one-horse open sleigh..."

"She's singing carols!" Paige snickered.

"Good grief," Ana rolled her eyes.

Pauline continued, "O'er the fields we go, laughing all the way—ha, ha, ha!"

"At least she's not freaking out about what might have happened to my dad," Ana pointed out. "Seems like that's been on her mind nonstop ever since your dad told us about it. Though I can't blame her; it's been on my mind, too."

"Bells on bobtail ring," Pauline carried on, then becoming louder to emphasize the next line, "Making spirits bright."

"I've been worried about *my* dad, too," Paige said tenderly. "I miss him," then, her voice quivering, "and Ret."

"We all miss Ret," said Ana, "but he's the one we should worry about the least."

Pauline finished the first verse, "What fun it is to ride and sing a sleighing song tonight!"

Now time for the chorus, Paige suggested with a smile, "Maybe singing will cheer *us* up, too."

"You know, maybe you're right, P," Ana grinned. Struck with an idea, she started improvising the familiar chorus based on whatever junk she happened to be sifting through: "Jingle bells, pasta shells, two new headphone jacks." Paige was laughing, so Ana kept going. "Dracula, a spatula, and..." then finding something unexpected, she questioned, "Little Debbie snacks?"

"Hey!" Pauline snarled from the bedroom. "Those are mine!" The caroling had come to an abrupt end.

"You hit the jackpot, Ana!" Paige observed, coming over to inspect the bounty.

"Girls!" Pauline warned, hastening to the kitchen. "Just nevermind those!"

"No wonder you haven't lost any weight, Mom," Ana realized. "Check out this stash!"

"Cosmic Brownies, Swiss Rolls, Oatmeal Crème Pies..." Paige announced.

"And look, Red Velvet Christmas Tree Cakes!" Ana cheered. "Sweet, I found my Christmas decoration!"

"That doesn't count!" Pauline declared, arriving in the kitchen. "Now unhand those cakes!"

"I can't believe this," Ana remarked. "You've been holding out on us. What other goodies are you hiding?"

"Thank you for your help, girls," Pauline calmly told them. "You're excused."

"Mom, you're supposed to be on a diet," Ana reminded her.

"One little treat isn't going to kill me, Ana," Pauline rationalized.

"Yeah, *one* won't," Ana returned, then reaching into the box to retrieve some of its contents, "but *nine* packs of Pecan Spinwheels might!"

"Mmm, Spinwheels," Pauline's mouth began to water.

"Mom." Ana glared at her in all seriousness, the roles of mother and daughter temporarily switched. "I thought we talked about this. You said you were going to make healthier choices, remember? I'm worried about you!"

"I know, I know," Pauline looked down in shame. "I'm sorry. I was doing pretty well for a few days, but sometimes I just need a little treat, that's all. There's nothing wrong with a little sugar, Ana. I mean, there's sugar in oranges, for Pete's sake. Am I not allowed to eat oranges now, too?"

"Ugh, *Mom,*" Ana grunted with a facepalm. "The issue isn't sugar; it's *how much* sugar. Sugars are carbs, and the body doesn't get rid of extra carbs like it does extra water—it stores them. So if you eat more carbs than you need, then you'll start gaining weight. So yes, there's nothing wrong with a *little* sugar, but do you see why there might be something wrong with a *lot* of sugar? If you eat like an Olympic athlete but live like a couch potato, then you'll end up looking like Jabba the Hutt. Sure, a treat every now and then is fine, but *every day?* I mean, how often do you eat these, anyway?" She held up a random package from the stash.

Calling the confection by name, Pauline searched for a loophole, "Do you mean Zebra Cakes in particular or just sweets in general?" Ana shot her an unamused glare. "Okay, I'll admit…lately it's become a little more frequent."

"Mother!" Ana complained with frustration.

"Don't get so worked up, dear," Pauline defended herself. "I had a flat belly when I was younger, but child-bearing and middle age have been hard on me. My beach body is no longer a priority."

"Is *that* what you think this is about?" Ana balked. "Mom, this is about your *health,* not what you look like in a bathing suit. Don't you want to be healthy?"

"Of course I do," Pauline replied, her previously positive attitude fading. "Look, I'm trying. I'm following the guidelines…" then eyeing the mini powdered donuts, "…for the most part." Paige smiled. "But my weight won't change." She threw up her arms. "What do you expect me to do, eat broccoli all day?"

Intrigued, Paige inquired, "What guidelines are you following, Mrs. Cooper?"

"Oh, you know, what we've all been told," Pauline explained. "Eat plenty of protein, choose clean carbs, drink lots of water, exercise more, avoid fats…"

"What's wrong with fats?" Paige questioned.

An awkward moment followed, as if Paige has just asked the obvious. She and Ana made eye contact and smiled. They had done a little research on fats since the lecture at school.

"Uh, what do you mean?" Pauline asked.

"Why should fats be avoided?" said Paige.

"Well, uh..." Pauline searched for a reason. "Well, because everyone knows fats make you fat, dear."

"How do you know?" Ana interrogated.

"They just do," was all Pauline could say. "It's in their very name, isn't it?"

Paige innocently laughed, "Well, that's silly— nothing more than a misleading coincidence, really. I'm not sure the words *fats* and *fat* can be used interchangeably here. That's like saying wearing shorts makes you short, which doesn't make any sense."

Paige had a point.

"I don't understand why fats have such a bad reputation—they're a necessary nutrient," Paige continued. "I mean, there are essential amino acids (or proteins) and essential fatty acids (or fats), but I've never heard of an essential sugar (or carbohydrate)."

Pauline, who lived on the simple-minded side of life, stared at Paige as if she was speaking a foreign language.

"Oh Paige, dear," Pauline sighed helplessly, "it's all so confusing to me. I tell you, the definition of what's healthy changes like the wind these days."

"I haven't really figured it out yet either, Mom,"

Ana said, "but until then, just cut back on the sweets, okay?"

"I know, honey." Pauline was speaking realistically now. "I've just been so stressed out lately. First the move to this dreadful Keep, now the uncertainty about your father. I mean, we don't even know if he's...if he's..."

"Still alive?" Ana hesitantly completed the sentence.

"Oh, don't say it!" Pauline finally broke down, pulling the two girls into an embrace like a mother hen. "Life is hard for all of us right now, but if we stick together, I know we can pass through it. Now," she clapped, wiping her eyes, "shall we resume our search for a Christmas decoration?"

"I guess so," the girls moaned.

"I know!" Pauline shouted. "Why don't you go explore the Keep? I hear those rooms are full of all kinds of stuff. You're bound to find something Christmassy." When the girls showed some reluctance, Pauline insisted, "Go on, it'll be fun." She escorted them to the front door, anxious to re-hide her stash of goodies in their absence (and make sure they hadn't found the eggnog). "Good luck!" she bade them as she shut the door.

"Ugh, this is so lame," Ana muttered, still standing by the door.

"Where should we start looking?" Paige asked.

"I say we just bring back some of that mistletoe," Ana suggested.

From inside the house, Pauline yelled, "No mistletoe!"

"Fine," Ana sighed, walking toward the main room of the 21st century floor.

"How about we visit a December 25th sometime in the past?" Paige proposed.

"What do you think this is, a Charles Dickens novel?" Ana teased.

"Very funny," Paige grinned. "Maybe we can find an antique ornament for the tree or something."

"Okay, but we should probably find a tree first," Ana joked.

The pair strode to the elevator in the center of the room and climbed aboard.

"How far back should we go?" Ana asked, stepping up to the controls and cracking her knuckles.

"Not too far," Paige said, "maybe just down one—"

Without any warning, the elevator engaged, freefalling like a rollercoaster ride at an amusement park. The girls were thrown into the air and then onto the floor.

"What did you do?!" Paige shrieked, trying to catch her bearings.

"I didn't touch a thing, I promise!" Ana yelled back.

They were plummeting, the floors zipping by so fast that they were all just a blur.

"Make it stop!" Ana cried out, struggling to stand up.

Paige crawled over to the control clock, its three hands wildly spinning counterclockwise. Trembling, she pinned all three of the hands together, and the elevator slowed to a stop. Its doors opened, and the girls eagerly spilled out onto solid ground, panting. They found themselves in another main room but on a different floor. Paige stared wide-eyed at the year painted in big, black letters on the wall.

"2500," she quietly announced, then added with profound gravity, "B.C."

The fact that they had, in a sense, gone back in time to four and a half millennia ago made their hearts pound even harder. Although they knew they hadn't *actually* left the present day (which was now 45 floors above them), the Keep had a way of making even the most non-threatening situations feel very disquieting.

Paige and Ana rose to their feet amid profound silence. Every wall and every hall—from the floor to each door—shone with the most intense whiteness imaginable, like a scene from another realm. Cold and stale, the air tasted like it hadn't been stirred in a couple thousand years.

"Do you think we should go back up to a more recent time?" Ana asked with noticeable uneasiness. "I mean, Christmas didn't exist 'B.C.'"

"Yeah, maybe you're right," Paige said, though not totally persuaded. "Still, I wonder if there's a reason we came here. You said you didn't touch the controls, right?"

"It was probably just a freak accident, that's all," Ana assumed, anxious to get back into the elevator. "Come on, let's—"

Suddenly, the girls saw something move out of the corner of their eyes. They glanced to the left just in time to see the figure of a man turn down one of the room's ten corridors.

"Okay, time to go," Ana quickly said, officially freaked out.

"Hold on," Paige pled, caution yielding to curiosity. "Let's find out who that was."

"Girl, are you crazy?!" Ana protested. Paige was already walking away. "Yes, yes you are." Ana unwillingly followed.

Paige walked to the place where she had last seen the unknown person. She entered the corridor and slowly started down it, the years of two decades stretching out on either side of her. Near the end of the corridor, a little ways down a hallway on her right, Paige noticed that one of the doors was open. She slowly headed toward it, Ana several steps behind.

"Hello?" Paige called out as she approached the door. "Is anyone there?"

No answer.

Paige was about to peer into the room but paused. Her sense of confidence (inherited from her father) had carried her to that door, but her inner voice of prudence (passed down from her mother) was keeping her from entering. She glanced back at Ana, who, with a look of terror on her face, was making all kinds of desperate gesticulations to tell Paige not to proceed. Although she was also nervous, the Coy child had the feeling that she needed to see what was in this room. And so, she took a deep breath and entered.

About the size of a small bedchamber, the room was mostly dark, the light from the hall casting a faint gleam inside. Paige stepped toward the center and pulled on the ripcord, illuminating a single, low-wattage lightbulb on the ceiling. There was no shortage of things to look at: idols from Mesopotamia, pottery from Egypt's Old Kingdom, examples of early Sumerian writing. Papyrus had just been discovered, and China was in the silkworm business. It was like strolling through the ancient civilizations section at a museum, Minoan art alongside Phoenician artifacts. There was even a fake tree in one corner. But the mysterious person was nowhere to be found.

"You okay?" Ana asked, peeking in from outside.

"Yeah, there's no one here," she said, somewhat disappointed. Ana breathed a sigh of relief.

Paige was about to leave the room when something caught her attention. On the left side of the far wall, there was an aerial illustration of Stonehenge, that prehistoric structure near modern day's London, England. Having done a report on the iconic monument not too long ago, Paige recognized the famous site immediately. However, the Stonehenge in the drawing looked very different from the Stonehenge of today. In the sketched version, none of the stones was missing or out of place. The image before Paige's face was a whole and complete Stonehenge. She wasn't sure what to make of it. It was either the original architect's blueprint of what Stonehenge looked like when it was built, or it was just a hopeful artist's rendition of what Stonehenge *may* have looked like when it was built. Whatever it was, it felt right.

As Ana roamed the room, Paige took a closer look at the curious painting. When viewed at a slight angle, the light revealed slight traces of ink where words had been handwritten on the drawing. Paige unpinned the parchment and held it in front of the lightbulb. Sure enough, the diagram was covered in notes, as if each stone of the henge had a certain meaning. Although the words were very hard to read and likely from a different language, Paige wondered if Ret or her dad might want to take a look at it.

Meanwhile, Ana was checking out the fake tree in the corner of the room. Halfway up its trunk, she thought she saw a pair of human eyes. She examined them with interest until one of the eyes twitched.

"AH!" she squealed.

"What?" Paige spun around.

"I think this tree just winked at me!" Ana explained.

"Oh Ana, it's probably just your fear playing tricks on your mind," Paige dismissed.

"Can we just get out of here?" Ana begged, already on her way out of the room. "This place gives me the heebie-jeebies."

"Alright," Paige obliged. She folded up the Stonehenge drawing and slipped it in her pocket, then turned off the light and closed the door.

"You know, we still haven't found a Christmas decoration," Paige pointed out, trying to keep up with Ana as they headed back to the elevator.

"Don't worry," Ana reassured her. "I'm sure my mom has found something by now."

Once inside, Ana immediately began to spin the controls clockwise, returning them to a more familiar time.

"Who do you think that person was down there?" Paige asked.

"It was probably just a trick of the mind," Ana smiled, using her friend's own words.

"Yeah, maybe you're right," Paige said.

Arriving at the 21st century floor, Ana stepped out of the elevator and made for her humble home, anxious to check on her mom.

"Oh, girls!" Pauline celebrated as the pair walked through the front door. "You're just in time!"

"For what?" Ana wondered.

"I found a decoration!" Pauline replied. She reached into a tall box and pulled out a porcelain statue of an angel. She stood a little shorter than the average person, her round face sporting an awkward smile between two rosy cheeks. The dress was the same color as butter, billowing around her body like a cumulonimbus cloud. A pair of golden wings completed the look.

"Oh," Paige said, trying to disguise her disgust. "It's so...so..."

"Hideous," Ana filled in.

"Isn't she wonderful?!" Pauline cheered, undeterred. "And look: she even lights up!" Sure enough, the pointy tips of an inlaid strand of lights could be seen poking through the porcelain. It was like looking at a three-dimensional Lite-Brite design.

"Even better," Ana fibbed.

"I can't wait to see what she looks like lit up, Mrs. Cooper," Paige said politely.

"Neither can I!" Pauline said, untangling the power cord. "Did you girls find anything?"

"Oh, we found something," Ana replied, recalling the winking tree.

"But nothing that was appropriate for Christmas," Paige added, recalling the Stonehenge diagram.

"That's okay," Pauline said as she searched for the nearest outlet. "This one is big enough for the three of us." Before plugging in the cord, she paused to utilize the teaching moment, saying insightfully, "You see, girls, this angel is the symbol of our lives right now: just when we thought all was lost, we found a little shred of hope at this Christmas season."

"That's tender," Ana mumbled.

"In fact, that's what Christmas is all about," Pauline continued. "I remember one year when—"

"Mom," Ana interrupted, "just plug it in."

"Oh, alright," Pauline said, her attention returning to the plug.

"Don't be such a Grinch, Ana," Paige kidded.

Pauline called out, "Okay, ready?"

"Ready!"

As soon as Pauline let the electricity flow, a part of the strand shorted and some of the lights exploded, causing the angel's head to break off and shoot from its body.

"AHH!" the three ladies screamed, shielding themselves as the head collided into the ceiling, taking a chunk of drywall with it. They dove for cover, trying to dodge the projectile as it chaotically bounced off the walls. They waited until the head rolled to a stop.

"Well, you're right about one thing, Mom," Ana remarked, combing bits of drywall out of her hair. "This angel sure is the symbol of our lives right now."

"At least she's still smiling," Paige observed, trying to look on the bright side after inspecting the statue's smoking head.

"Well, I give up," Pauline muttered dolefully now that her fragile optimism had exploded back into depression. "Who's up for some Honey Buns?"

CHAPTER 10

LONG LIVE THE
MUTANTS

"Nika?" Ret said, recognizing the name. "I know your brother!"

"You know Ivan?!" the woman replied, suddenly enthralled. "Do you know where he is?" In her excitement, she withdrew her hand from covering her face, revealing a terrible skin disease. It took Ret by surprise, a reaction that his sense of propriety couldn't quite suppress in time.

Nika's jubilant expression immediately faded. She looked away in shame.

"I'm sorry," Ret apologized.

"It's okay," she said sorrowfully. "I'm just not used to being around normal people." Ret didn't really understand what she meant by that, but he felt it best not to ask. Changing the subject, she inquired, "You've met Ivan? I haven't seen him since I was a young girl."

Ret took a deep breath and tenderly told her, "Sadly, Ivan is no longer with us."

"You mean he's…" Nika wondered, already suspecting the answer.

Ret nodded.

"Did he take his own life?"

"Oh no, it was an accident," Ret returned, "during a rescue mission."

"Hmm, well, he was one of the lucky ones then, I guess," Nika said. Again, Ret wasn't sure what that was supposed to mean.

"When I said earlier that I knew your brother, I was actually referring to your other brother, Sergey," Ret clarified.

"Oh," said Nika, less enthusiastic about her other sibling.

"He misses you," Ret informed her. "He hopes you'll come back soon."

"I miss him, too," Nika said, her confidence returning, "but not enough to go back." She walked past Ret as she headed out of the dead-end cleft in the rock. "I have to stay here; my people need me."

"Your people?"

"This is a land that nobody wanted, home to a people who nobody wanted," she explained, reaching the end and stepping out of the shadows. "Though we come from all walks of life, a common desire runs through each of us: a longing to be accepted." Then turning to face Ret, she asked, "Would you like to meet them?"

"Uh, sure," Ret said. Nika seemed pleasantly surprised.

Although a meet-and-greet wasn't exactly on his agenda, Ret didn't really have anything else to do at the moment. He secretly hoped Nika or her people might be able to tell him how to get back to ground level so he could get the Oracle from Mr. Coy, then return underground and collect the element.

"Okay, but I should warn you," Nika added as she led the way, "we're all a little…different." She stopped when they arrived at the hole in the side of the mesa, still blocked by the large rock that Ret had put there earlier to prevent Nika's escape.

"That's alright," Ret smiled as he easily rolled away the boulder without physically touching it. "So am I." Nika stared wide-eyed at Ret's abilities.

They stepped into the mouth of a large cavern, where the light was quickly swallowed by darkness. Ret, who in recent years had become somewhat of an expert in traversing dark passageways, conjured a flame to shed some light on the path ahead.

"You said your name is Ret?" Nika wondered after seeing Ret's self-produced flame.

"Yes."

"Any relation to the Ret Cooper who everyone is angry with?"

"That's me," Ret said with sarcastic pride.

"I thought so," Nika replied. "I've been here for years, but each new person who comes here keeps us relatively informed on what life is like back there."

"Yeah, I'm not too popular right now," Ret admitted.

"Great, you'll fit right in," Nika beamed.

"Then you must have heard your brother Sergey was recently elected president of Russia," Ret reported.

"Yes, I did hear that," Nika responded. "Better him than me."

"Sounds like you're doing the same down here," Ret pointed out.

Nika laughed, "Something like that."

Their route was a rough one, featuring frequent ducks of the head and slips of the feet. The air was cool and damp, and more than once Ret was pelted by a drop of water falling from somewhere overhead. The rock formations inside the cave were just as magnificent as the ones outside it, though for different reasons. Some were long and spiky, hanging from the ceiling like icicles of stone; others were round and stout, plopped on the ground and resembling scoops of ice-cream. Portions of the walls were frozen in ripples, below which sat pools of water so clear and still that their surfaces appeared made of glass. Everything had been splashed with the most colorful palette, and Ret could sense which minerals had left behind which colors: green from copper, yellow from sulfur, rust from iron.

The cavern was a natural wonder. It seemed to be the product of many things, yet one thing in particular: time. Ret felt it was ungrateful of himself to spend only a few seconds admiring stalactites and stalagmites that had likely taken hundreds of years to form. He wished he could take his time and spend a whole day—even a week or a month—studying the curtains and columns, the cave pearls and soda straws. But then he caught himself: he was starting to sound like a certain pesky Guardian named Neo.

The faint rays of light meant they were nearing the other end of the cavern. The path gradually opened up and leveled out until the two of them arrived on the other side. Nika stopped to let Ret take in the view. They were overlooking a great valley, in which was nestled an amicable settlement. Small homes dotted the floor, interspersed among lush, green farmlands. The quaint colony was completely enclosed by several grand mesas, which resembled a pack of elephants circled face-out to protect their little ones. Calm and inviting, the locale seemed a sanctuary.

As Ret followed Nika into town, he found it possessed a charm that helped him see past its primitiveness. There were no streets because there were no cars—no office buildings because there was no need. It was one of those heard-about but never-seen settlements where people still walked to places and talked to each other—where pace was slowed and time had stalled, and where everyone's favorite gathering place was the front porch. Peace and quiet grazed alongside horses and cattle, with a creek meandering through it all.

"What is this place, Nika?" Ret asked.

"Oh, just somewhere special," she replied with a gratified smile.

"It doesn't have a name?" Ret wondered.

"Of course it does," Nika told him. "I call it home."

"Where does the light come from?" Ret inquired, glancing up at the sky, or whatever it was. "It can't be from the sun since we're underground..."

"We're underground?" Nika marveled.

"Yeah, I'm pretty sure," Ret said. "That's how *I* came here at least. How did *you* get here?"

"Through the trilithon," Nika explained, "like everyone else."

"What's the trilithon?" Ret asked curiously. He figured if this trilithon thing was an entrance, then it might also be an exit.

"Oh, it's not much," Nika bent the truth. Her growing fondness of Ret prompted her to talk about something else. "Look, here they come!"

Eager to welcome a new arrival, the town's citizens were making their way down to the main drag as Nika and her guest were coming up it. She called everyone by name as she introduced them to Ret. There was Stephanie, who was missing an arm, and Davis, who had an extra thumb; Kelly, who was wearing an eye patch, and Paul, who had a withered hand. Of course, Nika only referred to them by name, not by malady, but Ret couldn't help but notice each person's ailment.

In fact, every single person he met had some kind of challenge. A man with severe burns was helping a woman with a terrible limp. Two deaf friends were speaking to each other through sign language, punctuated by an occasional moan. A blind woman navigated her way toward Ret with the aid of her long, white walking stick. Once there was no nose; twice a lazy eye—not to mention three pairs of crutches and four canes. One man took a break only to shake hands, then returned to pacing back and forth while conversing with himself. Another stuttered so dreadfully that Ret could hardly understand her. This person was fighting cancer, that one had frequent seizures, and two others had never been the same since their strokes.

But these were only the frailties that could be seen, for, as Nika explained, there were scores of other individuals whose troubles were not so obvious. These were the depressed, the anxious, the lonely—the mentally ill and socially awkward. One man often mixed words so refused to speak, while one woman never minced words and refused to keep quiet. Some were overbearing; others felt undervalued—these too loud, those too quiet. Disorders ranged from sleeping to eating, from handling stress to managing anger. A few had no self-esteem, others had too much. Still more had been labeled as unstable, bipolar, or downright obnoxious. From hyperactive to compulsive, it seemed everyone had been given an acronym, and if they didn't self-identify as ADD or OCD, then they were just plain ODD—odd. Yet all, in some way, had once been diagnosed as different and, from then on, treated as defective.

This was all a little much for Ret to take in. It reminded him of a visit he had made once to a nursing home, where he delivered some baked goods and played a few rounds of bingo but in the end was relieved to leave. His emotions then were the same as they were now: a harrowing mixture of sympathy and guilt. On one hand, he felt sorry for these people—for the lot they had been given—while on the other hand, he felt a sense of duty, like it was his job to somehow ease their burdens. In his mind, their imperfections were wrongs that needed to be righted—glitches that needed to be fixed.

"You okay?" Nika asked Ret after the townspeople returned to their labors.

"Sort of," Ret said with noticeable heaviness.

"You look a little overwhelmed," she told him.

"Yeah," Ret sighed.

"It's because we're different, huh?" Nika assumed.

After a moment, Ret replied, "I just need some time to think."

"That's fine, I understand," Nika said. "Take your time." She left him with a smile.

Pensive and troubled, Ret commenced an unhurried stroll through town. He was being bombarded by all kinds of emotions—some familiar, others new, and many not his own. He felt like a failure for not being able to collect the element. Confusion plagued his mind for being rejected by a Guardian, and resentment haunted his heart for being told he wasn't ready. Not to mention the aimlessness he was experiencing as he wandered this strange place with its strange people— people whose problems weighed on him. He wanted to help them—longed to cure them—but, for some reason, they neither solicited his pity nor requested his opinion. In fact, they looked perfectly content with their subpar lives. It seemed they had already accepted the things they could not change, and it bothered Ret that their infirmities no longer bothered *them*.

When Ret's path came to the creek that flowed throughout the settlement, he turned and began to follow its bank, hoping a peaceful walk with nature would soothe his soul as it usually did. He felt refreshed, admiring the flora and fauna while enjoying the merry weather, until he took a closer look at one of the flowers. It resembled a daisy but seemed deformed. Its petals were not uniform but of various sizes, and its dark center was more a warped oval than a circle. It looked odd and unnatural, but Ret figured it was just a different variety.

He inspected a few other plants and found similar situations: crazy leaves, contorted stems, stunted growth. Some had multiple shoots, others had exposed roots. These were maturing too early, those were blooming too late. The distorted shapes and twisted designs gave the landscape the look and feel of a Salvador Dali painting.

The trees were also victims of these surreal abnormalities. Limbs suddenly ended in decay and dust. Trunks had grown holes like Swiss cheese. Fruits were misshaped and discolored. Pine trees shed needles with knots and dropped cones with whiskers.

Even the wildlife had fallen prey to this phantom predator. There were fish with only one eye and butterflies with three wings. Ladybugs were every color but red. Bumblebees had extra-long stingers. A raccoon was missing a paw, the squirrels had no tails, and even the songbirds were tone deaf.

There was something fundamentally wrong with this place. It looked like something out of Willy

Wonka's chocolate factory. From its people to its plants, this was a land of mutation where nothing was normal because everything was different—and none of it in a good way. Could this place ever be cured?

Yes, cured. Was it not Ret's job to 'cure the world'? Was that why he stumbled upon this mutated place—to cure it? Was this what the Guardian had in mind all along? Ret already had some control over plants and trees; did that extend to other living things? He had regrown an apple, so how about an arm? Foliage, so why not phalanges?

Ret's mind began to run wild. If, in fact, the wood element's powers stemmed to the cellular level, there was no end to the possibilities. Would he be able to restore sight to the blind and hearing to the deaf? Could he correct chromosomes and reroute synapses? Had cancer finally met its match? Was DNA now DIY?

Ret was ecstatic. He ran to the nearest tree and placed his hand on its trunk. He concentrated on his scar and let its surging energy flow through the bark and into the branches. He instructed the tree to produce fruit, not the funny-looking kind that now encumbered its limbs but the true kind that it was born to bear. Soon, blossoms appeared, then fruit began to bud. But when it matured, it was just as mutated as the others.

Frustrated, Ret withdrew his hand and rushed to a flowerbed close by. He wrapped his fingers around a tulip stem, but its deformed blooms were not fixed and only multiplied like a Hydra. The same occurred with the daffodils and the roses. The mums stayed underdeveloped, and the lilies remained wilted. Ret plucked out a seed from a spent sunflower head and sprouted it in his palm, but the plant that emerged was just as mutated as its parent. In his anger, he grew the sunflower way beyond maturation until its head exploded, sending seeds shooting in all directions.

"Why can't I do this?!" he yelled. "Why can't I fix anything?" He fell to his knees in front of a large tree and slammed his fists into the dirt. He channeled his rage into the tree, causing it to swell until it had tripled in size. Then he fell on his back and laid on the grass.

Ret had reached a breaking point, desperate for change but incapable of it. He wanted to collect the element but was denied. He appealed for Neo's help but was spurned. He yearned to fix Nika and her people but couldn't. He attempted to cure their environment but failed. He was lost and lonely—purposeless and powerless. He didn't see the point in trying anymore.

Ret watched the shadows grow longer and longer until night fell over the land, the dimness of evening diminishing the details of everything. But instead of crickets chirping and owls hooting, Ret heard singing.

He stood and followed his ears to the town square, where the citizens had gathered for a variety show of sorts. Ret sat alone in the back as a group of school children finished their musical number. A poetry reading ensued. Next came acts of ballet, vocal and instrumental pieces, stories of personal triumphs, interpretive dancing, remembrances of deceased villagers, and even a bit of comedy. There were times of applause and laughter, interspersed with moods of sadness and tears, all against the backdrop of a warm fire.

Just when the night seemed over, someone in the crowd called out for one more performance. Obviously a favorite among them, the idea quickly gained momentum until Nika finally assented and took the stage. The audience cheered. A violinist joined her, knowing the routine. Nika waited for silence, then opened her mouth and, with the voice of an angel, sang this song:

> *I have a difference*
> *That makes me stick out,*
> *That's made me a reference*
> *For shame and for doubt.*
> *Though I've denied it,*
> *It's always still there.*
> *I try to hide it,*
> *But people still stare.*
>
> *They keep their distance*

And say words that sting —
That my flaw's existence
My own fault did bring.
So from life I've withdrawn,
And my friends I eschew,
Till hope's all but gone
And I hate me, too.

Yet what if mutations
Aren't meant for the host
But for populations
Who point fingers the most?
Maybe the reason
My difference won't budge
Is to teach them the lesson
To love and not judge.

For whoever said
Being different is bad?
It's in the scorner's head
Where that notion is had.
Since I could not rend
What they call my chink,
It might only end
If they change how they think.

So I'll be the mutant
That I could not nix,
Embrace my pollutant
That folks want to fix.
Soon the estranging
Will stop, and they'll see

That what needed changing
Was them and not me.

Long live the mutants,
The never-have-beens,
The outcasts and tangents
Who just don't fit in.
Long live our troubles
To keep pure our hearts.
Let's be the people
From whom the love starts.

As always, Nika sang the final verse once more, this time every mutant in the audience adding their voice to hers in singing the anthem they loved so much.

On that note, the evening ended. Feeling very small, Ret watched as the townsfolk got up to leave. These were the humble and homely—the cancered and crippled, the autistic and dyslexic—whose troubles ranged from upset stomach to Down syndrome. In a word, these were the mutants—the mess-ups when anatomy goes wrong.

Soon, only Ret remained, weighed down by his thoughts. It seemed the words of Nika's song had been meant specifically for him. He felt ashamed for the littleness of soul with which he had approached this town—a community that he had been bent on changing when he was the one who needed to change.

"Hey, handsome," Nika said, coming up from behind.

Ret exhaled with sadness and told her, "I think I need to go."

"Yes, well, the show *is* over," Nika joked.

"No, I mean leave this place—go back home."

"Oh," Nika said despondently.

"Can you show me the way?" Ret asked.

"If you want me to," Nika replied with disappointment, as if waiting for Ret to change his mind. When he didn't, she glanced at the dark sky and sighed, "If we leave now, we should be able to make it to the trilithon by first light."

Ret followed his guide through the shadows. There were no caverns to cut through on the journey this time, which was taking them to the far side of the valley. Where the farmlands ended, the brush of the desert resumed, growing ever sparser until their route became one of sand and rock. Ret could feel a slight incline to their path, and more than once he caught sight of a nocturnal creature.

After climbing a series of nature-made steps, they reached a landing that overlooked the valley. The first signs of light were just beginning to stir the expanse overhead.

"This is the trilithon," Nika announced.

Ret turned around to see what she was talking

about. There, in the center of a grassy plot, stood the trilithon, a solitary stone structure consisting of three great slabs of rock. Two of its pieces stood side-by-side, each about eight feet wide, five feet thick, and more than twenty feet tall. The third piece was a bit smaller in size, though still large, and had been laid across the top. The monument's post-and-lintel design gave it the appearance of a great doorway, even though the space between the two posts was only wide enough to admit one person at a time.

Ret slowly walked around the structure, admiring the massive stones that dwarfed him as Nika continued to speak: "It is the symbol of our way of life here. This stone," she said, touching the post on the left, "represents love of deity. And this one," touching the post on the right, "represents love of man. On these two pillars hang everything that we do," she added, pointing to the lintel across the top.

"Those are your only laws?" Ret asked. "Just love?"

"Just love," Nika answered contentedly. "That's what all other laws lead back to."

"I guess that makes sense," Ret said. "So how is this the way out of here?"

"Well, to be honest," Nika confessed, "I'm not a hundred-percent positive this really *is* the way out."

"What do you mean?"

"Since this is how we all got here," Nika explained, "we've always just kind of *assumed* it would take us back. But no one has ever tried it because no one has ever wanted to go back."

"Well, I guess it's worth a shot," Ret said, undaunted. Nika seemed a bit disappointed that her disclaimer had not deterred Ret's resolve. "How does it work?"

"If it works the same as how we got here," Nika said, "then you stand in the middle, and when the light appears above that ridge," she pointed to the top of the mesa on the other side of the valley, "the trilithon should take you to the other side."

"Like this?" Ret wondered, sliding between the two posts.

"Maybe," Nika chuckled, "but I was thinking more like this." She turned him ninety degrees so that he was facing frontwards. "You know, it'd be a little easier if your shoulders weren't so broad." Standing close together, they stared into each other's eyes for a long minute. Although Nika was a little older than Ret, she was very pretty, and her skin disease didn't stand out as much as it did when he first met her.

"I didn't realize how bright your eyes were," she whispered, their noses nearly touching now. "They're like sapphires."

Ret figured the growing light behind Nika was

accentuating his eyes. He brought his hand to her face to caress her cheek, but then his face clouded over.

"What?" Nika asked, automatically stepping back and covering the scarred portion of her face. "It's my skin, isn't it?"

"No, it's *my* skin," Ret replied with amazement, inspecting his hand and then his arms. "My skin is so pale—almost like it used to be." Ret's eyes widened at the possibility. He promptly pulled down a lock of hair from the front of his scalp and confirmed his suspicion: "And my hair is getting lighter again, too!"

"Again?" Nika wondered.

It was true: Ret's former appearance was returning. There was something about this land that was causing him to mutate back into his old self—his real self—a self that he had forgotten was a part of him. Now it was coming back, as if to remind him of his true identity.

It was in this moment when Ret came to a life-altering realization: he was a mutant. Yes, a mutant—not only in his appearance but also in his past and present, his hopes and habits, his family and fears. If anyone in this world was a mutant, it was him, for he was the most different of all. Oh what a hypocrite he was to have judged this land's people when he was one of them! Surely, this was where he belonged.

The first streaks of light were just peeking over the ridge across the valley—streaks that would, in some unknown way, purportedly take Ret back to where he had come. But just as the light fell on the trilithon, he stepped out from between its two posts and purposely missed his chance. He would not be going back; this was his new home.

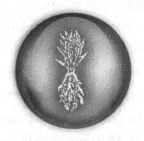

CHAPTER 11

MESSAGES OF WOOD
AND STONE

Back in the Siberian wilderness, at the bottom of the vast excavation site, Mr. Coy and Serge were pacing back and forth at the foot of the great tree, unsure of their next move. Several hours had passed since Ret had been dragged underground, with no indication of him returning any time soon. Although the Russian president seemed quite distressed about the situation, Mr. Coy was filled with more wonder than worry. He knew Ret was in the element's territory now, and so he didn't feel too uneasy when his repeated attempts to make contact with Ret proved futile. Still, night was approaching, and the falling temperature meant they needed to seek shelter.

"I think it's time I headed back to Moscow," Serge eventually said. "If you'd rather stay here, I'll give orders to the excavation superintendent to see to your needs."

"No, no," Mr. Coy replied, "I should get going, too. We've waited here long enough."

As they walked toward the helicopter, Mr. Coy tried to convince himself of his decision to abandon his vigil. Well aware that the Oracle was in his possession, a part of him wanted to remain nearby in case Ret came looking for it, if in fact the time to collect the element was drawing nigh. But he figured Moscow would be close enough for now.

Feeling slightly dejected and very unhelpful, Mr. Coy sat down in the cabin of the helicopter with a heavy sigh. Then, as he gave the pit floor one last sweeping gaze, he saw something he hadn't seen before: a small wooden sign, staked in the dirt by one of the tree's massive roots.

"What is that?" Coy wondered aloud, pointing at the sign.

"Shall we investigate?" Serge offered.

The pair quickly returned to the place of their watch and, in the twilight, read this brief message: *Ret is fine, call Paige.*

Now Mr. Coy was beginning to worry. Utilizing the helicopter's portable cellular tower to connect his call, he immediately took out his cell phone and dialed Paige's number, his heart pounding and mind racing. Where had this sign come from? Who had written it? And how did they know his daughter? With each unanswered ring, Mr. Coy was growing more and more concerned. He traced each letter of the sign's message with his eyes, over and over again. The words had not been written with ink but rather carved into the wood.

"Dad?" Paige finally answered, sounding somewhat groggy.

"Hi, sweetheart," Coy said with relief. "Are you okay?"

"Dad, it's five o'clock in the morning," Paige told him with a yawn.

"What have you been up to?" he asked, trying to find out why the mysterious sign had instructed him to call her.

"Not much," Paige responded, half asleep. "School's been out for the holidays."

"Is there anything you'd like to talk about?" Coy probed.

She had almost dozed off when she remembered, "Actually," perking up, "there is: Ana and I were exploring a really old part of the Keep the other day, and I found something that I wanted to show you."

"What is it?"

"It's a drawing of Stonehenge," she explained, "not how it currently is but either how it used to be or could have been. And there are all kinds of notes written faintly on it. I was thinking maybe we can go there when you and Ret get back?"

Mr. Coy was about to tell Paige to save the idea for later, but then he saw an entirely new message written on the little wooden sign: *Go there now.*

Coy and Serge glared wide-eyed at each other.

"Dad?" Paige said on the other line. "Dad, are you still there?"

"I...I think that's a great idea," Coy said, still in shock.

"You do?"

"In fact, why don't I meet you there?" he suggested, a bit robotic.

"When?" Paige questioned.

Coy hesitated for a moment, unsure of the sign's motives. Just then an invisible hand underlined the word 'now,' at which point Coy swallowed and told Paige, "Now?"

"Okay, great!" Paige cheered. "I'll get on the next flight. Can Ana come, too?"

Coy looked to the sign for guidance. A 'thumbs-up' symbol appeared.

"Sure," Coy told her. "I'll meet you at the airport in London, okay?"

"Okay, see you soon!" Paige concluded.

"Bye."

When the phone call ended, the sign showed a smiley face.

"What is going on?" Serge inquired with awe.

"I'm not really sure," Coy admitted, "but how soon can you get me to London?"

"You'll be on the first flight as soon as we return to Moscow," the president promised.

"Great," Coy said, stepping away from the sign. "Now let's get out of here."

Fairly creeped out, they anxiously returned to the helicopter, leapt inside, and shut the door. As the chopper's blades began to spin, Mr. Coy looked back to see if the sign's message had changed yet again. The sign was gone.

O   O   O

"Hi, Dad!" Paige called out after she and Ana spotted him at the airport.

"There's my girl!" he grinned, scooping her up in his arms. "Hello, Ana."

"Hey, Mr. Coy," Ana returned his side hug, gladly letting him carry some of their luggage.

The drive to Stonehenge gave the trio an opportunity to catch up on the recent past and strategize for the near future. The fact that Mr. Coy had arranged to get around by rental car rather than public transit allowed them to speak freely. He knew Lye had eyes and ears nearly everywhere, and he even wondered if the strange message from the wooden sign was leading them straight into a trap, which was why he wanted to visit the tourist spot in broad daylight when there were lots of other people around.

"I want you two always by my side," Mr. Coy informed the girls as they approached their destination. "No wandering off, understood?"

"Yes, sir," they replied in unison.

They parked the car and headed toward the site, walking side by side. It was a cold afternoon, the sun lost behind a dense blanket of gray clouds. Their faces stiffened in the cool air of a slight breeze, and the thick grass was still damp from a recent drizzle. Despite the gloomy weather, however, there was no shortage of visitors who had come to admire the famous wonder of the ancient world, its great sarsen stones towering above the crowds like llamas watching over herds of sheep. Trying to look as unsuspicious as possible, Mr. Coy led Paige and Ana to an empty space along the outer edge of the inner circle—at least, that's what the tour guide called it:

"And in this inner circle," the middle-aged woman told the group of tourists, "there are five trilithons." Dozens of sightseers took out their cameras to capture the majesty of the trilithons, those mysterious monoliths that, with their lintelled posts, looked like doorways to another time. The guide added, "Only three of the five are still fully intact."

It was true: the two trilithons on the left and the one on the far right all looked complete, each consisting of two giant vertical posts with a slimmer horizontal lintel on top. The other two trilithons, however, were in bad shape. Both the one immediately to the right and the one directly across from them had fallen apart, so much so that only one of their posts was still standing. Each of their second posts and their lintels lay broken on the ground.

The tour guide then directed everyone's attention away from the inner circle and instead toward the outer circle.

"In its day, it is believed that the outer circle made a full and complete ring around the inner circle," she taught. Well clearly, its 'day' had long since passed, for the outer circle was in about as bad of shape as the inner one. It had been built on the same concept, with posts lined up next to each other and lintels laid across their tops. Besides the stones being smaller, the only difference was that there was no break in the lintels along the top, making the outer circle one continuous structure — in theory that is, for most of it lay in ruins, strewn all over the grassy site.

In a word, Stonehenge was a disaster. As interesting as it was to meander among such history, the World Heritage Site was a wreck. If Ret had been there, he may have been tempted to tidy up the place — you know, just put a few stones back where they went (which he could easily do, of course, despite their enormous size). But even then, the monument would not have been complete, for many stones were missing from the site altogether.

Losing interest in the guided tour, Paige reached into her pocket and retrieved the aerial illustration of Stonehenge that she had found down in the 2500 B.C. floor of the Keep. With Mr. Coy and Ana peering over her shoulder, Paige unfolded it and positioned it until it lined up with where they were standing. They analyzed it for several moments, Mr. Coy regularly glancing around themselves to make sure no one was eavesdropping.

"Well, the drawing sure is prettier," Ana observed.

"Look how every lintel connects along the outer circle," Coy noted.

"Lintel?" Ana repeated the unfamiliar term. "Isn't that a kind of bean?"

"No, that's lentil," Paige corrected. "Lintel is a horizontal block that spans the space between two vertical supports."

Ana rolled her eyes, "Tomato, tomato."

Recalling the wooden sign's insistence that he take Paige to Stonehenge, Mr. Coy appealed to his daughter for her thoughts, "What do you make of it, sweetheart?"

Her eyes squinted in contemplation, she said, "The

thing that jumps out to me the most is the presence of a sixth trilithon in the drawing." She pointed to it on the paper. "It shows another trilithon right...," she said, stepping to the corresponding spot on the grass, "...here." The inner circle was more like a horseshoe than an actual circle, for there was a large gap at the end where she was standing. Or perhaps it was an unfinished circle, for Paige was getting the feeling that something was missing from the original design.

"Excuse me," she called out to the tour guide, folding up the drawing and returning it to her pocket. The lady, a prim and proper Englishwoman, displayed a revolting expression on her face, as if she had never been interrupted in her entire tour-guiding career.

"Yes?" she grimaced at Paige, raising one side of her upper lip, which caused her nostril to flare.

"Could it be possible that there used to be *six* trilithons?" Paige put forth. Several of the tourists began to mumble amongst themselves, intrigued by the idea. The tour guide had never been asked that question, and she wasn't sure how to respond.

"How do you mean?" she finally said.

"I'm curious why there is such a big, empty space on this side of the inner circle," Paige explained, extending her arms to partially span the gap. "Doesn't it seem like the perfect spot for a sixth trilithon?"

"I understand what you're saying," the guide told

her smugly, anxious to regain control of the tour, "but everyone knows Stonehenge has only ever had five trilithons."

"But how do we *know* that?" Paige persisted.

"We just do," she fleered, straightening her neck like an old buzzard. "All the experts agree."

"But just because a bunch of people believe something, doesn't mean it's true," Paige pressed. "'All the experts' used to think the earth was flat, remember?"

"Well, do *you* see any *remains* of a sixth trilithon? Hmm?" the tour guide shot back.

"No, but I don't see any remains of most of the outer circle either," Paige returned. The tourists were enjoying the debate. "All I'm saying is, could it be *possible* that there used to be a sixth trilithon?"

"Nonsense," the guide dismissed.

"But if the outer circle was originally a complete circle, why wouldn't the inner one have been, too?" Paige was winning over several of the tourists.

"I'm sorry, young lady, but you are disrupting my tour," the annoyed woman growled. "I'm going to have to ask you to vacate the premises."

Paige thought that was an unusually harsh ultimatum to give to an inquisitive tourist. Actually, it made her suspicious that someone might be trying to hide something.

"Come on, dear," Mr. Coy gently touched Paige's

shoulders from behind, "let's get going." The trio walked off, much to the delight of the tour guide, her face unflinching.

"But Dad," Paige protested on their way back to the car, "don't you see it, too?"

"Of course I do, honey," Coy whispered back. "But we weren't going to get very far, so long as that battleax was on duty." Once they had piled back into the car and closed the doors, Coy told them, "We'll come back late tonight, after the place is closed."

"Where are we going now?" Ana inquired as they pulled out of the parking lot.

Coy replied, "To get our costumes."

O   O   O

It was a few hours after midnight when Mr. Coy and his two accomplices returned to Stonehenge—well, the general area of it, that is, for like most people about to engage in not-so-legal activities, they made sure to park a fair distance away. The full moon cast a bright glow on the English countryside, and the air had turned bitter cold, which wasn't a problem since the three of them were covered in strips of synthetic fur.

"I can't believe I'm wearing this," Ana complained as she and the Coys covered themselves in material they had purchased earlier from a textile shop in town.

"Now remember," Mr. Coy told them, "we're trying to look like a family of deer, out grazing for an early morning meal." The girls pinned up their hair. "It's still dark enough that if we take it slow, we shouldn't provoke any security guards."

"What are the knee pads for?" Ana wondered.

"We'll be walking on all fours," Coy replied.

"And don't forget these," Paige said, handing the others each a fake nose, tail, and pair of pointy ears, which were actually just variations of party hats.

"You really think this is going to work, Mr. Coy?" Ana asked candidly.

"I think we've got a good chance," he answered, "especially thanks to *this*." He brought out a headpiece of fake antlers and secured it on his head. Then striking a pose, he said, "What do you think?"

"Oh dear," Paige unintentionally quipped at the unusual sight.

"I think you could double as the Exalted Ruler of an Elks Lodge," Ana remarked.

"Perfect," Coy cheered, locking the car and preparing to execute his plan. "Come on, let's get our deer on."

The fraudulent ruminants fell to their knees and began their unhurried crawl toward Stonehenge.

"We need to *walk* like a deer," Coy quietly advised, demonstrating his counsel by following no prescribed path and occasionally pausing. "We need to *think* like a deer." He craned his neck upwards as if alarmed. "We need to *act* like a deer." He put his face near the grass and pretended to eat it.

"Oh no," Ana refused. "I draw the line at eating grass."

It was slow going for the quasi quadrupeds. After passing the earthwork enclosure that encircled the site, they crossed the vast lawn until they finally arrived within the massive stones, which provided some degree of cover.

Still in disguise, they roamed the prehistoric site. Paige automatically returned to the empty space at the top of the horseshoe-like inner circle. She was drawn to it for some reason. She took out the drawing of Stonehenge and studied it again. The illustration showed a sixth trilithon, exactly where she was kneeling. With growing certainty, she suspected a trilithon did, in fact, once stand there. And if that was true, then it had been completely removed, for there was no evidence of it ever being there, unlike the two dilapidated trilithons in the circle whose remains lay on the ground. But who would have done such a thing? How? Why?

"Hey, girl," Ana whispered, arriving at Paige's side. "Is your fur starting to itch, too?"

"A little," Paige replied, without looking up. This was Ana's first opportunity to compare the two-dimensional drawing to the actual monument. She could easily see the distinction that Paige had made earlier during the tour: there were six trilithons on paper but only five in real life. Ana counted again. Something was missing. Where was the sixth trilithon?

One, two, three, four, five. Ana counted the remaining trilithons over and over again. One, two, three, four, five—then including the gap—six. Wait. Where had she seen this before? Her mind reached back to the health lecture at school. Then her focus changed from trilithons to food groups, and she had an epiphany.

"Hello, my *dears*," Mr. Coy joked as he joined the girls from behind. "Mind if I also take a look?" Paige held up the drawing for all to see.

The mystery of the missing trilithon was distracting the three of them from the approaching dawn. At their backs, the eastern sky was gradually growing brighter, rapidly burning up the low clouds. The fading darkness, however, meant the effectiveness of their costumes was fading, too.

"Freeze!" a threatening voice cried out. The mock mammals spun around in alarm. A security guard was running towards them.

Huddled together, the trespassers were unsure of what to do. Paige and Ana looked to Mr. Coy for guidance. Just when they were about to make a run for it, the first rays of the morning sun appeared on the horizon. A blinding light engulfed them from behind, and the trio disappeared.

CHAPTER 12

SUBATOMIC PROBLEMS

In an instant, Mr. Coy found himself in an entirely different setting. The grassy countryside that surrounded Stonehenge had been replaced by a rocky coastline along open ocean. Whereas a moment ago the sun had been rising behind him, it was now setting in front of him. A quick glance at his watch told him the date hadn't changed but that the time was nearly twelve hours later. When he turned around, he recognized his new location immediately. He was at Waters Deep.

Instinctively, Mr. Coy reached for Paige and Ana to protect them from potential dangers on this inhospitable island. But the girls weren't there. In fact, he didn't see either of them anywhere. He was about to go searching for them but immediately froze, figuring there were cameras all over the place. Then he realized he was still wearing his deer costume. He slowly fell to his knees and began to putter around, hoping the shadows of the approaching evening would help to obscure his true identity.

"Paige? Ana?" Coy whispered, as he made like a deer and dillydallied in the vicinity, despite the lack of vegetation. He was in an exceptionally stony area, close enough to the sea that he could feel the spray of the large waves as they crashed into the jetty-like shore. He had arrived in the vertical cleft of a large rock, much taller than him. As black as all the others, it was a single boulder that had been worn through in the center so that it was in the shape of a roughly square arch, like a crude and miniature version of the Arc de Triomphe in Paris, France. In fact, what it really looked like was a variation of a trilithon.

Still no sign of the girls, Mr. Coy began to meander inland, knowing he needed to keep moving in order to avoid drawing attention to himself. Although he did not understand how or why he had come to be at the Deep, he marveled at a strange coincidence: for many days now, he had been deeply concerned about Jaret. Was his friend dead or alive? Was he still Coy's secret link to Lye's inner circle, or had he been brainwashed again? More than once in the past few weeks, Coy hadn't been able to sleep at night, wondering if it was his duty to sneak to the Deep and rescue the captive Cooper man. He had always decided against doing so, but now here he was, on the wretched island. It was almost as if Stonehenge had known what was weighing on his mind and heart.

Night fell, and although the daylight faded, the warm temperature lingered, thanks to the many hot springs that dotted the landscape. A bright moon shone overhead, both revealing and concealing just enough. Mr. Coy was unsure of his next move. As much as he wanted to liberate his imprisoned comrade, he wasn't fully prepared to storm the bastille, and there wasn't exactly a neon sign that identified an entrance into the Deep's underground facility. Besides, he didn't know if Jaret was even on the island.

Coy was contemplating the idea of trying to figure out a way to get home when he heard a plane touch down nearby. It was a small plane, judging by the faint noise the tires made as they skidded along the ground. Mr. Coy hurried to find it, following the sound of spinning propellers. He arrived at a long field, which apparently served as a runway. Hiding behind a bush, Mr. Coy watched as the far end of the narrow airstrip began to lower into the earth, hinging at the other end and becoming a ramp that served as an entrance into the Deep's fortress. The plane bounced along as it rolled down the ramp.

"Not bad," Mr. Coy commented to himself as he observed the secret passageway, knowing he had a few of his own back at the Manor. "I like mine better, but not bad."

Reaching the end, the plane drove off the ramp and into the underground facility, at which time the ramp promptly began to close.

"It's now or never," Coy said as he leapt from his hiding spot. He ran toward the ramp, hoping to slip inside the ever-narrowing crevice along the nearest edge, but it was closing too quickly. He entered a full sprint, now more than halfway down the runway. His best chance at having enough room was at the far end. Just as it was about to seal shut, he angled his legs and fell on his side, gliding toward the gap like a baseball player sliding into home plate. The ramp closed. He had made it.

Well, sort of: his fake antlers had gotten caught, pinched between the ramp and the ground when they came together. Mr. Coy was stuck on the ceiling like a bat, hanging several yards above the plane. He was about to free himself from his headpiece when he was distracted by who got out of the plane.

"Welcome to Waters Deep, Mr. Zarbock," a pair of men greeted the world-renowned physicist, each extending a hand. Short and stout, they were identical twins, both balding and wearing oversized eyeglasses. Although Lionel wasn't exactly their superior, they were intimidated by him.

Spurning the handshakes, Lionel replied with displeasure, "Hello, Abacus," then addressing the other man, "Hello, Aloysius." Besides their parents, there were only two people who could tell the twins apart— every time, without fail: Lye and Lionel.

In a patronizing tone, Lionel said, "Lye tells me you Foxx twins could use some help." He began to walk away at a fast pace, knowing the twins would follow.

Mr. Coy was surprised by how uncordial Lionel was acting. It was very unlike him. Of course, he *did* look rather worn out, almost stumbling once or twice. Lionel chalked it up to jetlag, but Mr. Coy wondered if his true colors were bleeding through.

"We're doing the best we can," Abacus pled after catching up to Lionel, who he purposely stayed a step behind, assuming that was his place.

"What Lye wants done is no small feat," Aloysius sought for sympathy. "Most *countries* aren't even capable of doing it."

"Your excuses are disappointing," Lionel returned without mercy. "I can see why Lye is so frustrated with you two." The brothers looked down in shame as Lionel turned and led them down a hallway, out of sight.

Still dangling, Mr. Coy turned his attention to the pilot, who was the only other person in the room now. Coy not only needed to get by him unnoticed but was also counting on the pilot to break his fall. When the unsuspecting man exited the plane, Coy started to swing. Then, after the pilot closed and locked the cabin door, Mr. Coy aimed and unbuckled himself from his antlers, falling on the man and knocking him out.

"Thanks for the smooth landing," he told the unconscious fellow.

Coy shed the rest of his deer costume, then followed after the Foxx twins and their guest. With great caution, he tiptoed through the dark hallways, stepping lightly on the glass floor, which seemed to amplify the sound of his footsteps. He was in a high-tech wing of the Deep, a scientific workshop of sorts that pulsed with a tangible energy, like the turbine chamber at the base of a hydroelectric dam. A subdued, throbbing noise—this lair's heartbeat—was so pervasive that it seemed to reach in and beat Mr. Coy's eardrums.

When he could hear voices again, Coy reduced his speed to a snail's pace. Nearing the end of the hall, he crouched down and peeked around the corner into a spacious room. This huge and hollow underground cavity was bustling with activity. There were plumes of steam where hot metal was being cooled in cold water. There were flashes of light from heavy machinery fabricating specialized parts. The honking of big trucks competed with the beeping of forklifts. Deliveries were being made, and shipments were being sent. Some workers used power tools and were filthy, while others used computers and were unsullied.

Although Mr. Coy had an idea of what was going on here, his suspicions were confirmed when he saw what Lionel and the twins were standing in front of: the half-finished shell of an atomic bomb. Suddenly, Mr. Coy's heart began to race. He needed to get closer— needed to hear what they were saying. But how?

Just then, Mr. Coy heard someone coming from behind him. It was a worker arriving for his shift. Still crouched down, Coy pretended to be tying his shoe as the man strode by. He discretely watched the employee put on one of the white protective jumpsuits hanging up on the wall before entering an adjacent lab and getting to work. Mr. Coy did the same, stepping into and zipping up the suit, but instead of reporting to a lab, he headed toward Lionel and the twins, observing the different stations along the way.

The entire uranium enrichment process, from ore to fuel, was being carried out under a single roof. It began with a chemical reaction that turned solid uranium into a gas. The gas was then put into cylindrical tubes called centrifuges. About the size of a person, these tubes were then spun at super high speeds to separate the heavier uranium-238 gas molecules (which were much more prevalent, though useless for nuclear purposes) from the slightly lighter uranium-235 gas molecules (which were fewer but could be used for fuel or warheads). The spinning pulled some of the heavier particles to the edges, leaving the lighter ones in the center, which were then put into another centrifuge to be refined even more. Apparently, this process was repeated over and over and over again, for Mr. Coy could see hundreds of thousands of tubes lined up. Once the uranium was refined enough, another chemical reaction converted it back into a solid, and it was now ready for use. Money and manpower, space and skill — the uranium enrichment procedure required exorbitant amounts of each.

Arriving within earshot of his least favorite person and the identical Foxx twins, Mr. Coy turned his back to the party but tuned into their conversation, fiddling with some random devices to make it look like he was focusing on something else.

"Why is this taking so long?" Lionel asked with a hostile air.

"We're working day and night, sir," Abacus begged.

"That's not good enough!" Lionel sneered.

"Perhaps if we had more resources," Aloysius said, "then we could—"

"You have everything you need," Lionel retorted. "The creation of this bomb is Lye's top priority. We're running out of time."

"We will do everything in our power to have it ready for the attack on Coy Manor," Abacus pledged. Mr. Coy clenched his fists.

"This isn't for the attack, you fools!" Lionel scoffed.

"But I thought—" Aloysius started.

"But what?!" Lionel interrupted. "Lye has asked *me* to *lead* the attack on the Manor; don't you think I know what I'm talking about?" Mr. Coy gritted his teeth. "This weapon is for Ret. He has only one known weakness, and this is it. Why do you think Lye had you create the fission gun, hmm? That gun proved the boy's vulnerability. The Oracle is moving fast; Ret is already within reach of the fifth element. This bomb must be ready before the Oracle is filled."

By now, Mr. Coy had stopped tinkering. The mention of the attack on the Manor was bad enough, but the fact that Lionel was the one who would be leading it was even more irritating. And now Lye was building an atomic bomb to destroy Ret? Mr. Coy couldn't believe what he was hearing. He was livid.

"And so I ask you again," Lionel continued, "why is this taking so long?!" He banged his fist against the bomb's empty shell, the deep sound echoing throughout the room. "The only limitation I can see is you two," he pointed at them, "Tweedledee and Tweedledum. *You* are to blame."

"A thousand apologies, sir," Abacus besought, as if his life depended on it.

"Have you two mutinied also?" Lionel raged, his stress turning his hair grayer by the minute. "First, Commander Jaret tried to steal Lye's cane, and now the Russian president has defected." The twins gasped. "Is anyone still loyal to Lye? For all I know, that man over there has deserted us, too." Lionel pointed to the man in the white suit whose back was turned to them. "That man hasn't moved in ten minutes. You there, come here immediately."

Mr. Coy had been caught. Yet, strangely, he wasn't worried. There was something he wanted to do, especially after what he had just heard but really ever since he had met Lionel in the prison at Sunken Earth years ago. And Coy figured now was as good an opportunity as ever.

"You in the white suit," Lionel repeated. "I said come here!"

Mr. Coy looked down at the ground as if ashamed, then obediently trudged toward Lionel.

"You see, gentlemen," Lionel told the twins, "maybe if your workforce wasn't so lazy, things wouldn't be taking so long." Mr. Coy was getting more fed up with every step. "Watch how I take care of this problem."

His head still bent, Mr. Coy arrived in front of Lionel.

"And what do you have to say for yourself, scumbag?" Lionel mocked. "Are you still loyal to Lye?"

"That depends," Mr. Coy calmly replied, still avoiding eye-contact. Lionel and the twins were shocked.

"What did you say?!" Lionel threatened.

Mr. Coy finally looked up and said, staring squarely at Lionel, "Has Lye ever—*Ben Coy?*" Lionel's eyes bulged when he recognized the imposter, but before he could make a move, Mr. Coy punched him in the face. Lionel collided into the Foxx twins, and the three of them fell to the ground. Mr. Coy took off.

With a black eye and a bloody nose, Lionel yelled, "After him!"

Mr. Coy leapt over the railing and onto the ground floor, hoping his pursuers would lose track of him among the junk piles and various vehicles that crowded the lowest level. He slipped out of his suit and tied each arm to the raised forks of a parked forklift, making it look like he was making his escape by holding on and hanging between them. Then he jammed the lift's gears and sent it on a ghost ride, hoping the decoy would buy him some time.

Mr. Coy ran in the opposite direction. The entire facility was on alert, red alarms gonging every other second and bathing the place in splashes of red light. Although there were plenty of spots to hide, Mr. Coy knew he needed to get out of the room and fast. Off to the side, he saw a dump truck unloading a bunch of refuse into a kind of garbage chute. Mr. Coy ran over there, hid until the truck was through, and then jumped onto the chute. Like riding a playground slide, he glided down the slick track, using his arms and legs to slow his descent. When he neared the end, he came to a stop and hopped out.

He was in a junkyard of sorts. It was a sorry sight, the place where things go when they break down or burn up. Rusted refrigerators, jacked up automobiles, scrap metal, engines, computer hardware, tangled wires, even a Humvee—each in need of a quick fix or a long overhaul. Mr. Coy was in the market for a new set of wheels, something small and swift. Off to the left, between a truck with a cracked windshield and a van with a flat tire, he saw a four-wheeler. He ran to it. The service tag said it was in for minor body damage, but the key was in the ignition. Mr. Coy shrugged and climbed on, then turned the key and peeled out.

Meanwhile, in the chaos a few floors above, the runaway forklift had been seized. A mixture of personnel swarmed the vehicle. It didn't take long for them to realize they had been tricked.

"Find him!" Lionel announced, tearing Coy's white suit in half, which seemed to require all his strength. "He knows too much. Bring him to me—dead or alive, I don't care!"

"But sir," Aloysius countered, "only Lye approves of executions."

"Lye put me in charge," Lionel snarled. "Now find him!"

But Mr. Coy was on the move. He was speeding up and down the halls, taking whatever path would lead him up another floor, closer to the ground. He could see guards spilling into some of the halls, with more and more sirens sounding.

Despite the urgent situation, Mr. Coy came to something that made him stop. He had reached the end of another hallway, arriving in a circular hub where several other hallways met, and was startled by what he discovered in the center of the room. There was a glass tank, full of water, with a man inside. To Coy's horror, that man was Jaret. Attached to his face was a corded mask, supplying him with a limited amount of oxygen that was keeping him in this comatose state. The prisoner was in bad shape, clothed in nothing but spandex shorts and looking very pale in his liquid cell. A constant stream of air bubbles rose from the bottom of the tank, causing Jaret to bob up and down as if in a lava lamp.

The tank had been roped off, purposely placed in the center of the hub for display purposes. A placard at the base of the tank read, "The fate of all rebels." A scare tactic to instill allegiance in his minions, it was a typical teaching tool for Lye, who was battling more and more dissension these days.

Mr. Coy grabbed one of the rope stands and starting whaling on the tank. After a few hits, a crack appeared, accompanied by a fine mist. He directed all the anger of the night at the glass until he broke through, warm water gushing out. He was soaked but didn't care, reaching in and pulling out his dazed friend. Coy removed the oxygen mask, and Jaret took his first deep breath in days.

"Ben?" Jaret asked, his eyes out of focus and mind in a fog.

"Rise and shine, captain," Coy replied, setting Jaret on the four-wheeler.

"How are my girls?" Jaret said with concern, color returning to his face. "How are Pauline and Ana?" Just then, a round of bullets shattered the rest of the tank's glass, fired from a squadron coming up one of the hallways.

"Probably a lot better off than we are right now," Coy answered, sitting in front of Jaret and speeding away. "Any idea how to get out of this place?"

"Uh..." Jaret stuttered, trying to figure out where they were. "Turn right." Coy obeyed. "Now go full speed ahead."

"Into that wall?" Coy wondered.

"Don't worry," Jaret reassured him, "they're double doors disguised as a wall."

"Okay…" said Coy warily, increasing their speed.

Then, just before impact, Jaret added, "At least I think they are."

"What?!"

The captain was correct. Like something out of Coy Manor, the swinging doors parted down the middle, allowing the four-wheeler to pass through with ease. A short, dirt ramp immediately ensued, which they followed up to a small meadow on ground level.

"Looks like we're not in the clear yet," Jaret observed, eyeing the numerous guards that were popping up like gophers—some on foot, others on wheels, and still more in the air. Mr. Coy sped off.

"Where are you going?" Jaret asked.

"I know a rock that will get us off this island," Coy responded, glancing up at the sky, which was showing the first signs of morning.

"A rock?" Jaret gulped.

"Don't worry," Coy said, "it's a special rock."

"Okay," Jaret said, unconvinced.

Then, with both honesty and playfulness, Coy smiled, "At least I think it is."

The nimble four-wheeler cut through the thick forest like a hare, keeping ahead of the troops. The fugitives became nervous whenever there was a clearing, giving their enemies a chance for an aerial attack. When they came to an open stretch full of hot springs, Mr. Coy weaved in and out of the giant puddles like obstacles on a driving test. The helicopters fired, causing the pools to erupt like geysers and sending up walls of water.

"Yee-haw!" Mr. Coy shouted, surviving the assault and reaching the relative safety of another wooded area.

Soon, the vegetation grew sparse until it stopped, and the ground became pebbled until it was nothing but rocks. The pair ditched the four-wheeler and set off across the stones, which was difficult for the barefoot Jaret. In the dim light of the approaching sunrise, Mr. Coy could see the rugged archway through which he had come. He scanned the horizon; the timing needed to be perfect.

The two had just entered the cleft in the rock when a blinding light burst upon them—not the desired sunlight but instead a dreaded spotlight. One of the helicopters had found them from above. In a matter of seconds, dozens of vehicles poured out of the forest, guards jumping out and trekking across the rocky terrain toward their escapees.

"Come on, come on, come on," Coy muttered at the eastern sky. He knew the sun was on the verge of peeking above the ocean. If this was going to work, then he needed only another minute or two.

Suddenly, a special jeep arrived, driving across the rocks and stopping front and center. A guard opened the passenger door. Mr. Coy and Jaret were expecting Lionel to step out, but instead they saw Lye. He jammed his spirally-twisted cane into the rocks, his black robes and white hair blowing in the gentle sea breeze.

"There's nowhere to go, boys," the evil lord told them over a loud speaker. Jaret glanced behind, close enough to the edge to see the waves crashing. "I'm sorry it has to end this way," then he added, "Well, not really," followed by an evil cackle.

"Wait," Mr. Coy hollered back, struck with an idea on how to stall. "Don't we get any last words?"

"What?!" Lye barked.

"Surely you believe in proper execution etiquette," Jaret chimed in.

With a look of total annoyance, Lye sighed and shifted his weight to one side, saying, "Oh alright," then adding, "but don't even think about using your obnoxious 'Ever Ben Coy' catchphrase again...so overused."

"Dang," Coy mumbled to himself. Then, coming up with an alternative, he cleared his throat. Then he cleared his throat again. And again.

"Hurry up!" Lye ordered.

Mr. Coy swallowed and started to sing a familiar song, whose opening sentence was most appropriate, given the situation: "Oh, say can you see by the dawn's early light..."

"Enough!" Lye cried. "Open fire!"

But the American anthem's first line had bought them just enough time. The sun had risen, bathing the site in light. Coy and Cooper vanished, right before an onslaught of explosives rained down on the arched rock, blowing it to bits.

Lye raised his gnarled hand to halt the attack. When the dust and smoke cleared, he hurried to inspect the scene but found no remains of the bandits.

"Impossible!" he marveled.

Just then, the driver of the jeep interjected, "My lord," eager to share some news.

"Yes?" Lye hissed, understandably peeved. "What is it?"

"I've just received word of some unusual activity at Stonehenge," the driver reported, his cell phone still in hand. "Three individuals were seen trespassing there just hours ago. An eyewitness claims they disappeared out of thin air. Our undercover agent there has reviewed the surveillance video and identified them as Coy, his daughter, and the Cooper girl."

Lye's ugly eyes began to widen. His focus returned to the spot where Coy and Cooper had been standing— in a rock...an archway...which had looked a lot like..."No! A trilithon!" He had been unaware of its existence on his island. This was not the first time he had witnessed someone travel by trilithon.

"Well played, Neo," Lye growled. "Now it's my turn."

CHAPTER 13

THE NEOLITHIC
TRAVELER

Nika purposely went the long way on the trek back to town from the trilithon site. She had been pleasantly surprised when Ret chose not to return aboveground, hoping his decision had something to do with an interest in her. So she walked extra slow and utilized the time to ask Ret questions—you know, the personal kind.

But Ret had a few of his own questions to ask—the scientific kind.

"Why does everything here look so different?" he wondered of Nika, striding up to a tree when they stopped to rest.

"I think everything looks fine the way it is," Nika proudly replied.

"I mean, so do I, of course," Ret said apologetically. "I'm just wondering why it looks the way it does."

"Well, why do *you* look the way you do?" Nika returned.

That gave Ret an idea. He already knew why *he* looked different: the medical tests that he underwent when the Coopers first found him revealed he had a few more elements in his system than the normal human being—a finding that would be confirmed a few years later when Lye told Ret he had uranium in his blood. Ret thought perhaps the living things in this subterranean world looked different for a similar reason.

Ret held out his arm. He focused on the waves of light that were bouncing off his skin and then manipulated them as a microscope would, allowing him to zoom in on some of his cells. As he watched them, he noticed the presence of foreign substances that were causing the cells to behave in an unnatural way—the culprit of his unnatural appearance. Then he examined a portion of the tree's bark and observed a similar situation among its own cells. Could it be that this land had also been infiltrated by some kind of strange material?

"Things didn't always look like this," Nika said, appearing at Ret's side and slowly leaning towards him until their shoulders touched. "That's what I've been told, anyway. The elders in the village say their predecessors spoke of a season when everything started to change but never changed back." She caringly put her palm on the tree trunk. "It bothers them, but us of the younger generations? Not so much. We don't know any different—really, we don't know *different*."

"What do you mean?" Ret queried.

"Everyone is different, Ret," Nika said, holding his hand as they stood side by side. "Even back in the world where we came from, everyone is different from each other—some more than others, some less. Differences are largely shunned there; most people try to hide them in order to 'fit in' and be 'normal.' The truth is, being different *is* normal. We understand this here, and we still love each other—usually *for* our differences, sometimes *because* of them, and occasionally *in spite of* them. Some differences we can change and should; others we can't and shouldn't. Sometimes our differences are for us; sometimes they're for others. In the end, differences can either tear us apart or bind us together. Here, we choose to love."

"Me, too," Ret told her. Nika turned and stared at Ret longingly with her big, searching eyes. After a few seconds, he began to feel uncomfortable. "Well, that was a nice break," he said nervously. "We'd better be on our way." He paced away. Nika smiled.

As the day wore on, Nika probed deeper and deeper with her questions. Whenever the conversation was becoming a little too serious, Ret tried to change the subject.

"So…you never told me the source of your light down here," he reminded her.

Without an answer to give him, Nika said playfully, "You know what, Mr. Scientist? How about you tell me?"

"Okay," Ret shrugged. He shut his eyes tightly and turned to face the light source, then switched his sight into energy mode and did something he never would have done with his natural vision: opened his eyes and stared directly into the bright light. This time bending the beams of light like a telescope, Ret followed the rays to their origin.

"Looks like the source is a large deposit of molten rock," Ret spoke while staring.

"What?" Nika gasped.

"Apparently, this land is a giant air pocket in the earth's crust," Ret spoke his observations. "We live at the top—upside-down, which makes sense since the rock, though at the bottom, appears to be above us. So I'm willing to bet that during the day, when this part of the earth is facing the real sun, the rock heats up, causing it to shine very brightly. Then at night, the rock cools but is still hot enough to give off a gleam like the real moon. I even see smaller deposits, which explains why there are 'stars' here."

"Wow," Nika said with a flirtatious wink. "I'm impressed—*very* impressed." Ret blushed and quickened his pace.

The more that Ret played hard to get (as Nika assumed he was doing), the more she was attracted to him. But, unfortunately for her, the more time Ret spent with Nika, the more he thought of someone else: Paige. The two women were strangely similar, as Ret observed—partly in appearance but mostly in deportment: height and hair, eye color and skin tone, even the same sense of humor and penchant for deep discussion—to say nothing of each girl's infatuation with Ret. In fact, he had mentally mistaken Nika for Paige a few times already. And yet, despite their uncanny commonalities, one big difference overshadowed them all: simply put, Nika was *not* Paige. It was Paige who had always accompanied Ret on his adventures; Paige who had helped Ret collect the wind element. And so without her, something was missing. There was a void that no one else could quite fill. Yes, no matter how closely a replica, Nika could never and would never replace Paige.

With that in mind, Ret was not sure how to navigate his acquaintanceship with the amative Topramenov heiress. If this was going to be his home from now on, did that mean he would never see Paige again, making Nika the most likely runner-up? He knew Nika's feelings were fragile, and he didn't want to come off as insincere, but was he only drawn to her because she reminded him of Paige? It was all so confusing.

By the time they made it back to town, Ret was physically exhausted and mentally overwhelmed. Hiking to and from the trilithon on zero hours of sleep was one thing. Then add to that the lingering guilt for judging the townsfolk, the uncertainty of taking up residence in this mutant municipality, the stress of trying to rewire his brain to first accept people instead of critique them, the pressure to befriend Nika without giving her the wrong impression...not to mention a constant numbing sensation coming from the palm of his right hand.

O   O   O

"Wakey, wakey!" Nika sang the next morning as she barged into the barn where Ret had spent the night. "Time to get up, sleepyhead!" She knelt down at his side and picked bits of hay out of his hair as he rubbed his eyes back into consciousness. "I hope you're hungry."

"Starved," Ret said.

"Perfect!" Nika cheered. "Then let's go!"

Nika led Ret to a quaint little diner in the town square where they enjoyed brunch together. Apparently, word had spread overnight of Ret's decision to stick around, earning him a gracious "Welcome!" every few minutes, much to Nika's satisfaction. She was very proud of Ret's friendship, which she hoped was blossoming into something more.

"I'll meet you back here in a little bit," Nika told Ret as they returned to the square after their meal. "I told Ms. Montgomery I'd help weed her garden this afternoon. If you need anything, just let someone know."

"Okay," Ret replied.

"Don't get in too much trouble while I'm gone, handsome!" Nika called back as she hurried away, then blew Ret a kiss.

Ret stood in the square for several moments, unsure if he should catch the kiss or what. A man walked by, pulling two horses, and said, "Welcome." A pair of girls were seen carrying a batch of eggs; they waved and giggled. A tumbleweed blew by.

"Not bad, lover boy!" a familiar voice cried out from behind. Ret spun around.

"Neo?!" Ret asked in amazement, seeing the Guardian sitting nearby on a wooden bench in the shade. "What are *you* doing here?"

"I should ask you the same question," Neo smiled. "I take it you still haven't found a way out of this place?"

"Actually, I *did* find a way," Ret explained, stepping towards him. Despite the frustration of their initial meeting, Ret's attitude was now one of submissiveness, having since realized the Guardian had probably been right all along.

"So you left and came back?" Neo tried to understand.

"No, I never left," Ret informed him, employing the kind of humility when you have to eat your own words.

"You mean you've been here all this time?" Neo said with shock.

"Yes, sir," Ret responded somberly.

"Now why'd you do a thing like that, I wonder?" Neo asked, as if pleased.

"I don't really know why, exactly," Ret described, sitting next to the Guardian on the bench. "After I spoke with you the first time, I met this really nice person who brought me here."

"The gal who just blew you a kiss?" Neo poked.

Ret laughed, "Yes, her."

"Okay, go on."

"And, well," Ret thought, "while I've been here, I've learned some things."

"Oh?" Neo inserted. "Like what?"

"For starters, I never realized how judgmental I was of others until I came here," Ret reflected with a bit of shame. "I always thought I would 'cure the world' by curing its people—fixing them and changing them until they fit some kind of mold. But really, *I* was the one who needed to change—change my approach. I needed to stop judging people and start loving them. It's love that will 'cure the world.' So I guess that's what I've learned here: how to love."

"And how, would you say, does one love?" Neo asked, helping Ret to draw some conclusions.

"I'm still not sure," Ret confessed with a heavy sigh.

"Compare it to something," Neo suggested encouragingly.

"Okay, well…" Ret supposed. "I guess…I guess it's kind of like…like…"—then it came to him—"going for a scenic drive." A curious expression came over Neo's face. "You know, in a car." Ret wondered if Neo knew what a car was. "You *do* know what a car—"

"Yes, yes," Neo whispered, humored. This came as a surprise to Ret considering the Guardian had never left the site of his element, or so he assumed. "Carry on."

"So as I'm riding along," Ret continued, "the window begins to collect all sorts of dust and dirt, bug splatters and raindrops—maybe even gets a nick in it. In the past, these were the objects of my focus. I stayed fixated on trivial flaws because that was all my short-sighted perspective allowed me to see, and I wasn't going to change until the flaws were gone—a frustratingly miserable way to live since the flaws are on the other side of the window, completely out of my control. But then I came here and realized I had been missing the whole purpose of the drive. I was reminded that there was something better beyond the blemishes: the sky, the scenery, even the road. And so, like a camera lens narrowing its aperture, I was taught how to adjust my perception from the here-and-now to the big picture—how to see through the flaws. Of course, the imperfections are still present, but I'm no longer looking *at* them; I'm looking *past* them."

"I see," Neo said.

"So I guess that's how one loves, sir," Ret answered the Guardian's question, based on his own experience. "He learns to look past the problems and, instead, at the person. He does not present his love as something that must be earned or that is awarded only if certain conditions are met. No, truly unconditional love comes without caveat or qualifier. It just exists—freely given, always available, no matter what. And that is the true test in life: to see if we will love our fellow man, regardless of who they are, how they look, or what they do. Like the trilithon, all other laws hang on the law of love."

"Well said, Ret," Neo remarked, a broad smile forming on his grandfatherly face.

"That reminds me," Ret remembered, "how do you know my name?"

"I know a great deal about you," Neo replied. "I've been following you for a long time."

"What?" Ret asked. "How?"

"You know that trilithon that Nika showed you?" Neo said.

"Yeah."

"I built that," Neo explained. "Within it is a portal—a doorway to another time and setting. It has allowed me to travel extensively and," with a sly grin, "keep tabs on you. It is linked to several other similar structures that I have stationed in various parts of the world over the years—places like the Keep and Waters Deep." Ret's eyes widened. "The trilithon that Nika showed you actually belongs to Stonehenge, but I kept it here after Lye discovered it."

"Wait, wait, wait," Ret held up his hand, his mind suddenly overflowing with questions. He wasn't sure where to begin. "First of all, what do you mean 'travel extensively'? I thought each Guardian had to stay and 'guard' his element?"

"In many ways, it is the great tree that is the guardian of the wood element," Neo pointed out. "After your First Father scattered the elements, the wood element concealed itself within the complex root structure of the vast forest that lies above us at ground level—the largest forest on earth. After I found the element, I planted a single tree above it using a seed that the First Father gave me when he called me to be a Guardian. I expedited and controlled the tree's growth to make sure its roots grew around the element and then, as the roots expanded, completely enclosed the element, encapsulating it in a sort of air bubble within the roots. As a result of basically grafting the element into the tree, the element has transferred some of its power to the tree, making it indestructible. The tree cannot die, its root system is ever expanding, and its wood is impenetrable—as long as the element resides within it. So really, it is the tree that guards the element, which has permitted me to come and go as I please."

"So where exactly is the element?" Ret asked, well aware he would need to know that eventually.

"Somewhere in the great tree's root bulb," Neo loosely replied.

"Are you sure?" Ret interrogated.

"Pretty sure," Neo nodded.

"When was the last time you saw it?" Ret pressed, worried by the Guardian's uncertainty.

"Oh, it was centuries ago," Neo answered. "I wanted to make sure it was still within the root. It was easier then because, with each passing day, the root system grows larger and more complex, making it increasingly difficult to access the element chamber. But I *did* find it."

"Wonderful," Ret mumbled sarcastically.

"Don't worry too much, Ret," Neo reassured him. "The element *wants* to be collected. It wants to return to where it belongs inside the Oracle. This desire has been adopted by the tree, which is how it knows you are one with scars. You can expect it to help you when the time comes."

"Okay..." Ret said, not entirely convinced. He moved down his long list of questions: "So you've been to the Keep?"

"Oh yes," Neo returned. "I *created* the Keep."

"You did?!" Ret said incredulously.

"Son, I've been around a long, long time," Neo explained. "Early on, I needed a place where I could 'keep' a record of my doings—places I'd been, people I'd met, things I'd observed. That's what the Keep started out as: my personal filing cabinet, each room a drawer. The entire compound functions on the idea of time, including the elevator, which I designed. The facility itself is somewhat of a time machine, capable of bringing some semblance of the past to the present."

"But how did Lye take over the Keep?" Ret asked.

"Lye has forever been in relentless pursuit of the elements and their Guardians," Neo said. "He has eyes almost everywhere. It didn't take him long to learn I could leave my element. He would follow me—chase me, lay traps for me, hunt me down. I don't know how he learned about the Keep, but one day he took me by surprise and ambushed it. I had no choice but to flee. While under his control, Lye continued to use the Keep as an archival system, though for wicked purposes."

"Then you must be glad the Keep is no longer in Lye's control," Ret surmised.

"Very glad," Neo replied. "Lye may have found out about the Keep, but he has never detected some of my other secrets there, including the portal hidden in the cloven tree in the backyard bog, which has allowed me to visit there frequently. As soon as I learned the Stones had abandoned the property, I seized it and kept it from falling back into Lye's hands. I'm happy to see Mr. Coy has relocated there."

"I'd invite you to come and live with us at the Keep," Ret put forth, "but I know you will die once I collect the wood element."

"That may have been the case with other Guardians," Neo countered, "but I don't plan on dying anytime soon. I used to be able to stay away from my element for long periods of time without needing to return to it for rejuvenation. But as I began to grow old, my absences were cut shorter and shorter. Rather than give up traveling and stay confined down here, I set out to learn what I needed to do in order to extend my episodes away from the element. During these episodes, I had to rely on my physical body's health instead of the wood element's power in order to stay spry. Because it was an issue of time—*life*time—I wielded the element's influence and figured out how to live as healthy a life as possible so as to prolong my time and survive my trips abroad. After a few centuries, however, time eventually began to catch up with me. That was when I started wondering how Lye was staying alive. I tracked him down and discovered the island of Waters Deep, where I learned the secret to Lye's longevity and then made it my own."

"Which is…?" Ret asked in earnest.

"If I told you, it wouldn't be a secret, now would it?" Neo joked.

"Oh, fine," Ret rolled his eyes.

Neo chuckled. "Besides me, there has only been one other person who has figured out Lye's secret. That person was Helen Coy." Stunned, Ret made a mental connection, earning him an affirmative nod from Neo. Then Neo reached into his pocket and pulled out a small flask, whispering, "Lye doesn't know that I know." He shook the flask. "Hmm, getting a bit low. Looks like I'll be making a visit to the Deep very soon for a refill."

"Is there a portal at the Deep?" Ret questioned.

"There is," Neo answered, still proud to have installed one right under Lye's nose. "It is disguised as an archway of rocks. As far as I know, Lye is unaware of it. In fact, I don't think he is aware of any of the portals. Well, except for the trilithon that Nika showed you."

"How did Lye find out about the trilithon?" Ret asked.

"To answer that, I need to tell you how the trilithon came to be," said Neo. "It was no easy task to find where my element had hidden itself. I first had to learn about time, which is a complex concept. Everything in this world is subject to time, and because the wood element grants some ability to manipulate time, it means every-thing, in limited ways, can become subject to you and to me by virtue of time. This was key to finding the element. You see, time has its own dimension, which is all around us but cannot be seen by the natural eye. The past belongs to this dimension; it is where time goes after it has been spent—like the scenes on a film reel that have already been viewed: they still exist but have gone somewhere else. The wood element allows one to see into this dimension—to unwind the reel and review past scenes, so to speak."

Just then, Neo waved his hand, transforming the world into a sort of television screen. He began to slowly review the last few minutes that had just transpired. As if watching a recording that someone had filmed, Ret saw himself (in the past) get up from Neo's bench and walk backwards to the center of the town square. Then Nika reappeared, blowing the kiss and returning to Ret's side. Meanwhile, Ret and Neo (in the present) stood still, independent of the footage that was being replayed.

"How did you do that?" Ret marveled as Neo forsook his hold on the past and resumed the present.

"The dimension of time is related to the principles of energy," Neo explained. "I ran into Rado years ago, and he helped me to understand this idea." Ret recognized the name of the Guardian of the Wind Element. "Waves would not exist without the energy that they carry. Similarly, *we* cannot exist without time in which to do so. Wherever there is something happening, time will always be there not only allowing it to happen but also recording it. Think of the events of a day as bits and bytes of data—intangible like energy but still just as real. These are the data that occupy the dimension of time. To use an analogy, as the movie of life plays out, it is continuously being recorded onto the DVD of time, and the wood element is the remote control that permits you and me to go back and sift through the scenes."

"I might add," Neo continued, "that the movie of life is not a single disc—oh no. Every setting on earth— every classroom, every ballpark, every grocery store aisle—has its own 'disc,' constantly recording the footage that takes place within it. Here, I'll show you."

Neo snapped his fingers, overlaying the world around them with the crisscrossing lines of a grid. Ret watched Neo touch one of the squares—discs or "tiles," as he called them—in front of them, as if it were a screen. When he swiped to the left, an unbroken stream of video played out, replaying the past, as if a camera had always been positioned there. Ret saw what had taken place in that particular spot all day—from that moment to first light that morning, through the night, then the comings and goings of the various villagers who happened to pass by the day before. The faster Neo swiped, the faster the past rolled by.

"It's a lot more efficient to review multiple tiles at the same time," Neo said. With his finger, he outlined a large rectangle from his head down to his toes, three tiles wide and seven tall. Now when he swiped, all twenty-one tiles in the rectangle replayed at the same time, providing a much bigger picture. "Tiles can even be moved from their original spot," Neo pointed out, "but their original settings still remain, meaning they continue to record the activities of their first location even when they reside somewhere totally different." He placed his hand on the large rectangle and moved it an arm's length to the right, like how moving an icon on the desktop of a computer screen does not affect the program to which it is linked. Then he moved the tiles back, having never let go. "This is what makes portals possible."

Ret was in awe. As he sat there marveling, a townsman walked across the town square, from right to left. It transpired just like normal, but Ret saw it as if he was wearing eyeglasses with grid-patterned lenses, watching the man move from block to block. He touched the tile in front of him and replayed it to review what he had just seen: the man moved backwards from left to right across the tile. Then Ret touched the tile to the right and replayed it, picking up where the man had left off in his reverse walk from left to right.

"Keep in mind," Neo advised, "if you choose to visit the past, you do so as your present self. You can only *observe* your past self; you do not become it. This is important to understand. Many people, if given the chance, would go back in time and change their past, but this is against the laws of the universe. You cannot change the past. What's done is done." Neo snapped his fingers again, and the grid disappeared, ending their glimpse into the dimension of time. "But," Neo said with distinction, "you *can* learn from the past. That was how I learned the location of my element: by sifting through countless scenes of the past." Neo let silence prevail for a few moments, as if he had just given Ret an important piece of advice.

Neo resumed, "After securing the element within the tree, the tree began to take on a life of its own. Its roots stretched deep into the earth until they reached the air pocket that is this land. This presented a problem for me: the element was now out of range, in a faraway land that was impossible to get to."

"Except for me," Ret interjected.

"And me," Neo grinned. "It required intense searching of the dimension of time, but I eventually found the tiles that pertained to this land—a land lost in time. For ease of access, I bonded some of the tiles together in a rectangle like I showed you earlier, and moved them to an obscure spot where I could always find them: I chose an isolated plain out in the English countryside. Of course, tiles cannot be moved to a place where tiles already exist, so I had to switch the two sets: I removed tiles from England, placed this land's tiles there instead, and then filled the gap in this land with the tiles that I had removed from England. In short, I made a portal—two separate gateways, linked to each other, both in a place where they technically do not belong, capable of transporting things in real-time at the speed of light. In order to remember where I had put the English tiles, I placed them inside an existing stone arch, which at the time was on the other side of this valley where the trilithon now sits. I didn't have any stone arches to work with in the English countryside, however, so I built my own marker, consisting of two pillars with a lintel across the top. And with that, the trilithon was born."

"For a long time, this was how I traveled from the aboveground world to this one—trilithon to arch, and vice versa. Life was good. But then somehow Lye found out about my secret way of traveling. He did not yet know where the wood element was located but figured he would find out sooner or later if he followed me around enough. I feared the stand-alone trilithon was too obvious. I needed to disguise it somehow. I added five fake trilithons around the real one, then enclosed that inner circle with an outer circle—all patterned after the truths that I learned about how to optimize one's health and maximize one's time in life. Over time, I added other fake trilithons all over the English countryside to cause Lye further confusion."

"You built all of that by yourself?" Ret asked. "Trilithons are huge!"

"Actually, Heliu helped me before he found his element," Neo remembered fondly. "He moved those stones like they were feathers."

"Didn't people wonder what you were doing?" Ret inquired.

"That region was not populated then like it is today," Neo answered. "But as people began to settle there, yes, they were very curious about my monument. I'd come across their rumors and speculations occasionally. Some said it had to do with astronomy, others said religion. They even came up with a clever name for it: Stonehenge."

"For a while, my decoy worked, but Lye couldn't be fooled forever," Neo retold. "One day, when I went to the trilithon to warp to this land, he was there waiting for me. A fight ensued. Much of Stonehenge was destroyed. I tried to escape the area without warping because I didn't want to confirm any more of my secret to him, but the vicinity was too open to make a run for it. My only hope was to get away through the trilithon. Moments later, when sunrise came, I stood between the pillars, but Lye lunged for me. Although there was no room for him between the pillars, he latched onto my arm, which, as I learned, was enough for him to join the journey."

"We warped here together, arriving in the stone arch as usual," Neo detailed. "Apparently, my arm was not the only thing that Lye was touching when we were transported: the entire trilithon from Stonehenge came with us, too. But that was not my concern at the moment; I had to get rid of Lye. I purposely headed straight for the great tree, knowing it would take care of him. Sure enough, it did: as soon as Lye got close, the roots bound him and dragged him up to ground level. The tree knows who it does and doesn't want around."

"Sounds familiar," Ret muttered, remembering how the roots had done a similar thing to him.

"I knew Lye would try to come back," Neo picked up where he had left off. "To make sure he could not do so, I destroyed the arch that marked the portal into this land. I could not destroy the portal itself, so I left those English tiles with the trilithon and abandoned them, leaving the trilithon as a symbol of my folly. Not much later, however, people started showing up here randomly. They came on accident but for a purpose, each with the same story: they were outcasts, longing for a place where they could feel loved and accepted, standing at Stonehenge one moment and then here the next. This was when I realized the portal at Stonehenge was still there. It had not been transported with the trilithon when Lye followed me, as I had assumed. And because I had left the English tiles inside the trilithon, the two portals were still linked."

Ret loved listening to Guardians.

"Rather than put a stop to this, however, I let it happen," Neo said. "The people who were coming here needed what the portal provided: an opportunity to feel loved and accepted. At first, these valiant vagabonds were few. But over time, as I have traveled and installed more and more portals across the globe, the number of newcomers has increased dramatically. As I said, they come on accident but for a purpose. And no one has ever left."

"How does a portal decide where to send someone?" Ret asked. "Is it random?"

"Oh no, it is specific to each person," Neo described. "In a very real way, the portal is able to read a traveler's mind, and it transports him based on whatever he has been spending the majority of his time thinking about. Our thoughts run through our brains like pulses of energy, and, like a radio wave, there is infor-mation encoded in such energy. The trouble is, it is stuck in a person's brain and needs an external stimulus in order to access it." Ret thought of a neuroscope. "An intense supply of light is needed not only to read the electrical impulses in the traveler's brain but also to pixelate his physical composition, blast through the dimensional barrier, and then transmit him to his destination through the continuum of time. This is why the portals always face whichever way the sun rises: a sunrise—not even a sunset—is the only thing I have found so far that is capable of providing this kind of energy, and even then only because the rays are intensified when they bounce within each trilithon-like archway."

Ret sat silently for a few moments, his mind a bit overloaded.

"Sorry if I'm not explaining things very well," Neo apologized. "I'm a Guardian, not a scientist." He smiled. "Portals are a lot more complicated than my previous method of travel."

"What was your previous method?" Ret asked.

"Remember those cleats you used when you were searching for the fire element?" Neo reminded. "I designed those for Argo."

"Really?" Ret asked with awe. "What *haven't* you done?"

Neo laughed, "Like I said, I've been around a long time. Everything I know, I owe to the element."

"I was wrong about you, sir," Ret regretted. "I said you were the most *un*helpful Guardian I've ever worked with, but the truth is you might be the *most* helpful. I'm sorry I judged you before I got to know you."

"Apology accepted," Neo beamed. "Oh and by the way, you're free to collect the element now."

"I am?!" Ret choked.

"Yep, you're ready," Neo said. "You've learned what you needed to learn."

"How do you know?" Ret wondered.

"Because of the simple fact that you stayed here," Neo told him. "You did not have to stay. You could have gone aboveground and retrieved the Oracle, then returned here and collected the element—which you were so bent on doing when we first met. But you didn't."

"Because you told me not to," Ret reasoned.

"But you don't need *me* to collect the element," Neo reminded.

"Then why did you stop me?" Ret asked.

"Because I could tell you lacked something that I knew *would* stop you later on," Neo explained.

"You mean the Oracle?"

"No, I mean knowledge," Neo stated. "You needed to learn to see things not as they look or seem or appear but as they are and were and will be. You needed to develop the ability to view things through the lens of time so as to give your perceptions a whole new dimension. And if you couldn't even do this with people, then I knew you'd never be able to collect the wood element." Then, with a twinkle in his eye, he added, "Good thing you're a fast learner."

Although Ret had finally gotten the 'okay' to collect the fifth element, he suddenly wasn't too eager to do so. Things were following a horrifyingly familiar pattern: discover a hidden civilization, become acquainted with its people, develop feelings for their female leader—yes, this was Sunken Earth all over again. The next steps were to collect the element, send the land into irreversible meltdown, and then leave everyone to die—right? Sure, the Guardian had spared this land of Lye, but if he really wanted to save it, maybe he should have spared it from Ret. Although Lye ruined societies by taking control, it was Ret who destroyed lands by taking elements. At Sunken Earth, Lye had carved out the hierarchy, yes, but Ret had caved in the ceiling. Would Nika and her people suffer the same fate? Ret wasn't sure he could tolerate any more innocent blood on his hands.

"But what about the tests?" Ret put forth, looking for a way to postpone his procurement date with the wood element. "You know, to prove I've collected the previous elements?"

"I won't be conducting any tests," Neo stated. "I've been watching you for years; I don't need any more proof."

"Okay..." Ret thought. "What about the relic? Let's talk about that for a few minutes. Isn't there something that the First Father gave you to give to me?

"Yes, but I can't give it to you right now," Neo informed him, "not until after you've collected the element."

Ret sunk in his seat. This was all so different. He was so confused.

"You know, Ret," Neo said, "I'm getting the feeling you're not as jazzed about collecting the element as you were when we first met."

"I still am," Ret sighed, "but I'm worried about what will happen to the people down here. Do you think they'd ever consider returning aboveground?"

"Well, here comes your admirer now," Neo pointed out, seeing Nika bounding up the path toward the town square. "You can ask *her*."

Spying Nika, Ret wondered, "But what if she—"

But the Guardian was gone.

"Figures," Ret remarked with a frustrated smile. "The guy talks my ear off and then bails when I need his advice the most. Lame!" Just then, a large pinecone broke away from the tree above and struck Ret in the head—clearly an act of Neo.

"Hey, handsome!" Nika called out as she skipped toward Ret.

"Hi," Ret said, massaging his head.

"What've you been up to?" Nika asked, sitting next to him on the bench.

"Not much," Ret fibbed. Then he took a deep breath and said, "Nika, there's something I need to tell you."

"Yes?" she wondered with great interest.

Ret stared into her eyes, those windows of the soul. On the surface, he saw beauty and gentleness, even some mystery. But looking with the lens of time, he saw pain and heartache, even a general distrust. He couldn't ask her to return to the world that had cast her out. He knew how much she loathed it up there and loved it down here.

"All I wanted to say was," Ret changed his mind, "thanks for being such a good friend to me."

"Oh, Ret," Nika crooned, holding his hand. "Of course." She leaned in close and said softly, "There's something I want to tell you, too." Ever since meeting Ret, Nika had been wanting to kiss him. She figured now was as good an opportunity as ever to make her move. She brought her face to his, as if to whisper a secret, but then kissed him, taking Ret by surprise.

"Oh," Ret said with an awkward laugh.

"I'll see you tomorrow, sweetie," Nika said flirtatiously as she got up to leave.

"Yeah, see ya," Ret replied, now even more torn inside about whether or not to collect the element.

Not far away, hidden in the bushes, a young woman was observing this romantic exchange. She had recently arrived in this new land and was exploring her surroundings when she stumbled upon this happy couple in the town square. She immediately recognized Ret, overjoyed to have found him, as no one back home had known where he was or what he was doing. She would have ran to him right then and there, in fact, if it hadn't been for the stranger that had been sitting next to him, receiving his affection. She didn't know who this stranger was; all that mattered was that it wasn't her.

Heartbroken, Paige dragged herself back toward the trilithon through which she had come, shedding heavy tears with every step.

CHAPTER 14

THE SKINNY ON FATS

Ana opened her eyes to darkness. Although she didn't know where she was, it was obvious she wasn't at Stonehenge anymore. She took a few steps forward, sinking slightly into the moist and swampy ground. She could hear crickets chirping and see fireflies dancing. The bright moon overhead told her it was the middle of the night, while the mansion house in the distance told her she was at the Keep.

"How in the world did we get *here?*" Ana asked aloud. No one answered. "Guys?" She glanced around. "Paige? Mr. Coy?" But they were nowhere to be found.

Now a little scared and very much confused, Ana investigated her surroundings. She had arrived in the cloven trunk of a bald cypress tree. Tall and mature, it was one of many trees growing literally on the bank of the Keep's backyard bog, their large roots preferring the exceptionally wet soil. But unlike the others, this tree's trunk had split at the bottom, creating a sort of arched doorway. Actually, it looked a lot like a trilithon.

Just then, Ana remembered her ah-ha moment at Stonehenge, when she started to think of the trilithons as food groups. She hastened toward the mansion house to find her mother.

"Mom!" Ana yelled as she burst through the front door of the Coopers' modest dwelling on the top floor of the Keep. "Mom!"

"My word!" Pauline replied as she came out of her bedroom, half-awake and wrapping herself in her robe. "What is it—deer?" Ana was still wearing her deer costume.

"Long story," Ana said, throwing off her disguise. "Anyway, I think I figured out the truth about nutrition."

"Honey, it's two o'clock in the morning," Pauline protested with a yawn. "Can't this wait until later?"

"Just let me get it down on paper," Ana supplicated, "while it's still fresh in my mind."

Ana fetched a pen and some paper, then met her Mom at the kitchen table.

"Okay, this is a trilithon," Ana taught, drawing two posts with a lintel across the top.

"I thought a trilithon was a kind of race," Pauline wondered.

"That's triathlon," Ana corrected. "This is trilithon."

"Oh, got it," Pauline rubbed her tired face.

"There are five trilithons at Stonehenge," Ana said, drawing four more in a circle. "Three of them are fully intact, but two of them only have one post still standing. And then there's a big gap. That makes the inner circle."

"Looks more like a horseshoe, if you ask me," Pauline muttered.

"There's also an outer circle, but it has really fallen apart." Ana sketched a dilapidated outer circle around the inner circle. "Okay, now with that in mind, let's talk nutrition."

Next, Ana drew a triangle and said, "This is the Food Guide Pyramid. It has six groups." She divided the pyramid into six horizontal sections. "On the bottom is the biggest group: grains. Then come fruits and vegetables, followed by meat and dairy, and finally a small section for fats at the top."

"Where are you going with this, child?" Pauline inquired.

"Just hear me out," Ana returned. "A few years after the government published the Food Guide Pyramid, they revised it and called it MyPyramid." She drew a second triangle. "It also has six food groups." She divided this pyramid into six vertical sections. "Grains is still the largest, followed by vegetables and dairy, then fruits, and finally a much smaller meat group."

"That's only five," Pauline pointed out.

"Precisely!" Ana cheered. "Do you see this tiny sliver between fruit and dairy?"

"Hold on, I need my glasses."

"That's the fats food group!" Ana informed. "It's not even labeled."

"Okay...what are you getting at?" Pauline asked.

"One more graphic." Ana then drew a circle and said, "Most recently, the government scrapped the pyramid idea and came out with MyPlate. The big plate is divided into four sections: grains and vegetables are the largest, then a smaller wedge for fruit, and an even smaller one for meat." She split the plate into quadrants and labeled each. "Then there's a small side dish for dairy." She drew a small circle at the top right of the main plate.

Ana paused to let things sink in.

"That's it?" Pauline asked.

"That's it," Ana repeated.

"So what's your point?"

"Ugh," Ana groaned. "Mother, how many food groups do you see on MyPlate?"

"Five," Pauline counted.

"What happened to the sixth food group?" Ana said.

"It's missing?"

"Bingo!" Ana clapped. "The fats food group is

missing. It went from 'use sparingly' on the Food Guide Pyramid to not being identified on MyPyramid to totally gone on MyPlate. It's not even on the table anymore."

"So what does this have to do with Stonehenge?" Pauline asked.

"Think of each trilithon as a food group," Ana instructed. "The three intact trilithons are like the three food groups that have always been large and in charge: grains, fruits, and vegetables."

"Okay," Pauline said to show she was following.

"The other two trilithons, the ones that only have one post still standing," Ana said, "those are like the meat and dairy food groups: they keep getting smaller."

"Okay."

"And this big empty space?" Ana said, pointing to her rendition of Stonehenge. "That's where a sixth trilithon used to stand—or a sixth food group—until it was removed." Pauline glared at her daughter. "Yep, fats."

"What does all of this mean?" Pauline questioned.

"It means the secret to eating healthy isn't a pyramid or a plate—it's a balance," Ana concluded. "The diet that we have been taught to follow is out of balance. It has removed fats, reduced protein, and filled the gap with grains, fruits, and vegetables—which are all mostly carbohydrates or, when broken down, sugars. Our over-emphasis on avoiding fats has caused us to rely heavily on carbs and turn a blind eye to sugars. Ironically, our obsession with keeping our fats in check has left our sugar consumption unchecked. And look what it has done to our health! As a society, we are sick. In many ways, inside and out, we have mutated. Clearly, something is out of balance."

"So stay away from carbs, watch the sugar—is that what you're saying?" Pauline observed with a hint of offense.

"I'm not saying carbs and sugar are bad," Ana replied. "Grains are part of the balance. As much as it seems like it sometimes, this isn't an either-or battle between fats and carbs. The truth is, we need both. Neither is unhealthy—what's unhealthy is an imbalance of either. So what I'm saying is, we should pursue a more balanced diet, which, for most of us, will mean eating more fats and protein *at the expense of* carbs. This can be challenging in a culture where 'balanced' has been defined as 'low-fat' or 'non-fat'—selling points that are trumpeted on food labels. For example, next time you're at the grocery store, try to find a yogurt that has nearly equal amounts of fat, protein, and carbs. And all this because we've assumed fats will make us fat, which, though studies may suggest, no one has ever proven. I'm no scholar, but based on common sense, I don't believe fat makes us fat—carbs do. The body stores extra sugars; I'm not so sure it does the same with fats. Our logic should be flipped: we should be more concerned about our carb intake than our fat intake."

Pauline fell silent for a moment, as if digesting Ana's words. She looked back and forth at her daughter a few times, in deep contemplation. Finally she said, "So no more Cosmic Brownies, huh?"

"Oh, Mom," Ana sighed. "Think of it as a balance: if you know you're going to eat a lot of carbs at dinner, then go easy on them at breakfast and lunch. Or if you've got some strenuous exercise planned, that may justify eating some more sugar so that you have enough energy."

"But why would the fats food group have been removed, I wonder?" Pauline put forth.

"I'm not sure—maybe it was done on purpose, maybe on accident," Ana responded. "The answer usually comes down to money, doesn't it?"

"What do you mean?"

"I'm not aware of too many people who have gotten rich off of bacon and eggs," Ana said, "but breakfast cereals have certainly brought in a lot of cash in recent years, even though cereal, toast, and an orange hardly seem like a 'balanced breakfast' to me."

"You know, young lady," Pauline said with a proud smile, "maybe you're on to something."

Indeed, the self-taught health guru had a point. Perhaps a mere coincidence, the current condition of

Stonehenge bore striking similarities to society's current diet. What initially had started out as six food groups had been, over the years, reduced to just five. Though the grains, fruits, and vegetables trilithons were still intact, the meat and dairy trilithons had suffered some major blows, while the fats trilithon had disappeared altogether. With several of its foundational pillars missing, little wonder then that society's overall health, like Stonehenge, lay in shambles.

The two Cooper women spent the rest of the morning going through every food item in the kitchen. They cleaned out the cupboards and dumped out the drawers. They scrutinized the contents of the refrigerator and the pantry. Pauline had never been one to pay much attention to nutritional facts labels, but that was now a thing of the past. She was astounded to find that her kitchen wasn't very balanced.

By noon, the mother and daughter had come to a realization together: the difference between diet and lifestyle. Before, Pauline had tried to 'go on a diet' without changing her lifestyle, which only works for as long as the diet goes on. What she really needed to do, however, was make her diet a part of her lifestyle — make her way of eating her way of living. Then, whenever the Cosmic Brownies came out, she wouldn't have to reconfigure her diet but only make some quick adjustments, and then she'd be back on track.

While Pauline and Ana were cooking up a balanced lunch, Mr. Coy and Jaret appeared in the cloven tree trunk on the Keep's grounds. They had just arrived from Waters Deep, where they narrowly escaped death. Mr. Coy was puzzled why the Deep's trilithon had taken them to the Keep, until Jaret said, "Take me to my girls."

Coy led Jaret into the mansion house, down the elevator, and onto the twenty-first-century floor, where they hurried to the Coopers' place and knocked on the door.

"Dad?!" Ana shrieked.

"Jaret?!" Pauline squealed.

"My girls!" Jaret cried, taking them both in his arms.

"Oh, I'm so glad you're okay!" Pauline said.

"How did you get here?" Ana asked.

"Through a tree," Jaret answered with a bit of bewilderment.

"Me, too," Ana said.

"A tree?" Pauline gasped.

"Long story," Coy mumbled to her. "Actually, I first went to the Deep, where I rescued this big lug." He patted Jaret on the back. "Then we escaped right before Lye—" A look of concern washed over Coy's face. "Wait a minute, where's Paige?"

"She's not with you?" Ana returned.

"No," said Coy. "You mean she didn't come with you?"

"Nope," Ana replied.

A moment of silent pondering ensued.

"Ana, was this the first place you were sent to?" Coy asked. "To the Keep?"

"Yes, sir."

"What were you thinking about at the time?" Coy wondered.

"Um," Ana tried to recall. "Well, I was thinking of the trilithons as food groups and how excited I was to tell my mom about them."

"Hmm," Coy thought, as if solving a riddle. "Captain," he said, turning to Jaret, "what were *you* thinking about right before we were sent here from the Deep?"

"My girls," Jaret said, pulling both his wife and daughter into his side. "I wasn't sure you were going to get us out of there, Ben—figured we were done for. So I was thinking how nice it would be to see Pauline and Ana one last time."

"I see," Coy supposed pensively. "As for me, up until I was transported away from Stonehenge, I had been thinking about *you* a lot," he said to Jaret, "wondering if you were okay—still alive, even." Then, addressing the whole group, he said, "Well, folks, it seems to me that these trilithon-portal things transport you based on what you are most concerned about at the time—it sends you according to your desires. So, in the case of Paige, that means…"

"She probably went to wherever Ret is," Ana finished.

"Exactly," Coy said.

Jaret whispered to his wife, "Honey, have you lost weight?"

"Well, actually," Pauline said with a giggle, "no, but that's about change. I hope you like fats!" Jaret stared at her oddly.

Just then, there came another knock at the door. Everyone glanced at each other. Mr. Coy answered it.

"Leo!" Coy beamed. "How goes it, my boy?"

"Mr. Coy," Leo panted, as if he had just sprinted to the door, "there's something I need to show you."

"What is it, son?" Coy asked with seriousness.

"Remember that assignment you gave to me to search the Keep until I found something about a strange tree in Russia?" Leo explained to Coy. Leo leaned to the side to awkwardly wink at Ana.

"Yeah…"

"Well, I found something," Leo said.

"Take me to it," Coy requested.

"Yes, sir."

Leo led Mr. Coy to the elevator in the center room of the twenty-first-century floor, Ana following closely behind. They descended one floor, climbed out, and headed toward the corridor between the walls of the first two decades, on which was painted the years 1900 and 1910 in big black letters. Near the end of the corridor, Leo turned left into a hallway where the very last door on the left was ajar. Leo stopped outside and let Mr. Coy enter first.

The headlines caught his attention right away:

TUNGUSKA EXPLOSION ROCKS RUSSIA
MYSTERIOUS BLAST BAFFLES SCIENTISTS
POSSIBLE METEORITE STRIKES SIBERIA
UFO SIGHTING IN RUSSIA

"The opposite wall tells what really happened," Leo said. Ana had entered the room and was holding Leo's hand, forever a little creeped out by the Keep.

Mr. Coy turned around. The first thing he noticed was a blueprint of an atomic bomb. Next to it was the dog tag of the pilot who flew the plane that dropped the bomb. There were several schematics of the great tree— its height, girth, number of limbs, even the exact coordinates of its geographic location. Black and white photographs showed before and after scenes of the Tunguska River valley—before, a beautiful forest; after, a leveled wasteland. A picture of a massive mushroom cloud confirmed Mr. Coy's suspicions: the mysterious

Tunguska Explosion was the work of neither meteorites nor aliens but Lye, who dropped a crudely-constructed atomic weapon on the infinity tree in his effort to gain access to the wood element. In capital red letters, a final photograph of the bomb had been stamped UNSUC-CESSFUL.

"What is his obsession with nuclear power?" Mr. Coy mumbled to himself.

"I can show you more evidence in a few other rooms," Leo offered, "if you're interested."

"No, no, I think I've seen enough," Coy said. "Thank you for all your hard work, son." He put his hand on the young man's shoulder. "You've been very helpful." Leo smiled.

"So, what does this mean, chief?" Ana asked of Coy, as a sidekick would his superior.

"It means I've got a date with that cloven tree at sunrise," Coy answered. "If I think about Ret when I warp this time, it should take me to him. Then I can give him the Oracle, find Paige, and get out before Ret collects the element."

"Sounds like a plan!" Ana cheered. "Let's roll!"

"You should probably ask your parents first," Coy suggested.

"Oh alright," Ana agreed, as they left the room.

Pauline and Jaret needed little persuasion, knowing their daughter was in good hands with Mr. Coy.

In fact, the Coast Guard captain would have joined them had Pauline not pointed out that he should stay home to fully recuperate—or, as Leo joked to Ana, re-Cooper-ate.

There was no sleeping that night for Mr. Coy as he made preparations for their excursion. While everyone else went to bed, he stayed awake, too worried about Paige and what lay ahead. About an hour after midnight, he figured he had just about everything in order when he heard something on TV that caught his attention. He rushed into the other room to find that the regular programming had been interrupted for some breaking news:

> *Dr. Lionel Zarbock, renowned physicist and leader of the United Nations effort to stop Ret Cooper, was seen on the grounds of Stonehenge before dawn this morning. He was leading a large company of international soldiers, all on foot. Security personnel at the scene reported seeing Zarbock and his men disappear just moments ago at sunrise, after standing as a group in the large gap of the iconic monument's inner circle. It is believed Zarbock was acting on information that would lead him to the Cooper criminal, whose exact whereabouts remain a mystery. Reporting live from Stonehenge, I'm Katie Kline, Channel 4 News*

Mr. Coy's heart began to beat a little faster. Although this was breaking news for the world, it was bad news for him. Once again, Lionel was throwing a wrench in his plans. How did he know about the trilithon? And where was he going with an army? The situation had just gotten a little more complicated and a lot more dangerous.

But Mr. Coy had an idea. He grabbed his phone and urgently dialed a number. Time was of the essence. It just might work, but only if they moved fast. Sunrise was coming.

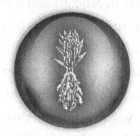

CHAPTER 15

TURNING THE PAIGE

It was happening again. She could sense herself getting caught in the downward spiral. With tears in her eyes and a lump in her throat, she cut a helter-skelter path through the woods back toward the trilithon, her pace hurried and desperate. Every pulse of her aching heart surged throughout her body, the sound of each beat in her ears making her deaf to the outside world. Her mind was swirling out of control, without her permission, but she was powerless to stop it—just like each time before.

Yes, Paige was falling into depression.

This was nothing new to the daughter of Benjamin and Helen Coy. For as long as she could remember, Paige had suffered from regular episodes of despair. At first, she assumed it was perfectly natural to be sad once in a while, but as she grew into adolescence, her moodiness worsened until, on her worst days, it would cripple her. On more than one occasion, she had overheard some of the Manor's staff and students discussing their own personal struggles with "depression," and each narrative sounded strikingly similar to what Paige was experiencing. But she didn't like the D-word. She would admit to *feeling* depressed occasionally, yes, but in her mind she didn't believe she actually *had* depression. She liked to think she was stronger than that. And most of the time she was. But sometimes she wasn't...

It always began with a trigger: something that set her unhappiness in motion—an unkind word or unmet expectation, a disappointing result or unpleasant thought, something she could not change about herself or the world. Whatever it was, it upset a delicate balance in her psyche—an unseen but very real (perhaps even chemical) equilibrium—and altered her mental and emotional stability. From there, the demon played dominos with her well-being, slowly consuming her every thought until there was no longer any joy to be found in anything. Pessimism pushed out simple pleasures. Hopelessness haunted every action. A prevailing pointlessness turned everything mundane. It was a chain reaction—the epitome of misery: inwardly ravenous yet outwardly silent, and all in her head.

Paige was a lot better at hiding her depression than dealing with it. She kept it completely concealed, putting up a false front of sunshine despite the gloom within. A fair amount of her despondency stemmed from her parents. Paige had no memories of her mother—only pictures, tear-stained from thumbing through them on hard days, which somehow gave her the strength to keep going, like a child admiring a hero. She could not say the same for her father, however. Until recently, no one had quite understood why Mr. Coy had distanced himself so drastically from his daughter. Like most children, Paige thought it was because there was something wrong with *her*—that she was a disappointment to him, an embarrassment. Now she knew it was for a much different reason, but the damage had been done, and, like most people, the mental pathways formed from the injustices of childhood continued to determine her self-worth and define her anxieties.

Well did Paige remember the day she finally went to see a doctor. It had been a rough week. She had lost the will to live (again), not so much a desire to take her own life as a wish to no longer exist—a lack of fulfillment and purpose in life that made it seem foolish to keep living. Each day that week, she had come home from school and gone straight to bed, hoping that things would be better in the morning. But they never were. By Friday, she was at a loss of what to do. Ashamed and afraid, she did not know who to turn to. Over that weekend, she mustered the courage to act, and then on the following Monday, she flagged down the psychologist who was guest-teaching at the Manor. He asked her a few questions, ran some simple tests, and then shared his diagnosis: the D-word.

"No, not me," Paige immediately thought to herself. "I *can't have d... d...*"

Then the psychologist handed her a prescription.

"Antidepressants?" Paige mentally balked. "I *don't need* those." The doctor handed her the prescription, but Paige hesitated in accepting it.

"There's no shame in needing help," the psychologist smiled lovingly, "only in not seeking help when you need it."

Those words were enough to convince Paige to pick up the pills. Still, it would be a few more days before she actually started taking them. She kept them where no one would see them, worried about the stigma of being "on medication." She tried the medicine for a few weeks, which was hardly enough time for it to kick in, but then stopped when she found an even better remedy.

"My name is Ana," the Cooper daughter introduced herself to Paige, who, at the time, was the newest student at their middle school. "Let's be friends!"

In no time at all, Paige found Ana to be the perfect prescription for her battle with depression. Ana's undaunted buoyancy never failed to lift Paige out of her doldrums. They laughed together, talked together, and just had good plain fun together. Paige had found her antidepressant—this time in the form of a person rather than a pill.

There was a side effect to Ana's friendship, however: association with her adopted brother, Ret. Although Paige quickly fell in love with the boy, she tried not to give in to her feelings, for she knew they came with the risk of disappointment if Ret did not reciprocate them—and disappointment was one of the triggers of her depression. But she just couldn't resist. She loved everything about Ret—his bright skin and eyes, his hair that was even blonder than her own, his good heart and innocent nature.

Most of the time, her slow-growing relationship with Ret staved off her depression, keeping the monster locked in its cage. But she knew opening her heart was like opening the cage door, making her vulnerable to another outbreak—like when they met Alana, the pretty princess of Sunken Earth. The thought of Ret pursuing someone else reawakened Paige's mental complex that day, and her deep-rooted feelings of inadequacy returned. She experienced similar distress when Miss Carmen came into the picture. Fortunately, these dives into depression were stopped fairly quickly each time because of something that Ret did to reaffirm his concern for Paige, and she was riding high (her highest ever, perhaps) after she helped him collect the wind element in Antarctica. Now, however, after seeing yet another female stranger steal her place at Ret's side, she was distraught like never before.

For Paige, the ups and downs of romance (especially the downs) affected her disorder more than anything else. The high-stakes emotion of love seemed to rock the teeter-totter of her inner zen with the heaviest hand of all. Some might call Paige a helpless romantic. Others might say she was unstable or obsessed. And perhaps that was true, for no matter how level-headed and straight-laced she appeared on the outside, she was still on the inside just a teenage girl—one who was turning out remarkably well despite her challenges. Plus, to her credit, there was something about this land that brought out the mutant in each of us. For, in some way or another, and whether we realize it yet or not, are we not all mutants?

And is that not what depression is—a mutation? A cancer of the mind, it invades something healthy and functional and reprograms it into something foreign and destructive. It ranks especially terrible because it has a way of feeding itself—gaining strength from the misery it causes, like how a hurricane intensifies while spinning above water. Paige was old enough now to know when the storm was brewing—mature enough to recognize the signs and try to avoid it, which always proved easier to attempt than to actually accomplish. In some sick way, the syndrome seemed to infect its victims with a venom that eroded their rationality—that mutated their desire to be free of the monster into a desire to befriend it.

Such was happening to Paige in this moment. She knew she needed to snap out of it, but the mutated part of herself produced a steady supply of depressing thoughts in order to keep itself alive. It had waited to flare up until she was worn down, knowing she was most susceptible when weak and alone, like a predator stalking its prey. Dizzy and delirious, Paige's march slowed to a stagger. She was mutating, and her will to fight was becoming weaker the longer it went on. She fell to her knees, her face flushed and awash with tears. It was over; there was no one to save her. Laying on her side in the dirt, she curled up into a ball as the unseen darkness closed in on her.

Depression was finally claiming her, once and for all.

But then, despite her blurred and squinted vision, she caught sight of something. Several yards away, she saw something shining brightly despite the onset of night. It was a large picture, positioned vertically among the trees. She thought it was a painting until its depiction moved. She slowly rose to her feet, intrigued by the screen and the strange scene that it was showing. It was obviously a foreign film, portraying things that did not belong in this wooded setting. Paige cautiously walked closer. It was about the size of a door, slightly taller and wider than herself. She peered inside, where there was no forest but instead a rich blue sky and a great grassy field. It was like a portal to another time and place.

Suddenly, a woman came gamboling through the grass, holding the hand of a small child. Paige's heart leapt within her chest: the woman was her mother, Helen. Then Paige recognized the child as a younger version of herself. She realized this was a scene from the past. She strode through the doorway and followed after the pair, who didn't notice her at all.

Mrs. Coy was even more beautiful in person than in pictures—at least in Paige's estimation. Slim and feminine, she was smiling from ear to ear as she frolicked across the field with her pride and joy. Paige the toddler was moving her little legs as fast as they could go, her curly blonde hair bouncing just above her waist. Their destination was a great sycamore tree, from which was hanging a simple wooden swing. Paige had seen this swing before—in an old photograph, one of her most treasured—and, judging by her mother's yellow skirt, this may have been the exact day when it had been taken.

"Will you push me, Mommy?" young Paige asked sweetly as they approached the swing, her favorite pastime.

"Of course, sweetheart," Mommy obliged. She lifted her daughter onto the wooden seat, made sure her little fingers were gripping each rope, and then commenced the ride with a gentle push.

The child cheered, crying, "Higher, higher!"

For a long time, the pair played together in the afternoon sunshine at the old swing under the big tree. With wonderful enthusiasm, Helen entertained her girl. She pulled her forward like a train and backward like a rollercoaster. She reached from behind during the upswing to tickle her tummy, or sat underneath and laid back just in time to avoid the downswing.

"Do 'Walking Along'!" the toddler requested.

Helen knew precisely what that meant. She stood to one side and, pretending not to see the swing coming towards her, started to unsuspectingly 'walk along,' purposely pacing back and forth in front of the swing's path. Each time it whizzed by, she quickly leapt out of the way, narrowly escaping a strike from the swinger whose arms and feet were outstretched to try and bump her mother. The closer the call and sillier the reaction, the bigger the grin and louder the laugh. Most of the time, Helen dodged her, but sometimes she allowed a direct hit, much to the swinger's glee.

There was something infectious about the pure joy of a child. It was an antidote for depression. Current-day Paige observed from the sidelines, soaking up the happiness that was radiating from her younger self. She couldn't help but feel good inside. The gladness was difficult to deny—a smile impossible to suppress—the warmth swelling within her ridiculous not to welcome.

In time, Helen grew tired. She sat down at the base of the tree, leaning against its wide trunk. Without someone to push it, the swing gradually slowed until it stopped. Young Paige hopped down from her seat, trotted over to her mother, and sat in her lap.

"I love you, Mommy," the child whispered, hugging her tightly.

"I love you, too, Paige," Helen replied, straightening the girl's curls.

"You're my best friend."

"You're my best friend, too," the mother stated.

"I wish we could be together all the time," young Paige said.

"But we *are*," Helen told her. "In here." She brought her daughter's hand to her chest.

"That's your heart," young Paige giggled, feeling her mother's heartbeat.

"You are always with me in my heart," Helen said. "And *I* am always with *you*," she placed the girl's hand on her own chest, "in *your* heart."

"But I mean *together*," the youngster emphasized, "not just in your heart."

"I know, darling, I know," Helen pulled her in close. "But there might be times in life when we can't be together." She thought of her beloved brother Peter, who died during a special ops mission for the U.S. Navy. "There was a time in my life when I was very sad because I couldn't be with someone I loved anymore."

"You mean Uncle Peter?" young Paige wondered, having heard her mother speak of him often.

"Yes," Helen said, her voice shaky. "I was sad for a long time. Meeting your dad helped a lot, but it wasn't until I had *you* when I began to feel completely happy again. I love my little girl." She drew her in even closer.

It was clear by now that these people from the past could not see the person from the future who was in their midst. Paige went and sat down next to the pair, knowing she was invisible to them.

"So," Helen carried on, "if there's ever a time when we can't be together and you are feeling sad, I want you to promise me something."

"Yes, mommy?"

"I want you to be strong," her mother said.

"Strong like Daddy?" young Paige asked, holding up her little arms in a muscle-man pose.

"Daddy is very strong," Helen smiled, "but I'm talking about something different. This is a strength that comes from inside—from here." She pressed her finger to the child's heart. "So when you're feeling sad, just look inside your heart because I'm always with you in your heart."

"And *I'm* always with *you* in your heart," the girl returned.

"That's right," Helen said, her eyes moist. "We'll always be together, and we'll help each other to be strong. Promise?"

"I promise," whispered both the past and present Paige, the latter watching the tender exchange and answering as if her mother was speaking to her right now.

Just then, a sound was heard a good ways behind Paige. She turned around to see her father striding through the grass, coming to join his wife and daughter. There was a camera in his hand. He looked so young.

Young Paige yawned and laid her head against her mother's chest, listening to her heartbeat.

Helen wrapped her arms around her and then, while still looking off toward her husband, said, "I love you, Paige." Although Helen was really watching Ben as he drew nigh, current-day Paige was sitting directly in her line of sight so that for a moment it felt as though her mother was looking her in the eye, saying those comforting words to her not only in the past but also in the present.

"I love you, too," Paige told her, speaking in unison with her younger self, then her present self adding, "I miss you."

"Be strong," Helen whispered, cradling her child as Mr. Coy's footsteps grew louder. "I'm always with you." Paige placed her hand over her heart. "In your heart."

Snap. The entire scene disappeared. Paige found herself back in the forest, which was growing brighter from the first rays of dawn. Her stroll through the past had occupied the entire night. Confused, she glanced around, then nearly fell over when she saw a man sitting on a bench nearby.

"Who are you?" Paige questioned timidly.

"I am Neo," the older gentleman told her politely, "Guardian of the Wood Element."

"Oh," Paige said, taken by surprise, "it—it's a pleasure to meet you, sir."

"Likewise," Neo replied, "though I've known you for a long time."

"You have?" Paige asked with a bit of alarm. "How?"

"It's a long story—I'll let Ret tell you about it sometime," Neo said. "Remember that person you and Ana saw in the Keep recently—the one who led you to the room with the Stonehenge diagrams?"

"Was that you?" Paige queried, sitting next to him on the wooden bench.

"Yes, indeed," Neo answered. "And how did you like the glimpse of the past that I just gave you?"

"You did that, too?" Paige questioned with growing amazement. Neo nodded.

"Now, my dear, it's time to make your *depression* also a thing of the past," the Guardian counseled. "I believe you've battled it long enough."

"I know," Paige confessed. "I've tried, but I just can't seem to get over it."

"That's because you're not doing it right," Neo told her sensitively. "Your approach is missing something—or, I should say, some*one."*

"Who?" Paige wondered with great interest.

*"Any*one," Neo said. "You can't do it alone. You need help. Tell someone about it tell anyone about it. When you feel yourself starting to spiral out of control, tell them and ask them to help you. Depression thrives on loneliness but flounders with companionship—surely you know that."

"Yes, I do, but who?" Paige asked. "I feel like no one will understand—that they'll just think I'm strange."

"Give people a chance; they may surprise you," Neo advised. "Might I suggest starting with Ret?" Paige's head fell at the idea.

"Why should I talk to *him?"* she put forth, her good-hearted nature ruining her attempt at sounding scornful.

"Now, now," Neo gently warned. "The guy at least deserves a chance to explain himself, doesn't he?"

"Yeah, I guess you're right," Paige admitted.

"Of course I am," Neo clapped. "Now off you go."

With that, Paige stood and took a few steps forward. "Be strong," Neo added, borrowing the phrase from Helen.

Paige smiled and, glancing back, said, "Thanks, but I—"

But the Guardian was gone.

"Hmm," Paige hummed. "All I was going to say was I don't know the way back to town." Suddenly, a line of trees off to her left parted, showing a clear path to take. "Guardian of *wood* is right," she remarked to herself as she started down the path.

Though nervous to confront Ret, Paige was in much brighter spirits than she was a few minutes ago. Such was the nature of her disorder: it came suddenly and consumed quickly but could be dispelled just as rapidly with the right intervention. She was grateful that Neo had come to her rescue, and she appreciated his wise advice to seek out someone—anyone—who could interrupt any of her future descents into depression. With renewed hope, she hiked through the woods until she found the trail that would take her back into town, feeling, for the first time in her life, as though she finally possessed what had been missing in her quest to control her mutation.

Still new to this strange land, Paige kept a quick pace in her trek back to town. She was unsure of what creatures might be wandering in the woods, the thickest patches of which were quite shadowy despite the daylight. The slightest sound scared her. She wished Ret was with her.

Paige's worried heart took courage when she saw the figure of a man on the path ahead.

"Excuse me?" Paige called out to him. "Can you help me?"

The man did not move, his back still facing her.

"Sir?" Paige said with growing uncertainty in her voice.

Slowly, the man turned around. He was wearing a black robe, the hood concealing his face. He started to step towards Paige.

Startled, Paige began to walk backwards, but after only a few steps, she bumped into something. She spun around to find another person in a black robe. Paige screamed, but as soon as the sound left her mouth, the person held up a hand and silenced the sound waves. Paige glared wide-eyed at the hand, which bore the marks of two illuminated scars—identical to Ret's.

Paige rushed to her left, but a third cloaked person cut off her escape, followed by two more on her right. By now, the first mysterious man had joined the huddle, surrounding Paige on all sides. Despite her squirming, the five strangers bound her hands and feet and carried her away into the woods.

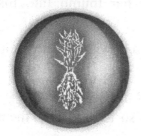

CHAPTER 16

SERGE PROTECTOR

Apparently, there was a rooster somewhere in the old barn where Ret was staying. It probably would have woken him up the next morning, had he been asleep. But he wasn't. In fact, he hadn't slept a wink all night.

"Rise and shine, sweetheart!" Nika caroled as she strode into the barn a good while later, like she had done the day before. "I know you need your beauty rest, but sleeping past noon seems like plenty of—oh." She was surprised to see Ret was already awake. "Hello, Ret," she said with a bit less enthusiasm. When his gaze remained fixed on the nearby window, she knew something was troubling him.

Nika slowly approached Ret. She could see him massaging his right palm. He did that a lot, she had noticed. She quietly sat down next to him in the hay, reached for his right hand, and took over as masseuse.

"What are these markings on your hand?" Nika curiously asked as she pressed her thumb into his palm.

"They're scars," he answered without emotion, still not turning to look at her.

"How did you get them?" she questioned, childlike.

"I wish I knew," Ret said, "so I could give them back."

"Do they hurt?" Nika wondered.

"On the inside," Ret told her.

"They look like symbols," Nika assessed, leaning in for a closer examination. "Do they have any meaning?"

"They tell me where the elements are," Ret explained.

"The elements that you have to collect?" Nika deduced.

"Yeah," Ret said softly.

"Why is our old world mad at you for collecting elements?" Nika tried to understand.

"Because it's destroying their world," Ret said.

"Oh," Nika said with subdued shock. "Then why do you do it?"

Ret sighed with heaviness and replied, "Because I have to." A moment of silence ensued.

"Why is this scar brighter than the others?" Nika asked, referring to the scar on the far left side of his palm. "This one that looks like a tree?"

Ret finally turned to face her and said with soberness, "Because its element is *here*."

Nika froze. She was connecting the dots.

"The great tree," Nika whispered to herself as she analyzed the scar. "The element is in the great tree?" Ret closed his eyes and nodded. Nika released his hand and immediately became defensive.

"So that's why you're here?" she interrogated, her eyebrows furrowed with suspicion. "That's why you stayed? To collect your element?"

"Not exactly," Ret said pathetically, his temperament steady. He suspected such allegations.

"So you're using me?" Nika continued to jump to conclusions. "Using me to get to your element? And then what—steal it and leave us all to die?" Her words were growing more acrid by the moment. "You're just like all the others." She turned away, then brought her knees to her chest and wrapped her arms around them.

Nika had not always been so distrustful of others— in fact, quite the opposite was true. Once upon a time, she believed people were innately trustworthy and that no one would knowingly hurt someone else. But that was long ago, in a land far away, before a series of tragic experiences in her life taught her to believe otherwise—the first of which occurred when she was rejected by her own household as a young girl. That disownment had left her crushed, and so in order to protect herself from getting hurt like that again, she subconsciously began to cast up walls between herself and others—walls of distrust, bitterness, and cynicism. Initially, the walls were short and thin, but with each act of unfairness and prejudice that was thrown at her, those walls became taller and thicker.

For this reason, Nika's accusations did not bother Ret. He knew her assumptions of his motives struck a familiar nerve within her that sent her insecurities into panic mode. She had let down her walls for Ret, but now that he was within them, she feared the past was happening all over again. In short, her reaction was the manifestation of her mutation.

"I never said I was going to collect the element," Ret told her.

Nika turned to face Ret and said, her antagonism melting, "You're not?"

Ret shook his head, "No." Nika detected consider-able disappointment in his voice. "I can't—I don't even have the Oracle."

"The Oracle?" Nika inquired.

"It's the sphere that houses the elements," Ret clarified. "It has the same markings on it as my hands. When someone with the scars holds it," he cupped his hands together, "it aligns itself with the scars and opens into six wedges, then each wedge closes around an element. But I don't have it—Mr. Coy does."

"Who's Mr. Coy?" Nika asked.

"It doesn't matter anymore," Ret said with visible sadness.

Ret's words indicated that he had made up his mind. His body language, however, told a different story. It was obvious that he wanted to collect the element—that his sense of duty, no matter how unwanted, was pulling him in that direction. But, for some reason, he was yielding to his mind this time instead of his heart. No wonder he looked so heart-broken. Notwithstanding the relief she felt at his decision, it pained Nika to see Ret in such despondent spirits. She wondered if there was a way for Ret to win despite the apparent lose-lose situation.

"If the element is in the great tree," Nika postu-lated, "then collecting the element would only destroy the tree and nothing else, right?"

"The tree is the backbone that holds this whole place together," Ret returned. "Its roots run everywhere. Once the tree goes, everything will cave in on itself." Nika winced at the thought. "It'd be like removing the skeletal system from a human body."

After a few moments of thinking, Nika came up with another idea: "You can control the elements, right? Remember when we first met and you rolled away that boulder without even touching it?" Ret nodded. "How about you collect the element and then keep this place from caving in on itself?—you know, hold it together? It's basically one big rock, after all."

"Who do I look like? Atlas?" Ret glared at her. "I can't hold it together—there's too much water—in the dirt, in the plants—and that's the one element I don't control yet. Besides, even if I *could* prevent this place from imploding, what would *keep* it together? Without the tree, this place is toast."

"Maybe you could collect the water element first and then come back for this one?" Nika sheepishly suggested.

"That's going to be the hardest element of all to collect," Ret sighed. In his frustration, he got up and started to pace around the barn. "I don't even *want* to collect elements. It's just a game—it's not the goal."

"Then what's the goal?" Nika wondered.

"It's this!" Ret insisted, holding up his arms to signify his surroundings.

"A smelly old barn?" Nika joked, hoping it would get Ret to smile.

With a stifled laugh, Ret said, "No, I mean this land—your people."

"My people?"

"Yes," Ret reaffirmed. "It's your way of life here, just as you told me: love of deity and love of man— everything else hangs on those two laws. And because of that, look what you have: peace, acceptance, freedom from strife. What you *don't* have are the problems that plague our old world: greed, tyranny, selfishness. *That* world has been set up incorrectly. The people there work for money, but the people here work for others. And because everyone here works to meet each other's needs, everyone's needs are met. That's why I stayed here—because *this* is what I've been searching for. This is what's missing. This is the goal. If there's one element that will 'cure the world,' it's love—it's this place. I can't destroy it; I want to propagate it. I want to take it back with me and graft it into my languishing world in order to save it."

"You want us to go back?" Nika asked with absurdity. "To the world that cast us out? Why should we do that?"

"Because they need us," Ret answered.

"What do you mean?" Nika questioned.

Ret returned to the pile of hay and sat down next to Nika before continuing, "We are given differences to teach us how to love. I used to see them as opportunities to judge, but now I know they are really opportunities to love. We have done the world a great disservice by removing ourselves from their society. If we truly love them, we will go back and return to them the opportunity to love." Looking her in the eye, he pled, "Would you do that?"

Nika blushed. It was hard for her to say no to Ret.

"Would we ever be able to come back?" Nika hoped. "After our job is done? Or if it doesn't work?"

"Of course," Ret told her. "By not collecting the element, this place will remain safe and sound." Suddenly, Nika seemed much more willing.

"Then I guess it's worth a try," she said.

"Great!" Ret cheered. "Thank you." He hugged her.

"I would do anything for you, Ret," Nika said tenderly. Staring into his eyes, she tilted her head and moved to kiss him.

Suddenly, there was a commotion heard from outside. Before their lips met, Ret sprang up from Nika's side and stared out the window. A large company of military men was marching into the town square. The townspeople were scurrying out of the way, shutting themselves indoors. Alarmed, Ret hurried out of the barn.

"What is it?" Nika called out, sensing trouble and getting up to follow. "What's going on?"

Ret ran out to the square, firmly planted his feet in the dirt, and unflinchingly faced the approaching brigade. His fearlessness faded into puzzlement, however, when he saw who was leading the group.

"Lionel?" Ret wondered aloud.

"Ret!" Lionel exclaimed, rushing toward him with a warm embrace. "I'm so glad I found you."

"What are you doing here?" Ret asked.

"I'm here to help you, of course," Lionel said affectionately.

"Help me with what?" Ret queried.

Lionel leaned in close and whispered, "Collecting the element."

"Oh," Ret sighed, "well actually—"

"Shh," Lionel said softly. "It's okay, I know."

"You know?" Ret asked incredulously.

"Yes," Lionel repeated. "You're right: we have to be very careful about this. That army back there," he motioned behind him, "they're expecting me to *stop* you from collecting the element—the whole world is, in fact. But I *want* you to collect it. I've come up with a plan that will allow us to collect the element even while it looks like I'm trying to stop you. Just do exactly what I say."

"But Lionel," Ret protested, "I don't—"

"Trust me, Ret," Lionel reassured him. "It'll work."

"But—"

Lionel spun around and announced to his forces, "As promised, I have led us to the Cooper criminal, and he has agreed to cooperate." A few cheers emerged from the group.

"Criminal?" Ret mouthed to himself. He could see the worried faces of townspeople pressed up against the windows, watching the proceedings.

"Now Ret," Lionel loudly addressed the accused, employing a sterner tone than just a moment ago, "hand over the Oracle."

"What?" Ret asked, stunned by the request.

Lionel discretely nodded at him, a subtle reminder to just follow along.

"But I—I don't have it," came Ret's truthful reply.

"Oh, Ret," Lionel laughed. "It's okay, just—"

"I'm being honest," Ret avowed.

"Ret, give me the Oracle," Lionel said, his patience growing thin.

With more conviction, Ret repeated, "I said I don't have it."

"Give me the Oracle, boy!" Lionel shouted, echoing in the square.

Lionel's angry words seemed to ring a bell in Ret's mind, for suddenly a strange (though increasingly familiar) scene flashed before his eyes. For a split second, he was taken back to a moment in time when he was aboard a burning ship, amid billowing smoke and howling wind, with someone yelling those same exact words at him—someone who looked very little like Lionel but a lot like...Lye?

"Ret!" Lionel screeched, shaking Ret from his memories.

Confused, Ret shrugged his shoulders and shook his head, unsure of what Lionel wanted him to do. Ret was shocked by his friend's behavior. Was this all part of the act?

"Argh!" Lionel growled with frustration. He turned around and barked to his men, "Search the town!"

"What? No!" Ret countered.

"Leave nothing untouched!" Lionel instructed.

"Stop!" Ret begged as the soldiers fanned out, charging through the doors of houses and stores.

"I know it's here!" Lionel told them, ignoring Ret's pleas.

Ret grabbed Lionel by the arm and asked pitifully, "Why are you doing this?"

"Like I already told you," Lionel answered, "the entire United Nations is counting on me to stop you. As their emissary, I am against you. But as your friend, I want to help you. This is an incredibly difficult position for me to be in, but I'm doing it for *you.*" Nika emerged from the barn and wandered within earshot.

"You're doing it for *me?*" Ret questioned.

"The whole world is against you," Lionel explained, "but I control the international effort to stop you. So although I need to make it look like I'm trying to stop you, I can also ensure that you collect the last two elements." Nika didn't like the sound of that. "I am your key to filling the Oracle! I just need you to do exactly as I say."

"Ret doesn't want to collect the elements," Nika inserted matter-of-factly, stepping to Ret's side from behind. "He told me himself."

"Nika..." Ret quietly scolded her.

"Who are you?" Lionel sneered.

"I am the leader of these people," Nika boldly declared. "I would ask that you and your men leave immediately."

"I'm not leaving without the Oracle," Lionel threatened.

"Ret doesn't have it," Nika told him flatly. "Now leave at once!"

Lionel stared at Nika with suspicion and asked, "Did Ret tell you that, too?"

"Yes," Nika replied, unsure of Lionel's reasoning.

"I wonder what else Ret has shared with you," Lionel wondered with an unsettling smile.

Just then, one of Lionel's men arrived with a status report: "We've looked everywhere, sir. There's no sign of the Oracle."

With displeasure, Lionel glared at Nika. Her confidence buckled under his penetrating gaze. She instinctively covered the scarred portion of her face.

"Bring her," Lionel commanded his soldier, who promptly grabbed Nika.

"Where are you taking me?" Nika demanded, futilely wailing on the soldier's armor.

"Wait!" Ret called after Lionel, who was striding away. "What are you doing?"

"Ret!" Nika cried for help.

Lionel stopped in the center of the town square and proclaimed, "Listen well, mutants." The frightened citizens peeked from behind doorjambs and windowsills, trying to make sense of their ransacked homes. "Somewhere in this town, there is a sphere called the Oracle. I know you know what I'm talking about. I want it, and I'm going to kill you one by one until I get it—starting with your leader."

"Lionel!?" Ret said with perplexity. "What has gotten into you? You're like a different person."

"Restrain him," Lionel said. A pair of guards seized Ret.

"You know what I'm capable of," Ret warned him. "Don't make me—"

"I'm waiting," Lionel told the town.

"These people are innocent," Ret implored. "They don't know anything about the Oracle."

"*She* does," Lionel said of Nika. He pulled a gun from his soldier's holster.

"Please don't hurt them," Ret besought. "These people have been nothing but good to me. They're my friends."

"These aren't people," Lionel mocked. "They're mutants—worthless, ugly mutants." Many of the townsfolk looked down in shame. "They're a scourge to our society. I'll be doing us all a favor by ridding the world of them." He raised the gun in the air.

Ret had had enough. He had tried to reason with his so-called friend Lionel but to no avail. He wasn't about to let the innocent get hurt.

Ret focused on the gun in Lionel's hand. Made of metal, he knew he could easily manipulate it. But before Ret could do anything to it, the gun suddenly flew out of Lionel's hand. Someone had shot it. Lionel jumped in alarm, inspecting his hand to make sure it was unharmed. He angrily spun around and demanded of his men, "Who did that?!"

"I did." Everyone turned to look across the square at the brave stranger.

"Well, well, well," Lionel said with disgust. "If it isn't Sergey Topramenov."

Nika's eyes bulged to hear her brother's name. She looked at Ret, who nodded with an equally surprised smile.

"Let her go," Serge ordered, his gun still aimed and ready, "or you'll be next."

Lionel laughed and asked defiantly, "You and what army?"

Suddenly, masses of Russian infantrymen poured into the square, surrounding Lionel's men.

"This one," Serge answered after his men had finished assembling.

With a disgruntled grimace, Lionel exhaled and instructed his soldier, "Release her."

Nika rushed to Ret's side.

"Are you okay?" he asked.

"Yeah, I'm fine," she told him.

But Nika's attention was focused on something else. She looked across the square. Someone was watching her. It was her brother. Despite the presence of two locked-and-loaded armies, there was silence throughout the town as the two siblings stared at one another. Separated since childhood, they were both in awe—the brother that his sister was still alive, the sister that her brother cared enough to find her. They slowly stepped forward, the sound of their footsteps heard by everyone.

"How did you find me?" Nika asked, clearly moved.

"I've been searching for you since the day you left," Serge replied lovingly.

Serge was about to hug his long-lost sister, but she turned away with the shame of a leper. She brought her hand to her face to cover her unsightly scar. Delicately, Serge pulled her hand away and then, without any hesitation, used one of his own to caress her face.

"I've missed you so much," Serge said softly with tears in his eyes, "my beautiful sister." They embraced.

"I love you, brother," Nika whispered in his ear.

Ret was touched as he observed the reunion. He stepped toward Lionel and, still profoundly confused by the man's actions, said, "You should probably leave."

"You're right," Lionel sighed with feigned dejection as he dragged himself back to his troops. Ret turned to join Nika, just in time to miss the evil grin on Lionel's face that meant he wasn't leaving just yet.

"Serge!" Ret rejoiced as he approached the siblings.

"How good it is to see you again, Ret," Serge replied.

"Thanks for your help," Ret said with relief. "How did you get here?"

Just then, the sound of a gunshot filled the air. Taken by surprise, everyone leapt and then looked around. One of Lionel's men fell to the ground, struck by the bullet. A Russian solider was guilty, his gun still smoking. Serge's speechless scowl demanded an explanation.

"It wasn't my fault!" the solider confessed. "Something moved my finger—I swear!"

Lionel rushed to his fallen soldier, then indignantly grunted, "Dead." Heated murmurs spread throughout his men. "What are you waiting for?" he addressed them. "Attack!"

The square erupted in gunfire—Lionel's forces sending a barrage at the Russians, Serge's forces firing back in defense. Doors were splintered and windows shattered as chaos engulfed the scene, everyone running for cover.

"Nika? Serge?" Ret said aloud, searching for the siblings amid the pandemonium. As he scanned the area, he saw Lionel leave his men and sneak out of the square. He was up to something, and Ret was going to find out.

"Ret!" Nika shrieked, pulling him into the bushes where she and her brother were protecting themselves from the onslaught.

"You alright?" Ret asked.

"Yes," Serge answered.

"What do we do now?" Nika besought.

"Nika, I need you to get your people out of here right away," Ret told her. "Take everyone to the trilithon, and wait there until sunrise. Tell everyone to be thinking about a place called the Keep—it's where I live. You'll be safe there until I can clean up this mess and bring all of you back here. Okay?"

"What if we're spotted?" Nika worried.

"Serge, can you spare a few men to go with them?" Ret asked.

"Of course," the president promised.

Ret got up to leave.

"Wait!" Nika stopped him. "Where are you going?"

"I've got some business to take care of," Ret told her. Before Nika could object, Ret had already left to pursue Lionel.

Serge and Nika prepared to emerge from their hideout. They froze, however, when the nearby bushes began to tremble. Serge leaned in front of his sister, shielding her from whatever enemy had found them. He held out his gun, ready to shoot. A man's head popped out of the bushes. It was Mr. Coy.

"Ben!" Serge breathed with relief, lowering his weapon.

Mr. Coy spit out a leaf that had gotten lodged in his mouth and then asked, "What happened?" He seemed displeased. "An actual battle wasn't part of the plan."

"I'm not sure," Serge told him. "It seems one of my men fired on Lionel's forces, but I know my men—they never betray orders."

Just then, two more heads appeared in the bushes.

"Ana, Leo," Coy addressed them. "Any sign of Paige?"

"Not a trace," Ana answered, defeated.

"Who's this?" Mr. Coy wondered of Nika.

"My sister, Nika!" Serge beamed. "The one I told you about, remember? Can you believe it?"

"Incredible!" Coy cheered. "How do you do, madam?" He mistook the branch on his head for a hat but still tipped it with all chivalry.

"Where's Ret, Mr. Coy?" Leo wondered.

"Wait, *you* are Mr. Coy?" Nika interjected. This was the man who had the Oracle, according to what Ret had told her just recently.

With an air of pride, as if pleased to be well-known, Coy returned, "You've heard of me?"

"Yes," Nika answered. "Ret told me about you."

"You know where Ret is?" Leo asked.

"He was here just a moment ago," Nika said.

"Where is he now?" Ana wanted to know.

"I'm not sure," Nika expressed. "All he said was he had some business to take care of."

Mr. Coy, Ana, and Leo stared at each other, all thinking the same thing, and said: "The element."

Nika didn't like the sound of that.

Mr. Coy turned to Ana and Leo and said, "I'll go after Ret. I need to give him the Oracle so he can collect the element. Odds are he'll lead me to Paige."

"I'll go with you," Nika interrupted. Coy glanced at her quizzically. "I—I know the way to the great tree. I can get you there safely."

"Very well," Coy agreed, somewhat reluctantly.

"So what do *we* do?" Ana queried.

"Ret asked Serge and me to get all of my people to the trilithon by sunrise," Nika explained. "He said we should be thinking about a place called the Keep?"

"That's where we live," Leo added.

"Right," said Nika. "Can you help my brother do that while I take Mr. Coy to Ret?"

Ana and Leo looked to Mr. Coy.

"As soon as I get the Oracle to Ret," Coy told them, "he could collect the element at any time, which means this whole place will be caput." Nika looked away, stung. "Your safest bet is to do what Ret said and get to the trilithon."

"What about you?" Leo asked.

"As long as I find Ret, I should be okay," Coy replied.

Ana looked at Leo and took a deep breath before saying, "Alright."

With gun in hand, Serge peeked out of their hiding place and looked around, then said a moment later, "The coast is clear." He stepped out.

Before joining Serge, Ana grabbed Mr. Coy's hand and said soberly, "Just please find Paige."

"If I can't find her, then Ret will," Coy assured her.

Leo pulled Ana along, leaving Mr. Coy with Nika.

"Which way did Ret go?" Mr. Coy asked.

"That way," Nika pointed, "but let's go this way." She started in the opposite direction.

"Why?" Coy asked with concern.

Nika said, "It's a shortcut."

CHAPTER 17

THE REVENANTS

Nika led Mr. Coy down a series of alleys, around a couple of farmhouses, and then safely out of town. She was heading for a little-known passageway through the towering mesas that encircled the valley—not the cavern through which she had brought Ret just days ago, but instead a narrow cleft between the cliff sides. Carved out of the rock by running water, this ancient stream had long since dried up, leaving behind a bed of smooth stones and soft sand. It was a straight shot to the desert on the other side—truly a shortcut, as Nika had promised.

Picking up on Mr. Coy's sense of urgency, Nika kept her pace fast and words short as they traversed the dried riverbed. Still, Mr. Coy frequently gazed upwards to admire the incredible shapes and varied colors of the gorge, stretching several hundred feet above them.

Clearly, this land was not only lost in time but had been made by it, too.

When they reached the end of the cleft, Nika leaned against the canyon wall and poked her head out. The vast desert lay before them, quiet and still. She looked to the right and then to the left, scanning the vicinity like a mouse preparing to venture from the safety of its hole in the wall. The late afternoon heat was obscuring her vision as it rose in waves from the ground, swaying like cobras under a snake charmers' hypnosis.

"What do we need to watch out for?" Mr. Coy whispered.

"Everything," she replied soberly. "The desert is a mysterious place. You never know what you'll find here—or worse: what will find *you*."

"Where do we go from here?" Coy questioned.

Nika pointed to the massive root bulb of the great tree, resting on the desert floor like a prehistoric squid, its giant arms extending out of sight in all directions.

Coy stared at the bulb curiously and then realized, "You mean we're upside-down?"

"Our world may be upside-down," Nika remarked, "but our society is right-side-up." She resumed their journey, though Mr. Coy stayed back for a moment, pondering her words.

They blazed a trail through the desert brush, dodging ant hills and snake burrows. In the distance,

Coy could see plateaus and buttes dotting the level landscape like islands in a sea of sand, their tops so flat and sides so chiseled that they seemed to have been constructed from Legos. Overhead, he watched in wonder as this land's sun grew dimmer and dimmer until it *became* the moon.

Nika paused at the edge of the expansive plain that surrounded the root bulb. The vegetation was sparse in this beach of rock where the great tree's main roots slithered football-fields apart before meeting at the bulb. In the twilight, Mr. Coy searched for any sign of Ret.

"There!" Coy said softly. Not far from the base of the bulb, there was a small cloud of dust, as if someone was disturbing the soil. "Come on!"

Coy was leading Nika now as they hurried across the plain. As they drew nigh, they could see the figure of a person within the haze, moving great amounts of earth away from the roots with nothing more than a wave of the hand. Mr. Coy knew only one person who could move dirt like that.

"Ret!" Coy called out. "I'm so glad we found you."

The individual immediately stopped and turned to face Mr. Coy.

"I've come to give you the Oracle," Coy added, still striding forward.

A moment later, however, the dust in the air began to settle, revealing a hooded individual. Mr. Coy came to an uneasy halt.

"I don't think that's Ret," Nika pointed out.

"Are you the Guardian?" Coy asked.

"Give us the Oracle," the cloaked man answered, his voice eerie and monotone.

"Us?" Coy queried. Suddenly, two more hooded figures emerged from behind. Taking a step back, Coy demanded, "Who are you?"

"Give us the Oracle," the spokesman calmly replied, "and no one gets hurt." Ready to accept the sphere, he held out his right hand, the palm of which had three glowing scars that were identical to Ret's.

"Scars," Coy said to himself, alarmed. "You have scars." He glanced at the three antagonists slowly stepping towards him. "Show yourselves!"

"First, the Oracle," the man reaffirmed.

"Over my dead body," Coy defiantly told him.

"How about hers?" the man put forth, motioning to his left. Coy and Nika looked to find two more hooded individuals who were tightly gripping a squirming Paige, who was tied up and gagged.

"Paige!" Mr. Coy shouted. "Let her go!"

"Give us the Oracle," the stubborn man restated.

Mr. Coy clenched his teeth and sighed with displeasure. Whoever these hoodlums were, they reeked of Lye. He could see his noble daughter shaking her head as he contemplated the terms of the exchange. It was clear these marauders were not leaving without the Oracle, and if they could, in fact, wield the elements, then Coy figured it was wisest to free his daughter while he still had the option to do so.

Nika's heart sank when she saw Mr. Coy, with great heaviness, reach into his front pocket and retrieve a curious and colorful sphere. She was willing to bet these mysterious thugs were much more bent on collecting the element than Ret was and that they cared little for her people or their town. It was all she could do not to intervene.

"Here," Coy said with disgust as he tossed the ball to the man. "Now let her go!" The pair forsook their ransom, and Paige fell to the floor.

Coy ran to his daughter and asked, "Are you okay?" Nika used her pocketknife to cut the girl's bands.

"Oh Dad," Paige cried with great sadness, "why did you give it to them?"

Mr. Coy was about to explain his actions when he saw a flicker of light from across the desert, followed by the faint sound of cackling thunder. The small light was coming towards them, zooming across the sand at great speed.

"What is that?" Nika wondered.

They watched as it drew closer. Very soon, the bright moonlight revealed a man in black flowing robes, riding a white cane like a witch's broomstick, propelled by an electric current.

"Lye," Mr. Coy said with a mix of irritation and worry.

The dark lord slowed as he approached the scene, then leapt from his cane and continued on foot in one fluid motion.

"We have it, my lord," the hooded man nearest to him reported.

"Then what are we waiting for?" Lye growled. "Earth," he called out to the man who had received the Oracle from Mr. Coy. "Dispose of these vermin." Lye motioned to Nika and the Coys. "They are no longer of any use to me—for now."

"As you wish," the man replied. He flicked his hand, creating a large ripple in the sand.

"Surf's up," Lye told the trio with a sinister grin as the wave picked them up and transported them all the way back to the cleft in the mesas.

When the wave finally died, Paige immediately got up and started heading back to the root bulb.

"Hang on there, young lady," Mr. Coy stopped her, grabbing her by the arm.

"We have to go back," Paige protested. "They have the Oracle."

"Actually, they don't," Coy informed her.

Confused, Paige asked, "What?"

"They *think* they have the Oracle," Coy explained, "but what they really have is a fake." Relief washed over Nika.

"But—how?" Paige wondered.

"I had a replica of the Oracle made after we got back from Sunken Earth, way back when," Coy retold, "not quite as expertly crafted as the original, of course, but close enough to at least buy us some time if we were ever in a pinch. I've carried it with me on all of our adventures since—figured it might come in handy someday. And I'd say it did just that today, wouldn't you, darling?"

"You're one of a kind, Dad," Paige couldn't suppress a smile.

"Just living up to the family name," he proudly replied. "I learned a long time ago to always make a duplicate of the thing your enemy desires most."

"Thank you for rescuing me," Paige said.

"So do you have the real Oracle?" Nika asked.

"Indeed," Coy told her, pulling it from his back pocket. "Now all we need to do is find Ret and give it to him."

"Actually," Nika interjected, "Ret told me he has no intention of collecting the element."

"What?" Paige gasped.

"Why not?" Coy asked.

"Because he doesn't want to destroy this place like all the others," Nika relayed, earning hard stares from the Coys. "Wouldn't you agree?"

"Excuse my effrontery," Coy said after a moment of careful thought, "but how do we know you're telling the truth?" The souring situation was bringing out Nika's mutation. Her walls were going up.

"It's obvious, isn't it?" Nika stated with a bit of attitude.

"What do you mean?" Paige asked, suspicious of this mistress.

"Ret could have left this place days ago," Nika said, trying to sound resolute despite her petty reasoning. "I showed him how to do it. But he stayed—for my people, for me."

"For you?" Paige gulped.

"He belongs here," Nika continued. "This is his home now."

As the Coys contemplated Nika's words, Paige's memory was jogged. She had seen this woman before. Sensing Paige's glare, Nika covered her face and looked away.

"You're the woman I saw sitting with Ret on the bench in the town square, aren't you?" Paige asked. "The one who kissed him?"

"Yes," Nika admitted. "What's it to you?"

"Because you're not the only one with feelings for Ret," Paige said, more crestfallen than threatening. Nika's defensiveness suddenly melted.

"You...you also have—" Nika asked, her former firmness fading.

"Yes, very much so," Paige disclosed, "but this isn't about you and me—it's about Ret. So let me ask you something: when Ret told you he wasn't going to collect the element—if that's really what he said—did he look happy about it?"

Nika remembered how downcast Ret had been earlier that day when she came to him in the barn. She shook her head, "No."

Paige stepped towards Nika and, looking her in the eye, said with a hint of heartbreak, "If you really care for Ret, you'll help him collect the elements. He doesn't want to, but he knows he has to. Don't make it any harder."

Just then, a deafening roar rattled their ears. About a mile up the mesa, something had blasted through the base of the vertical cliff side, sending out a great spray of rocks.

"That's the entrance to the cavern," Nika observed. She and the Coys saw someone step out of the mouth and then take off running at the speed of wind.

"Ret!" Paige cheered.

"What is he doing?" Nika wondered.

"Pursuing Lye, I bet," Coy said. "Come on, let's get out of here." He made for the cleft.

"But Dad," Paige refused, "we can't just leave. Ret needs our help."

"I know, child," Coy told her, "but I'd say the three of us are pretty ill-equipped at the moment to face Lye and five of his minions who apparently can also yield the elements. I think our best bet is to meet back up with Serge and his men and then devise a plan." Mr. Coy's realism seemed to squash Paige's romanticism. "Besides," Coy added, "if it's true that Ret does not want the element to be collected," he glanced at Nika, "then we need to get the real Oracle as far away from the tree as possible." He returned the sphere to his back pocket.

Paige looked back at the root bulb, longing to be there to help Ret. But she knew her father spoke the truth. She took his hand and followed him into the cleft, her head down.

"You coming, Nika?" Coy called back to her.

Nika hadn't moved. She was still thinking about what Paige had told her—that if she truly cared for Ret, she would help him collect the element. She was caught in a dilemma, convicted by her own conscience.

"Yes," she replied, disappointed in herself. She entered the riverbed, dragging herself a few steps behind the Coys and wondering if there was yet a way to make things right.

"Once we get to the trilithon," Coy strategized aloud, his voice echoing off the steep canyon walls, "we'll confer with Serge and get his input. Then, on our way back to the tree, we'll stop in town and search for any survivors."

"How can I help?" Paige asked.

"You can help Ana and Leo get all of Nika's people through the trilithon at first light," Coy explained. "It'll be no easy task getting that many people through in such a short window of time. We're sending everyone to the Keep until we clean up this mess. Isn't that right, Nika?" There was no response. "Nika?" Mr. Coy and Paige spun around. Nika was gone.

"Where'd she go?" Paige questioned. "She was right behind us a minute ago."

Mr. Coy checked his back pocket. It was empty.

"She took the Oracle," Coy announced, not altogether displeased. "Looks like your words convinced her to change her mind." He put his arm around Paige, then noticed her frown. "What's wrong?"

"*I* should be the one helping Ret," Paige confessed.

"I'd say you already did," Coy reassured her. "If that woman gets the Oracle to Ret and he collects the element, then it'll be thanks to you." Paige smiled. "Come on, sweetheart." They continued to head for the trilithon.

O   O   O

Ret slowed his whirlwind and alighted on the sand in front of the six cloaked individuals gathered at the root bulb.

"Where's Lionel?" Ret asked, arriving with a gust of wind.

"It's good to see you, too," Lye playfully hissed, his robes blowing in the breeze.

"What did you do to him?" Ret demanded to know.

"You mean the man who blackmailed you in front of all your mutant friends?" Lye laughed.

"He was only trying to help me," Ret defended his friend.

"And then caused the cavern to cave in on you?" Lye added.

"You can't fool me," Ret snapped back. *"You* did that—I saw your lightning bolt strike the ceiling, even from the other end of the cavern."

Lye shrugged and acknowledged with satisfaction, "Guilty as charged."

"Now tell me what you did with Lionel." Ret was inching closer to Lye's hideous face.

"He is none of your concern."

"Tell me!" Ret yelled. In his anger, he summoned a fireball and hurled it at Lye. But, to Ret's great surprise, it was met by an equally powerful flame, the two ricocheting into the night. Ret shrunk back in shock as a hooded person emerged from the shadows behind Lye. Ret could see scars on the person's hands, one of which was still smoking.

"What's this?" Ret asked. "Another one of your clones?"

"Actually no," Lye stated. "Something better: one of your relatives." Ret's eyes widened. "You see, after my clone failed, I got to thinking—why go to the trouble of cloning you when my prison is full of members from your family line? They're just like you but so much more agreeable."

"You're lying," Ret said.

"For once, I'm not," Lye guffawed. "And then I thought, why stop there? Everyone knows five is better than one." Four more hooded figures emerged from the shadows, scars in hand. "And instead of training them to become like *you*—jack of all trades, master of none—I commissioned each to become an expert in one of the five elements that you've collected for me so far." The five each produced a symbol to show which element they had mastered.

"Sorry to disappoint you," Ret said smugly, "but I'm not here to collect the element. I don't even have the Oracle."

"Of course you don't," Lye grinned. "I do." He held up the sphere that Mr. Coy had surrendered.

"How—how did you get that?" Ret asked in amazement.

Lye explained, "Your Coy friend gave it to me—"

"Mr. Coy would never..."

"—In exchange for his daughter," Lye finished. "Love—such a weakness."

"What did you do to Paige?!" Ret bellowed.

"Relax, Romeo, she's fine," Lye said before adding, "this time, at least."

"The Oracle doesn't belong to you," Ret snarled.

"You know, you're right," Lye amused himself. "Here." He lobbed it to the hooded man who had mastered the wood element. "It should stay in the family."

"They are *not* my family," Ret asserted.

"Sounds like you've got some catching up to do," Lye wheezed. The quintet shed their cloaks, revealing three men and two women with hair, skin, and eyes as bright as Ret's, though of various colors. "Call them what you will, but I call them revenants." They began to walk towards Ret. "Enjoy your reunion." Lye turned to the revenant with the Oracle and bade, "Come on, Wood." The two of them made for the root bulb. "We've got an element to collect."

"No!" Ret objected. He lunged forward to stop the pair, but the four remaining revenants blocked his path. Ret took a step back and glared at his familial foes. They were poised and ready, waiting for him to make the first move.

With a grunt, Ret blasted the revenants with a gust of hurricane-force wind, and with that the family feud was underway. The wind revenant immediately countered the attack by removing the energy from the air and then funneling it back at Ret, who absorbed it into his palm. The revenants separated, encompassing Ret on all sides and besieging him simultaneously. The arena erupted in elements—landslides and earthquakes, fireballs and lava flows, heavy chains and sharp swords, bright lights and gamma rays. Earth, fire, ore, and wind—Ret quenched everything that was thrown his way.

The gang decided to team up instead of split up. The earth revenant lobbed rocks into the air like a skeet machine, then the wind revenant propelled each one with a supersonic burst of wind. The projectiles were extremely difficult to dodge, coming so fast that they exploded upon hitting the ground.

Meanwhile, the ore revenant, a brute of a man, jammed his hands into the ground, sifting through the sand and attracting all kinds of metals to them like magnets. He brought them out covered in flecks and fashioned them into a heavy wire, which he began to swipe at Ret like a whip, passing it through the fire revenant's superhot flame with each swing to make it temporarily pliable.

Ret had no time to strike with his own attacks. The revenants truly were experts in their respective elements, conjuring things that Ret had never even imagined, from dust storms to laser beams. The fire revenant was supplying the spark to ignite the earth revenant's gun powder in order to shoot the ore revenant's bullets-turned-heat-seeking-missiles under the wind revenant's direction. It was four minds against one. Alone, they were manageable; but together, they were unstoppable.

Ret was growing weary. He would just quell one threat when a new one would arrive. There was time neither to rest nor to think. His senses were being over-loaded. His adversaries were working as a single team now. Ret saw them exchange glances and then nod, as if they were about to execute a much-rehearsed plan. Then they struck. In an instant, the field erupted in walls of sand, which were melted and blown into glass. A blinding light appeared, intensified by the glass and bouncing off it at all angles, forcing Ret to shut his eyes. When he opened them, he found metal cups clasped around his hands, limiting his powers. Then he was pinned to the ground.

The excitement subsided. Ret, his face in the sand, finally had a moment to think. This was like fighting his clone all over again—futile and going nowhere. He needed now what he had needed then: something unique to him that would give him the upper hand. Last time, it had been Paige. What could it be this time?

Just then, a tiny root emerged from the sand near Ret's face. Like a worm, it silently wiggled for a second or two, just long enough to get its point across, before sliding back into the ground. Ret's gaze shifted to the other roots in the vicinity—the large and mighty ones. That was when he realized the wood revenant had fled with Lye. As powerful as these four revenants were, they were not complete. Something was missing.

Ret could beat them with the power of wood.

Suddenly, four roots shot out of the ground, wrapped themselves around each of the revenants, and yanked them away from Ret. He rose to his feet and commanded more roots to peel away the metal from his hands, which they did with impressive strength. Ret was back in business.

Each of the four revenants devised some way to break, burn, or blow their bands away, but Ret was ready for them. He enclosed the earth revenant in a cage of briars, so tightly that he couldn't move without getting severely poked. Next, he doused the fire revenant in a tangled mess of seaweed and then cast up an entire field of extra tall grass around the ore revenant, who was soon as lost as a child in a corn maze.

Ret was about to turn his attention to the wind revenant when he was thrown to the floor. Though back on his feet in an instant, he was soon punched in the face and kicked to the ground. He looked around, but his attacker was nowhere to be seen. Then he saw footprints in the sand, coming towards him. Ret knew what was going on: the wind revenant was manipulating the waves of light to make herself invisible.

Ret sent a gust of wind towards her, spraying sand in her eyes. He quickly turned around and outlined a series of tiles in the dimension of time. He bonded them together and rolled the scene back to a random moment in the past.

Ret had just turned around when he was tackled. He switched his vision to energy mode and found the wind revenant leaning over him.

"You'll never get the best of me," she threatened. "I'm the cleverest of them all."

"We'll see about that," Ret countered.

Using his legs, Ret launched the woman behind him, directly through the tiles and into the past. Then he rolled the scene back to the present, sealing her inside.

"I'd like to see your cleverness get you out of *there*," Ret remarked.

With the four revenants detained, Ret hurried towards the root bulb, hoping it wasn't too late to stop Lye and the fifth revenant from collecting the wood element.

CHAPTER 18

MUTANT WOOD

Leaving four of his revenants behind to keep Ret occupied, Lye hastened toward the great tree's root bulb, the wood revenant right behind him. Nothing could stop them from collecting the element now—or so they thought. They abruptly halted when they found a man standing in front of them.

"And just where do you think you two are going?" the calm-mannered man asked.

"Well, if it isn't Neo," Lye scoffed, "the part-time Guardian. Tell me, old friend, done any vacationing lately? I'd love to see pictures."

"We're not friends," Neo retorted, "and you know very well the great tree can detect you a mile away."

"That may have been true in the past," Lye said, "but this time I brought an acquaintance." Neo stared at the revenant. "Turns out he and his scars are just the trick in tempering this troublesome tree. I'd say he must have been a lumberjack in his former life—before I brainwashed him."

"You'll never reach the element," Neo pledged.

"Hmm, let's see," Lye poked. "I've got the Oracle, he's got the scars—looks like the only thing standing in our way," Lye's countenance fell, "is you." Without warning, Lye shot a lightning bolt from his cane, but Neo, expecting as much, caused a root to latch onto the base of it and tweak it, sending the bolt zigzagging into the night sky.

Neo grinned and teased, "You missed."

"I may not be a match for your green thumb," Lye jeered, "but I do have something you want."

"Oh?" Neo doubted. "And what's that?"

Lye reached inside his robe, retrieved a flask from the chest pocket, and said, "This." Neo glared at him curiously. "I know how you've been staying alive all these years, Neo." He shook the contents of the container. "And you've been stealing it from me—right under my nose."

"Not bad, huh?" Neo beamed.

"Well not anymore," Lye shot back. "I know about the portal that you installed on my island." Worry seized Neo's face. "You can thank Ben Coy for that. And if you or he or anyone else so much as sets one toe on my island again, you'll be dead before you can blink." Neo swallowed hard. "So consider this flask your only hope of surviving because after I collect the element tonight, this tree will be dead—and so will you. Unless, of course, you'd like to fight me for it."

"If I must," Neo said through his teeth.

Lye handed the Oracle to the wood revenant and instructed him, "Go and collect the element while I take care of this grass stain of a Guardian." The revenant rushed off. Lye turned to face Neo, who was slowly pacing around him in a half-circle. "Alright, spinach breath. Give me your best shot."

Just then, Neo transformed the plain into a watermelon patch.

"Really?" Lye looked at his opponent pitifully. "Is that the best you can do?" From behind, Neo sent a watermelon crashing into the back of Lye's head. He fell to the ground, seeds stuck in his beard. "Enough of this child's play," Lye seethed. He rose to his feet, but the watermelons were now as large as cars, and Neo was nowhere to be seen.

"I don't have time for your games," Lye growled, walking through the field in search of his rival. He shot a watermelon with a lightning bolt, causing it to explode, followed by another. Lye was too busy smashing melons that he failed to see the little vine that had crawled up his clothes, reached into his robe, and filched the flask before slithering away. "Come out and face me like a man." Another watermelon exploded.

"Okay."

Lye spun around to find Neo behind him, clutching the flask.

"I win," the Guardian smiled victoriously.

In his anger, Lye rolled one of the watermelons directly onto Neo, knocking the flask from his possession.

"*Water*melon was a poor choice of produce, plant man," Lye derided as he regained the flask.

Lye's jubilance faded when he felt the ground at his feet rumbling. He scarcely had time to react as Neo sent a full-fledged forest of great and towering trees surging up through the sand. Engulfed in the treetops, Lye was taken into the sky. Neo wasn't far behind, carried into the canopy with the help of vines that he lengthened and shortened as desired. He found Lye stuck in the branches, hanging by his robe. Pulling and tugging, Lye struggled to free himself until he managed to straddle his cane, emit a powerful bolt, and break free. The evil lord flew through the trees, dodging the limbs and vines that Neo was growing and throwing in his way. In a desperate effort to escape, Lye broke through the canopy but enjoyed smooth sailing for just a moment before the living forest reached for him and swallowed him whole. Lye crashed and tumbled to the ground.

Furious, Lye stood and erupted in electricity, sending currents in all directions that reduced the entire forest to splinters. Then he vaporized the organic material, condensed it into water molecules, and sprayed it at Neo with the force of a geyser. Neo was propelled several hundred feet backwards, where he lay lifeless on the ground.

Lye strode past Neo without showing any concern, determined to join his revenant and collect the element. Without the wood revenant at his side, however, Lye now had a much bigger problem on his hands than the Guardian: the great tree.

Lye was approaching the root bulb when he heard a bone-rattling moan, like the call of a large whale. Alarmed, he glanced around, then panicked when he saw a massive root in the sky, directly overhead and falling fast. Lye turned back and leapt out of the way as the root came crashing down, creating a tidal wave in the sand. Lye rolled away, then braced for another attack. The entire tree was aware of his presence now. Every root was awake, swooping in the air like the tentacles of a sea monster and colliding into the ground, transforming the desert sand into an ocean of deadly dunes.

Just as all the roots were coming at him, Lye ran full speed toward the bulb. Like a warrior charging into battle, he held out his cane and shot a colossal current of electricity into the air. With great effort, he kept the flow of power constant. Great bands of electricity burst from the main conduit, keeping the roots at bay. As he neared the entrance to the root bulb, he saw the tree sending out smaller roots along the ground in an effort to trip him up, but Lye stretched out his hand and shot electricity from his fingers, repelling them.

After centuries of trying to subdue the infinity tree and claim its prized element, this was the closest that Lye had ever been. He sprinted toward the entrance, cane in hand and still surging with immense power. He thought he had succeeded when dozens of roots came flying out of the bulb. They collided into Lye's chest, knocking the wind out of him and driving him back. His lightning beam ceased. The roots dragged him out a far distance and left him sprawled out on the desert sand, not far from where Neo still lay. As always, the tree had won.

A moment later, Ret appeared at the scene. He checked on the Guardian, who was badly hurt but still breathing. The same could be said of Lye. The wood revenant was nowhere to be seen. Ret knew he had to stop him from collecting the element. He ran towards the root bulb and, upon reaching the entrance, hurried inside.

Though dark, the root bulb surged with a palpable energy that gave off a subtle luminescence. Ret felt like a flea inside a ball of yarn. There were roots all over the place, swooping every which way and branching off in every direction like enclosed waterslides. Some roots were very large and straight; others were quite small and twisted. It was the most maddening kind of maze—one where he could go anywhere.

Based on what the Guardian had told him, Ret had to remind himself that the great tree was not the element but only its protector, born from a seed that the First Father had given to Neo when he was called to be a Guardian. Neo had personally grown the tree around the element, sealing it somewhere inside its root structure, which, as Neo pointed out, had become more and more complex with the passage of time—though 'complex' was quite an understatement, to which Ret could now attest. He wished there was some way he could roll back the clock and see what the roots looked like in their younger years.

Fortunately, he could do just that.

But someone had already beaten him to it. Off to the right, he saw a doorway to the past. The wood revenant had been here.

Ret studied the tiles. Whatever year their footage belonged to, it was a time when the root bulb was much smaller, so much so that when Ret stepped inside, the floor was no longer made of roots but dirt. Ret hadn't wandered far when he saw another open doorway. He looked inside, where he found an even smaller root bulb.

It would be three more doorways until Ret caught up to the wood revenant. He was standing with his back to Ret, swiping the tiles of yet another doorway. As the years flew by, the root bulb shrunk more and more until, at last, the element came into view. He reversed the scene to the time immediately prior to when the great tree fully enclosed the element in its roots, leaving just enough space for him to reach in and procure it. He passed through the doorway, sphere in hand.

Ret's heart leapt in his chest. It was now or never. He ran after the revenant.

"Stop!" Ret cried. He waved his hand to manipulate some of the roots of the bulb, hoping they could knock the Oracle from the revenant's hands, but the roots did nothing. To Ret's surprise, they wouldn't budge.

And then it was too late. Cradling the Oracle, the wood revenant held it under the wood element and waited for it to open.

But nothing happened.

He tried again. Still nothing. He held it higher. Nothing.

"Why isn't this working?!" he cried.

Suddenly, Ret knew why. It was the same reason why the roots hadn't obeyed his command.

"We can't change the past," Ret said, standing behind him, "but we *can* learn from it." It was something Neo had taught him. "You used the past to learn where to find the element, but it cannot be collected in the past because the past cannot be changed." Ret hadn't known this before; he was simply learning it in this moment.

They were both too distracted, however, to notice the appearance of a new doorway in the room. Like a window in mid-air, scenes from some other time period flashed by until they stopped. The figure of a woman could be seen through them. She had recently been sealed in the dimension of time and was manipulating the tiles from within the other side.

"Thanks for the tip," the woman said, passing through the doorway that she had (cleverly) created.

Ret turned around to find the wind revenant.

"You," Ret said, stunned. "But how did you—"

"I'm a fast learner," she said, punching Ret in the face and knocking him to the ground.

Using the knowledge that Ret had imparted, the wood revenant turned his attention to the tiles that portrayed the wood element. This time, he rolled the clock forward, all the way to the present. When he finished a moment later, he was still standing in the past but now looking at the element in present day.

Once again, he held the Oracle under the element, but, like before, nothing happened.

"Nothing's happening," the wind revenant observed.

"I'm trying," the wood revenant said, now thoroughly frustrated. "What's wrong with this thing?"

"Let me see that." The wind revenant grabbed the Oracle and looked at it closely. She tapped the wedge that housed the wind element. In doing so, she chipped off some of the paint. She rubbed off the rest of it. The sphere was empty.

"This isn't the real Oracle, you fool!" she roared. She shattered the replica over the wood revenant's head, rendering him unconscious.

"Where is it?!" she bellowed at Ret, who was still dizzy from this woman's punch. "Where's the real Oracle?" She blasted him with a gust of wind, sending him rolling across the room.

"I—I don't know what you're talking about," Ret confessed.

The wind revenant picked him up by his shirt and threatened, "You'd better give me the real Oracle, or I'll send you so far back in the past that—"

Just then, a strange noise was heard from across the room. It sounded like someone was watching a movie.

"Nika?" Ret wondered when he saw his friend. "What are you—?" She was clutching the real Oracle. Distressed, Ret looked to the tiles where the element should have been, but it was gone, replaced by chaos. In that moment, Ret realized Nika had followed him into the root bulb and used the unconscious wood revenant's hands to collect the element.

There was no time to explain. Although the post-procurement bedlam was presently nothing more than a few tiles, Ret knew it was currently playing out in real life. They needed to get back to the present.

"Come on!" Ret yelled.

"What about them?" Nika asked, looking back at the wind revenant, who was dragging the wood revenant along. "Should we help her?"

"Don't worry," Ret told her. "She's clever."

They went back the way they had come, returning through the doorways that had taken them to the past. The past was totally unaffected by what was occurring in the present, but when they stepped through the last doorway, they were thrown into the madness. The root bulb was in a state of upheaval, shaking terribly with entire roots shriveling in seconds. Soon, Ret had no choice but to produce a strong wind and fly the rest of the way out of the bulb.

Once outside, Nika watched in horror as her homeland disintegrated. Mesas cracked and crumbled before her eyes. Beautiful buttes that she had come to cherish were reduced to rubble in no time at all. The tree was not so much dying as reversing its growth process, calling back its glorious roots, leaving the land without support.

Ret ran to find Neo. Despite being on the verge of death, the Guardian was dragging his own frail body towards Lye, who was being aroused from unconsciousness due to all the commotion. Neo reached for the flask, uncorked it, and began to pour its contents into his mouth. But before the life-saving liquid reached him, Lye used his power over water to redirect it into his own mouth, consuming every last drop.

"Rest in peace, Guardian," Lye cackled menacingly.

Neo collapsed on the ground, his last hope of survival gone.

With renewed vigor, Lye ran off to find his revenants and congratulate them on procuring the element.

"Neo!" Ret called out, falling to his knees at the Guardian's side.

"Nevermind me," Neo rasped. "The relic!" Too weak to lift his hand, he used one finger to point back at the great tree. Ret watched as the last of its roots returned home. Ret ran back to where the root bulb had been just moments earlier. There, in the soft sand, was a seed—the same seed that the First Father had given to Neo so long ago. Ret picked it up. What once was a great tree was now a relic.

Ret returned to Neo's side, but his eyes were closed. A smile graced his face. Ret knew what that meant. His heart sank. It was never easy to lose a Guardian.

"Look!" Nika shouted. She was pointing at the sky. It was almost first light. "If we hurry, we can make it to the trilithon."

His eyes moist, Ret walked away with Nika, leaving the Guardian's body in the charge of the elements.

"Well done," Lye told his revenants once they had regrouped. "Now let me see the element."

The wind revenant hesitated before fearfully reporting, "We don't have it."

"What?" Lye angrily asked.

"The Oracle was a fake," the wood revenant explained. "That woman had the real one." He pointed to Nika, running across the plain with Ret. "She used my hands to collect the element."

"Argh!" Lye howled, infernally miffed. "Fire," he barked at the revenant, "set the land ablaze. Wind, blow the smoke so that it blocks the sun." They obeyed. In an instant, the parched desert went up in flames.

Ret and Nika stopped when they found themselves surrounded by fire.

"Perfect," Lye said to himself when Nika was standing still. He aimed his cane at her and fired a bolt of electricity, which struck her square in the back.

"Nika!" Ret exclaimed when she collapsed to the ground. He fell to his knees and cradled her. "Stay with me!" he told her shakily. She looked just the way Ivan did when he was struck by an energy blast by the guards at Sunken Earth. "Nika, say something!"

With her last breath, she whispered, "Thank you for teaching me to trust again." She caressed Ret's cheek with her hand. "I love you." Then her eyes rolled back in her head, and her body fell limp.

"Nika!" Ret cried. She was dead.

Ret could hear Lye's evil laugh. He looked back to see the dark lord and his revenants heading into the past through a doorway that they had made, where they would escape this land's demise.

"You may have gotten the element, Ret," Lye yelled, "but you didn't get the sunrise."

Ret looked up at the sky. The smoke from the brush fire had veiled the sun in blackness, blocking its power to send anyone through the trilithon.

"Ta-ta!" Lye rejoiced as he fled into the past.

Ret flung Nika over his shoulder and took to flying. Great chunks of the ceiling were crashing down to the ground. The mesas that had once encircled the valley were crumbling like sand castles. He could see the town being rattled to pieces, as if the houses and stores had been built with Lincoln Logs. Ret knew he had only a few minutes, at best.

In the airwaves, he could hear the desperate cries for help from the hordes of people who were stranded at the trilithon.

"Is it too late for the sunrise?" Paige wondered.

"I'm afraid so," Mr. Coy told her.

"What do we do now?" Ana asked.

Leo grasped her hand tightly.

"Look!" one of the soldiers shouted. Everyone in the group strained to see what was flying towards them. Ret had flown through the smoke, heading for the trilithon.

"It's Ret!" Paige exclaimed.

"And he's got Nika!" Serge pointed out.

Ret extended his hand and used his power over energy to conjure the brightest light he could summon. With amazing whiteness, it shined like a second sun, prompting everybody in the crowd to shield their eyes.

"Everyone grab someone!" Mr. Coy shouted. "Ret made his own sunrise!"

In an instant, the entire gathering vanished, transported through the trilithon.

Just then, a terrible tremor shook the platform where the trilithon stood, causing the posts to fall over and the lintel to crash to the ground. But Ret knew the trilithon was merely the sign of the portal—that the portal still remained. Dodging falling boulders, he held onto Nika and flew as fast as he could. With his self-made sunrise still beaming from his hand, he sailed directly into the portal and disappeared.

CHAPTER 19

MOURNING IN THE EVENING

In the blink of an eye, a multitude of people appeared on the back lawn of the Keep's mansion house. A mix of soldiers and mutants, they looked around at their new surroundings with confusion, some still shielding their heads from the falling debris that was now a world away. Their emotions were as varied as their backgrounds: relief for escaping with their lives, heartache for those who weren't so fortunate, devastation for losing their homeland, worry for what the future might bring.

Just then, a loud thud was heard near the cloven trunk of the bald cypress tree that marked the time portal on the Keep's grounds. Everyone turned to find Ret hovering over Nika's lifeless body. A poignant sadness seized every heart as a profound silence fell over the gathering, interrupted only by Ret's weeping. Unsure of her place, Paige brought her hand to her quivering lips and fled to her father's embrace. Ana leaned into Leo's shoulder. Serge wept openly. Jaret and Pauline came running through the backdoor of the house but abruptly stopped when they saw what was happening.

After a few minutes, Ret slid his arms under Nika, picked her up, and gently laid her body at her brother's feet.

"It was Lye," Ret told him somberly. "I'm so sorry."

"As am I," Serge replied haltingly, wiping his tear-strewn face. "At least I got to see her one last time. Thank you for reuniting me with my sister."

Ret returned the gratitude with a slight bow and then looked into the crowd. Everyone was watching him. He knew which of them were Nika's people because their cheeks were wet with tears. In their eyes, he saw longing for their lost land and also love for their late leader, though now bereft of both. Truly, they had suffered great loss.

But Nika had a heart that was too great to be bested by death. Her legacy would live on, beating in the heart of each of the people she touched, including Ret's. She had achieved the purpose of life—to develop uncondi-tional love—and, remarkably, she did it despite (and perhaps on account of) being a victim of its opposite. She understood that although it is easy to love a friend, it can be hard to love a stranger (especially an enemy) because that love must come from within—it must start with you. So it was with Nika. She, who had every excuse to be bitter and cruel, chose instead to be what she herself had wished from others. In life, she loved her people. In death, she loved Ret. And, through it all, she was the person from whom the love started.

Ret could think of no better tribute to Nika than to sum up her existence using her own words. He took a few steps back and, speaking primarily to her people, boldly declared:

> *Long live the mutants,*
> *The never-have-beens,*
> *The outcasts and tangents*
> *Who just don't fit in.*
> *Long live our troubles*
> *To keep pure our hearts.*
> *Let's be the people*
> *From whom the love starts.*

Despite Ret's quivering voice, his eulogy seemed to bolster the sagging spirits of every mutant in attendance. Shaky smiles started to defy stubborn sorrows, and flickers of hope began to take root—a hope that they would surely need in the difficult days ahead. For, once again, they were strangers in a strange land, with nothing more than the clothes on their backs and the love in their hearts. It was this love, however, that Ret was counting on, for if it had cured *their* world, then it just might cure *the* world.

To keep the optimism going, Ret sprouted wild-flowers in the grass around Nika's body, then expanded it to the entire back lawn. Serge plucked the brightest bud he could find and set it on Nika's chest. One by one, her people followed, each honoring the woman they loved so dearly, until a beautiful bouquet lay at Nika's feet.

While everyone was distracted, Ret quietly slipped away from the scene. Just before he disappeared among the trees, Paige saw him out of the corner of her eye and snuck away to follow after him. When she finally tracked him down, she wasn't surprised where she found him: walking on the beach.

"Hey," she tenderly said, striding up next to him.

"Hey," he smiled back. "I was hoping you'd find me." Paige was silently relieved when Ret reached to hold her hand, as she had not been entirely sure of the status of their relationship these days.

"It's nice to see your true colors are back," she pointed out, referring to how Ret's skin, hair, and eyes were unusually bright again.

"Thanks," Ret chuckled. "Something about that land brought out the mutant in me."

"My dad told me Lye dropped an atomic bomb on the infinity tree a century ago to try and get to the element," Paige retold, "so it was probably leftover radiation poisoning that did it to you." Ret responded with a melancholy nod.

After a moment, Paige said, "I'm sorry about Nika."

"Me, too," Ret replied. "She was a good person."

"She seemed to really like you."

"What makes you say that?" Ret asked with a subtle grin.

"I saw her kiss you once," Paige said playfully.

"Oh, that," Ret blushed. "I didn't know she was going to do *that*."

"Smart girl."

"We were just friends," Ret reassured her. "I think she wanted us to be more than that, but I didn't. In fact, whenever I was with her, I couldn't stop thinking about *you*."

"Really?" Paige wondered, inwardly giddy.

"Yeah," Ret said. "I felt kind of bad about it, actually. I never told her, of course, but it's true."

"Well, *I* couldn't stop thinking about you, too," Paige confessed, grabbing Ret's arm with her other hand. "I missed you—a lot."

"I missed you, too," Ret told her. "And now I'll miss Nika. She was a great help to me, Paige. She was exactly the friend I needed at the time. She taught me how to love others."

"She sounds like a hero," Paige observed without any jealousy.

"She was," Ret nodded. "After all, *she* was the one who collected the element—not me."

"She did?"

"Yeah," Ret repeated. "She followed me into the root bulb and used one of the revenants' hands to do it. I still don't know how she got the Oracle."

"She took it," Paige filled in, "from my dad."

"I wonder why," Ret put forth. "We had both agreed not to collect the element."

"I...may have said something," Paige slyly inserted.

"Oh? Like what?"

"I told her that if she really cared about you, she would help you collect the elements, not hinder you," Paige recalled. Then with remorse, she added, "So I guess it's my fault she's dead, huh?"

"No," Ret quickly interjected, "it's *Lye's* fault."

"Well, I can't say I blame her for doing what she did," Paige said. "I'd have done the same thing if my dad hadn't stopped me."

"I'm glad he did," Ret said.

"Why?"

Ret stood still and stared into Paige's eyes. "Because then it might be *you* lying in the grass back there." He slipped his hand behind her head, her curls between his fingers. "And I couldn't live without you, Paige."

"I couldn't live without you either, Ret," Paige whispered. Then he did what she was hoping he would do. He brought his lips close to hers and kissed her. When he finished, she pulled him back and kissed *him*. And, for a moment, nothing else seemed to matter—no worries or fears, no Oracle or Lye, no elements or problems. Just Ret and Paige, together.

And then that moment ended. When Paige opened her eyes, she was stunned by what she saw in the distance. She blinked several times to make sure she was seeing things correctly. Out on the ocean, there were ships—many ships. These were not barges carrying goods or sailboats watching whales—no, these were battleships and aircraft carriers, with more and more coming out of the far-off haze every minute.

Ret noticed Paige's fixation and asked with concern, "What is it?" He spun around. His heart sank at the sight. "They're here to destroy the Manor."

"Oh no!" Paige cried. "What should we do?"

"We need to tell your dad," Ret answered, "now."

Paige reached into her pocket and groaned, "My phone is dead."

"It's okay," Ret told her. "I'll text him."

"No, text Ana," Paige instructed. "My dad doesn't always check his phone right away."

With a wave of his finger, Ret sent off a beam of light with the words of his text message encoded on the waves. A second later, back at the mansion house, Ana's phone vibrated. She took it out and found this message from Ret:

Tell Mr. Coy to come to the beach ASAP

Ana rushed to find Mr. Coy, who was speaking with the Russian president.

"Well, my friend," Coy said, "I can't thank you enough for dropping everything and coming here with your army. We couldn't have gone up against Lionel and his forces without you."

"You are very welcome," Serge replied. "I'm just glad we made it here before sunrise."

"As am I," Coy agreed. "But tell me, how *did* you get here so quickly?"

"It was just after nine o'clock in the morning when you called me," Serge detailed. "By the end of the hour, we were airborne."

"But it's over 5,000 miles from here to Moscow," Coy pointed out. "How did you travel so far in just a few hours? You essentially flew into the past!"

"Let's just say your country isn't the only one with hypersonic aircraft," Serge said with a clever smirk.

Impressed, Coy responded, "If I ever need to fly in excess of Mach 5 speeds, I know who to turn to."

"Anytime," Serge promised, "but I'm afraid Lye also has such capabilities. It will be a long time before I forgive myself for ever conspiring with that madman."

With a hearty slap on the back, Coy beamed, "I'd say your aid to us today was more than enough restitution."

Just then, Ana approached Serge and politely said, "Sorry to interrupt, your royal-ness," then turning to Mr. Coy, "but I have an urgent message for you." She showed him the text from Ret. Coy excused himself from Serge and hurried off across the lawn, then through the bog and into the low-lying marshland that preceded the beach. Even before reaching the sand, however, Mr. Coy learned why Ret had summoned him. Wide-eyed and open-mouthed, Coy stopped as soon as he saw the ships—dozens and dozens of them, with more coming. Thanks to his service in the Navy, he could distinguish the destroyers from the raiders—the frigates from the corvettes. Assault ships sailed alongside capital ships, even torpedo boats and submarines. Based on the flags waving above each deck, it seemed nearly every nation in the world had launched a craft to aid in the attack.

Meeting up with Mr. Coy, Ret remarked, "Seems a bit excessive, if you ask me," referring to the over-whelming number of vessels.

"I'm sure even *one* of these would get the job done," Paige observed.

"This isn't just about getting the job done," Mr. Coy inserted dryly. "It's about proving a point. Lye wants to show us that the world is against us. He is trying to scare us into giving up."

"But we've got Serge on our side," Ret optimistically pointed out. "Maybe *he* can help us."

"In future battles, perhaps," Coy said dismally, "but not this one."

"But there's metal," Ret persisted, surveying the battlefield. "And there's sure to be lots of fire. I might be able to repel some of the attack."

"I don't want to start a war, Ret," Coy countered definitively. "It's too late for the Manor."

"But—"

"The Manor is just a house," Coy shot back, his own heartache accidentally sullying his tone. "It's nothing more than a bunch of walls. We already removed everything of significant value, and we don't want our foes turning on the Keep. Now promise me you won't intervene."

Ret looked down, then glanced at Paige. Though also disappointed in the situation, she squeezed Ret's hand to tell him not to fight her father on this one.

"Yes, sir," Ret said softly.

Like serried troops, the warships surrounded Little

Tybee Island, their number growing more ridiculous by the minute. The smaller-hulled boats crept closer to the shore than their larger counterparts, with even grander battle-cruisers looming in the deeper waters. The clicks and clangs of heavy machinery traveled on the wind as captains and crews readied and aimed their canons and guns.

A moment later, Ana arrived with her parents and Leo, their moods subdued and mouths muted by the ominous scene that lay before them. They joined Ret and the Coys on the beach, huddling together in the twilight.

Suddenly, a flash of light appeared from the deck of a large guided-missile destroyer, floating near the back of the fleet. A second later, an ear-splitting sound filled the air, giving the onlookers on the beach a jolt. They watched the missile trace a slight arc in the sky before flying over the Manor's front gate, through the double doors, and into the semicircular entryway, where it exploded. Ret winced. Pauline gasped. Every eye spied on Mr. Coy, whose face held firm.

The first punch thrown, the international armada erupted in gunfire. A flurry of bombs and bullets rained down on the Manor, which, with its state-of-the-art defense system relocated to the Keep, stood utterly helpless to retaliate. Round after round of rockets and shells mercilessly pulverized the vacant establishment, which soon became engulfed in flames and smoke.

With a wide inlet of water between them and the onslaught, the Coopers, Coys, and Leo gazed in relative safety but total horror as Coy Manor was destroyed—a piece of themselves being destroyed with it. Pauline thought of the studatory where Ret interpreted the prophecy on the piece of parchment for the first time. Ana recalled the planetarium where she had taken a ride on Mercury and almost gotten singed by the sun. Leo's mind was in the courtroom where he had delivered his stirring case about things real and unreal. Paige remembered when she and Ana used to practice volleyball in the Manor's sports complex. Ret was thinking of the savanna where Conrad, astride a rhino, once rescued him from a hungry cheetah.

But those were just memories now. A missile collided into the bell tower, where Ret had received his first carillon lesson from Mr. Coy. Underwater torpedoes had finally caused the seawall to give way, releasing into the ocean the aquarium where Ret had come face-to-snout with a pack of tiger sharks. The Manor's beautiful grounds now lay scorched and blackened, the lagoon empty and charred. Like the finale of a fireworks show, one last wave of ammunition exploded on the scene until, with an audible sigh, the underground hangar succumbed, swallowing the property and sending up a great cloud of ash and smoke that signaled the end of Coy Manor.

Their mission complete, the ships began to retreat, leaving behind an inferno whose flames lit up the skies so brightly that it appeared the sun was rising instead of setting. The seawater around Little Tybee Island looked much disturbed as it poured into the Manor's many underground chambers.

True to his word, Ret stayed out of the struggle, despite his desire to engage. Paige caressed the top of his hand as compliment for his restraint, then wiped away a tear from her eye. There were still no signs of sadness from Mr. Coy. Meanwhile, Jaret's eyes were glued to a pair of binoculars. Perhaps the Coast Guard in him, the captain was getting a closer look at the departing ships.

"Pauline, look at this," he said in hushed tones, handing the binoculars to his wife. "Does this man look familiar to you?"

After a quick look, Pauline replied, "Of course, dear. It's Lionel." She kept her voice quiet, knowing such a name would only aggravate Mr. Coy even more in this difficult moment. She passed back the binoculars.

"Why does that face ring a bell...?" Jaret thought to himself, following Lionel's face until his ship sailed out of range. Jaret may have made the crucial connection right then and there had he not been purposely, though only partially, brainwashed after unsuccessfully trying to steal Lye's cane.

Pauline turned to the youth and said delicately, "We best be heading indoors. We don't want to catch a cold." The group began to make its way to the Keep.

Except for Mr. Coy. He waited until he was alone and then, no longer needing to be an example of strength, buckled under the weight of his emotions. He fell to his knees and wept. He had loved the Manor, not so much for the foundation that it stood on as the principles that it stood for. Yes, it was just a bunch of walls, as he had said, but it was what had happened within those walls that had transformed that house into a home. Truly, Mr. Coy put the heart in hearth.

In the midst of his grieving, Mr. Coy saw the sand in front of him begin to move. It swelled and swirled until a small structure took shape, like a sand castle. Then it grew—and grew and grew until a miniature replica of Coy Manor stood in the sand.

"We'll rebuild it," Ret said, admiring his handiwork as he returned to Coy's side. "We'll rebuild the Manor—maybe not here, but somewhere." He helped Coy to his feet. "Someday, there will be a Coy Manor in every major city in the world."

"Thanks, Ret," Mr. Coy smiled, sniffling. "I hope you're right." Then he took one final look at the remains of the Manor and never looked back.

Ret took the Oracle from his pocket and held it out in front of himself for Mr. Coy to see. Naturally, their attention turned to the wood element, the sphere's newest member. It was not the color of old bark but rather of the fresh center of a large tree trunk: white with an almost unrecognizable tinge of beige, like that of piano keys or the cue ball of a billiards table. It was the purest piece of wood, the source of all other plant life.

"Five elements down," Coy sighed.

"Only one more to go," Ret added brightly.

Ret stared at the palms of his hands. There was only one unlit scar remaining, on the far right side of his left hand. But it had been illuminated once before, of course. In fact, for the first time, he already knew what the next scar symbolized.

"Where are we headed next?" Coy asked.

"To the very heart of Lye," Ret said gravely, looking out to sea. "Waters Deep."